DOWN COUNTRY

Lorne Tepperman

Rock's Mills Press
Rock's Mills, Ontario • Oakville, Ontario
2025

Rock's Mills Press
www.rocksmillspress.com

Edited by Elizabeth Sheldon.

The name Rock's Mills Press and its styling in Rockwell Bold is a registered trademark, used under license by the publisher, 16336442 Canada Inc.

For retail, library and bulk orders, please contact the publisher at customer.service@rocksmillspress.com.

RAVE REVIEWS FOR *DEADLY DONATION*, FIRST BOOK IN THE RACHEL TILE MYSTERIES

"Tepperman has hit a home run!" —Bruce McGregor, author of *GPS Wealth* and *GPS Millionaire*

"[Rachel Tile is] an out-of-the-ordinary protagonist who thinks too much—and not enough." —Rick Blechta, award-winning author of the Pratt & Ellis Mysteries

"A cracking good read! Lorne Tepperman keeps the pages turning." —Lars Osberg, author of *The Age of Increasing Inequality: The Astonishing Rise of Canada's 1%*

"If you like 'whodunit' crime fiction in a Canadian (read Toronto) setting, there is much to savour in this densely plotted saga." —Julian Tanner, author of *Teenage Troubles*

"A powerful and mesmerizing gamble of a book, seen with the wise eye of a master observer!" —Murray Pomerance, author of *A King of Infinite Space*

"*Deadly Donation* is much more than a whodunit. It is a thoughtful meditation on truth, consequences, character and life's meaning." —Michael Adams, author of *Sex in the Snow* and *Fire and Ice*

"Lorne Tepperman, a retired academic, draws on years of experience studying crime, gambling, and family relations in crafting this neo-noir thriller." —Rosemary Gartner, co-editor of *The Oxford Handbook of Gender, Sex, and Crime*

Books by Lorne Tepperman from Rock's Mills Press

The Rachel Tile Mysteries
Deadly Donation

Nonfiction
Why You Buy (with Megan Markus)
Canada's Place: A Global Perspective (with Maria Finnsdottir)
Consumer Society (with Nicole Meredith)
Outsights: Inequality from Inside and Out (with Nicole Meredith)
Flows: A Network Approach to Social Inequality (with Sally Chiang)

I

I'm a night owl and maybe you are too. If so, you know the pattern. We walk through our duties as attentively as possible. We do the day job and the housework, keeping the family lovingly at bay. Once or twice a day we fall into a short, mild coma. The world gets murky and we have to take a break. Then, after the sun goes down, we get a second wind. We start our real day and get our best ideas. That's when we think, plan, and imagine.

That part of the day—our real day—is intense and productive, and usually solitary. I spend most of this 'second day' in my home office, writing books and planning lectures. Time flies by. One day slides into the next, one week into another, summer into fall, fall into winter. The years pass in an orderly, blurry procession.

I also spend part of my 'second' day in bed, falling asleep (or failing to fall asleep), dreaming, waking up with new ideas, recording those ideas, then falling asleep again. That makes my bedroom a workplace. Maybe, the most important room in my life.

And my bedroom hasn't changed much. I mean, since Daniel left to live in Picton with a casino greeter. If you visited, you'd still see a queen-sized bed and two end-tables, each holding a lamp and alarm clock. A dark wooden dresser, with a traditional Indian painting over it. Oh yes, and blinds on the north-facing windows that never let in much light.

A comfortable and familiar bedroom where I wake up every

morning (and many nights). Even when I dread waking, as I did today.

I was dreading a replay of what happened last year. I didn't think I'd make it through that difficult time. But I did. And after a summer vacation that seemed far too short, here I was again. Back to teaching. Back to running the School of Criminology at Strachan University, here in Toronto. Waking up to the first day of the new semester.

I'd try to make this year better than last. Not necessarily more relaxing, but less frightening. Maybe, I'd succeed.

Was I mentally ready for this new academic year? Not a bit. But that's life. When you're running at top speed—say, you're Usain Bolt and can run 38 km per hour—life is still going by you at 40 km per hour. And that little bit makes all the difference. So, in my imagination, I can run faster, like Wile E. Coyote. But in reality, I can't do it. I'll never run any faster than my present speed. Which is my top speed.

I'd promised myself this year would be slower, easier, less scary than last year. But today didn't start the way I was hoping. Around 7 a.m., my 'daytime' started with a jolt. The telephone rang loudly and wouldn't stop. Sitting up with a start, I bumped my head on the night table. "Damn, I hate that thing!" I shouted at no one in particular. I rubbed my head. Drops of blood coloured the palm of my hand.

My forehead hurt like hell, and I leaped out of bed to bandage the cut. "To hell with the telephone!" I shouted. Then, in my rush to the bathroom, I stubbed the big toe on my right foot. That slowed me down to a walk. I stopped to rub my forehead, then my toe. Forehead, then toe, hobbling all the way.

I was still half asleep. And I'd been dreaming—or was it thinking?—about the rise of violent 'patriotism' in the United States. About an article I was writing on the role of anger in politics. An article titled 'Rage Against the Dying of the Light.' Propelled by the re-election of Donald Trump south of the border, it was the seed of my next book. I'd already imagined the cover photo. A picture of that 'patriot' who'd invaded the Capitol Building on January 6, 2021. The shirtless one with buffalo horns on his head. A 'Proud Boy,' I remembered. Or maybe one of those Q-Anon guys.

I already knew I'd have one extra duty this year. I'd have to help my colleague, Donny Foster, reintegrate into the School routine. Donny had suffered a mishap last year. Well, worse than a mishap. He'd been in Texas studying the Devlin Crew—a gang of car smugglers—when someone murdered his wife. I'd have to help him return to teaching. So, last year was bad for me, as I told you. But it was much worse for Donny.

If I could trust the bathroom mirror, that cut on my forehead was deep. Deeper than I'd realized. I put a second bandage over the first one, then massaged my aching big toe. Hearing the phone ring again, I rushed to answer it, this time nearly stubbing my other big toe.

Someone who might have been in China wanted to clean my heating ducts. "I don't have heating ducts," I told him. "Goodbye!" I slammed the phone. I'll have to get rid of that landline. Nothing but duct cleaners and political pollsters, these days.

Slow down, I told myself. I went downstairs and ate my usual breakfast—an apple, a muffin, a smidge of yogurt, and two cups of coffee—then showered very carefully. Careful not to make my forehead bleed again. Then, I dressed not quite so carefully, grabbed my briefcase, and jumped into my car. All this, very quietly, since my beloved teenage son, Josh, was still sleeping. His first class wasn't until two in the afternoon. You do the math.

For a moment, in the cool fresh air, I felt invigorated, even enthused. As usual, I strapped myself into the car, nice and snug. But I've never liked driving through rush hour, as I'd have to do today. At rush hour, half of everyone in the GTA was driving down Yonge Street in front of me. So, after a few minutes on Yonge Street, I went to Plan B. I winkled through a series of side streets, breaking a few traffic rules in the process. After only ten minutes, I arrived on Avenue Road. There, the other half of everyone in the GTA was driving downtown.

To make the drive feel shorter, I listened to an audiobook, also as usual. Louis-Ferdinand Celine's *Death on the Installment Plan*. Yes, Celine was a fascist and an antisemite, so don't bother bawling me out. That guy could write like a devil. Maybe he was The Devil, for all I knew. Still, that very amusing, very shocking book made the commute go faster.

And I positively adored my Ford Bronco. Most of the cars in my neighbourhood are classier—BMWs, Teslas, Lexuses, the occasional Mercedes. But that's why I like my Bronco. It makes me feel slightly proletarian—at least not showy. A Bronco is the kind of car a proletarian might buy. A proletarian with a fair bit of cash, of course.

Then, there's the O.J. Simpson factor. Remember when half of the police in Los Angeles chased O.J. down that freeway to arrest him for killing his wife? Well, he was driving a Ford Bronco. After O.J.'s notorious escapade, Ford stopped making Broncos for more than twenty years, before bringing the model back in 2021. So, driving my four-year-old silver Bronco through rush hour traffic made me feel, a little, like a renegade proletarian. Which, in these awful days of Donald Trump and Elon Musk, is … well, an act of mild protest. At least, for a Canadian.

I know, that's silly. The thing is, little flights of fancy take my mind off the rush of time. Also, off my bloody forehead, throbbing toe, and today's traffic jam. Above all, they took it off what I most didn't want to think about: the start of the new school year.

After thirty-five long, distracted minutes, I arrived. Strachan University is a big, sprawling campus with lots of buildings, new and old; also, lots of green space. A lovely old campus, really, though too large to be homey. I parked in an overpriced parking garage, walked the two blocks to my office at the School of Criminology. And who should I meet, also going in the front door, but Donny Foster himself.

"Welcome back, Donny. I'm sorry for your trouble last year. I'll do everything I can to make this year easier for you," I said in what I hoped was a kindly, parental tone.

He nodded and smiled. "Thank you. I appreciate that." Then he continued to his office, just down the hall from my own.

Donny, as every criminologist knew, was famous. He had many followers. The older ones showed him grudging respect. The younger ones copied his mannerisms, trying to win his support. He had charisma, at least in his students' eyes. Many of the young women found him charming. And now, with his dabbling in AI, he had even more admirers.

Yet Donny was also middle-aged. It showed in his short frame, soft from years of sitting at a computer. His slouched shoulders, the too-tight suits. He looked older than his fifty-five years. Naturally he tried to mask it. That wide-brimmed fedora, for instance. He must have thought it made him look rugged, like an adventurer, a man who explored the world. The vest he wore had trinkets—chains with attachments, a Phi Beta Kappa key, a Mensa medallion. They were supposed to make him look urbane.

Like everyone else, Donny wore a mask. But it was a good mask. It made him popular.

My secretary was already in, drinking coffee, opening the mail, and moving paper around her desk. I said hi, and we made small talk for a few minutes.

"What happened to your head?" she asked me.

"A small argument with my bedroom furniture," I said. Keep it light, I thought.

"Yeah, that happened to me last month. Duct cleaners, right?"

"Yeah, duct cleaners," I admitted.

Then we talked about what she'd done during the summer, what I'd done, how bad the traffic was, how unpredictable the weather. We needed better coffee for the office this year, would she look into it? That kind of thing.

Exhausted by trivia, I entered the inner office, where I did my 'daytime' work. I took off my coat, sat down at my desk. Put my feet flat and steady on the floor. But still struggled to silence the noise in my head. I was actively trying to forget Donald Trump, and the woman who'd died in Texas, Donny Foster's wife, Melanie. And my other duties at Strachan University.

My forehead still throbbed from the bump. But that pain was nothing compared to the pain of work ahead. First, there'd be the simple fact of lecturing. This was my first day back after a lovely, productive summer break. My Introduction to Criminology course was due to meet for the first time today.

Now, don't get me wrong. I love teaching. It's really simple, and there are only four steps to success. Write the textbook, make the students read a chapter each week, lecture about whatever interests me that week, and relate it to what the students have just read.

I write the textbook precisely so I won't have to lecture about the boring bits. The point of an undergraduate lecture is to display enthusiasm. To model curiosity. To show students what 'the life of the mind' looks like. That's what students need from a living teacher, I think. And that's what I give them. That's my grand strategy.

In this first week of school, few will have done the assigned reading. They're still shopping for courses. So today, in my first lecture, I'll welcome them, review the course syllabus, tell them how they can get an A, give them a short lecture on basic stuff. Easy-peasy. After fifteen years of practice, I could do that in my sleep. Correction: would (almost) do it in my sleep, today.

2

Just before ten, I strolled over to the lecture hall, three blocks away. With minutes to spare, I stood watching more than six hundred students jostle into Cudney Hall. Rowdy, fueled up from their summer vacation. I'd have to tamp down the energy in this large, multilevel space.

Cudney Hall was named in honour of the candy baron Alvin Cudney. He'd donated $200 million for the naming right. Cudney had made his fortune from a candy invention that, incredibly, no one had imagined before. A metre-long red licorice rope Cudney had named "the Whippersnapper." Kids loved eating the ropey candies after first whipping one another for minutes on end. Within a decade, Cudney made hundreds of millions of dollars from this rosy confection, a dime at a time.

Around the world, thousands of other students were tuning in on Zoom. By staying home and taking their Strachan degree online, they'd avoid the full, in-person tuition, which many lately were finding a little too steep.

I hadn't dressed up for my first class of the year. Just the usual: a tailored green shirt, black slacks, and a charcoal hoodie. Sporty, smart casual. But I'd washed my short red hair the night before, so I looked okay.

Some men have claimed to find me attractive. I'm slightly taller than the average woman—in fact, a little taller than the average man. I'm also slender and my reddish hair falls straight and soft around my face. I don't care about my looks, but a few men have told me—well, Robert, for example—that I'm beautiful. Robert is the man I fell in love with last year. He liked my high cheekbones and large, expressive eyes. At least, he said so.

I was there when Robert was murdered, and I won't tell you much more about him. Not today.

Here's what I see when I look in the mirror: a pale, thin, fit forty-two-year-old woman, with small freckles. Also, slightly damp ginger hair that frames my face. That will have to be enough for my students and the rest of the world.

"Hello, everyone. I hope you're doing well," I told them. "Welcome back from summer vacation. And don't mind the bandages on my head. Just a small household accident. I assure you, my brain's still working. Today, to get us started, I'm going to introduce a few basic ideas. Things you have to know if you're going to understand criminology this year.

"Let's start with the idea of 'rules,'" I said. "Every group, every organization, and every society has rules—lots of rules. Social scientists disagree about why we need rules, and how many rules we need. But there's no denying that, in societies, we need rules. So, we make them and enforce them. Rules give us a basis for conformity. They make life predictable. And we enforce rules to control what sociologists call 'deviance.'"

Next, I defined deviance, giving them examples from our

own society. "But understand that what people consider deviant in one group, or organization, or society, is not always deviant in another. And views about deviance are changing all the time." Again, I gave examples.

"And since there are different kinds of deviance, and different degrees of concern about them, there are different kinds of rules. Most criminologists would put society's rules into three categories: informal norms, formal rules, and laws." Again, I gave examples of each of these, drawn from present-day Canadian society.

"Now this next bit is important: criminologists are mainly—perhaps, only—interested in studying crimes. And crimes are violations of the law—not violations of informal norms or formal rules. We're going to talk a lot about the law in this course. About why people make laws, how they make laws, and how they try to enforce our laws. So, I will have a lot to say about the police, the courts, and lawyers.

"Criminologists also talk about how and why laws change. Whether, for example, people's attitudes change before or after the laws change. For example, whether people's attitudes about marijuana changed—liberalized—before or after lawmakers legalized the possession and use of marijuana.

"And that discussion gets us into the study of law-making, a topic with a long history in criminology and other fields. People who study law-making ask questions like, what is the connection between law, morality, religion, and politics. And why do some societies consider law-making a subfield of religion, while other societies separate the law from religion." Again, I gave examples.

"Finally, I'll talk about science and the application of scientific thinking to law-making. At our university, we consider criminology an applied science, and I agree with that idea.

But what do we mean by 'science'? How is science different from common sense or popular belief? How do researchers 'do' science? How do courts and lawmakers apply criminological findings to everyday social and political issues?

"Finally, what are the results of all this thinking? Does the application of criminological research work well or badly in the real world?" Again, I gave two examples—one, an apparent success and the other, an apparent failure.

"In this course, you'll come to understand why criminology, at its best, is a social science. At its most useful, it helps governments make good laws and enforce them in wise ways. You'll also come to understand the limits of our field. The reasons we can't apply every finding of criminological research to the real world. I'll also touch on the consequences of making mistakes when we apply criminological research.

"Now, normally, I'd have you write a short essay, 500 words, about what I've been telling you today. We'll do that at our next lecture, on Thursday, so be sure to bring your laptop or paper and pens. Meanwhile, please do the required reading before Thursday's lecture. I'll see you back here in about 46 hours."

The students had liked my lecture, and I got a small round of applause. A majority would be back on Thursday for my next lecture. A small percentage would drop the course. Too much reading, too much writing, too boring, whatever. Not enough like *CSI* or other TV depictions of criminology. No mention of criminal profiling, for example.

Still, my lecture had gone better than expected. As I returned to my office, I felt excited and relieved. I was fully awake, ready for the next installment of Day One at the Truth Factory.

Back at my desk, I took time to review my schedule for the fall term. I'd teach my undergrad Introduction to Criminology course every Tuesday and Thursday, from ten until noon. My graduate seminar on theories of rage and guilt would meet on Wednesdays, also from ten to noon. There'd be regularly scheduled faculty meetings on the last Thursday of every month, from four to six. Otherwise, my time was unscheduled, unpredictable.

This Thursday, the first of the term, there'd be a social mixer—faculty and graduate students—from four to six. My secretary had already ordered the food and drinks, and I looked forward to seeing everyone. To doing an inventory of 'my people.'

After a quick lunch, I was back at my desk when Altan Asker popped his head in the door. Altan was my new teaching assistant, a doctoral student from Turkey.

Before today, I'd only met Altan briefly, once or twice. I'd been out of town for the summer while he was settling into his new life in Toronto. We'd never really had a conversation. But the Graduate Director had chosen him as my TA. Altan had the qualifications and needed the job. Before coming to Toronto, he'd written a Master's thesis about honour killings in his home country. And remember, I study the role of rage in crimes of violence. Since honour killings are crimes of violence, there's a natural fit with Altan's interests.

In fact, Altan had come all the way from Turkey to work with me. I'd get to know him well. But first, I needed to break the ice.

"We haven't gotten acquainted yet," I said. "Can you stay for a short conversation?"

He approached my desk, nervous but eager, then held out his right hand. I shook it, firmly and enthusiastically.

Altan was much shorter than me, maybe a head shorter. A small, delicate-looking young man with Mediterranean features and a Mediterranean complexion.

"Thanks for making the time," I said. "How are you settling in?"

"Oh, fine, thank you," he said cheerily. "What happened to your head, Professor?"

"Nothing dramatic, I assure you. A small argument between me and a piece of furniture."

Contrary to what I'd expected, Altan wasn't shy. Not at all. In fact, he opened the conversation with what I learned was one of his favourite gambits. "Professor, you may be interested to know I was named after a famous Turkish warrior of the 15th century. I forget his real name, but the troops nicknamed him Altan Asker. Out of respect for his bravery and cunning. The name in Turkish means 'Red Dawn'—that's Altan—and 'Soldier'—that's Asker. So, I am a soldier who attacks at the break of dawn. Enemies, beware." He grinned after he issued this absurd warning to absent enemies, and to me.

Pleased at having launched the discussion, he waited for my reply. He was testing me for suitability. Trying to find out if I was as crusty and self-absorbed as his former supervisor in Istanbul. Happily for Altan, I wasn't.

"That's good to know," I said. "You must feel proud of your famous name. From now on, every morning I will watch out for your attack."

After pausing a few seconds, I changed the topic. I didn't intend to discuss the reasons my own parents had named me 'Rachel.'

Instead, I told him my thoughts about teaching, my past interests, and present enthusiasms. He told me about growing up in Izmir, then studying in Istanbul, which he called a 'magical city.' We agreed to meet briefly once a month to discuss the introductory course. We'd also meet whenever he needed my advice. Or, as it would turn out, whenever I needed his.

3

The next couple of days were social days as well as work days. Another lecture was scheduled for Thursday morning, though few of the students would have done the assigned reading yet. That left me free to talk about anything I liked. And because I was thinking about Melanie Foster's death in Texas, I'd lecture about something Donny Foster had written. About the gang of car smugglers he'd studied.

At ten to ten on Thursday, I strolled three blocks to the lecture hall. When everyone had settled in, I cleared my throat into the microphone, then began. I had their attention.

"Hello again, everyone. I hope you're doing well. As you can see, I'm down to one bandage on my head. So please, no more gifts or get-well cards." I smiled to show I was joking.

"Today, I'm going to talk about organized crime and the problem of 'role strain.' This will put a little flesh on the theoretical bones I outlined Tuesday. You'll see that even lawbreakers follow rules—in their case, unwritten rules. But *their* rules are often like *our* rules—the rules of law-abiding people.

"You learned about 'role strain' in your introductory sociology course, but if you can't remember, I'll remind you. Role strain is 'the stress or strain an individual experiences when a single social role requires incompatible behaviours, expectations, or duties.' I showed them a slide with this definition printed in large, block letters.

"That's the formal definition. But now I'll say the same thing in simpler words. Role strain is the anxiety a person feels when she's expected to behave in two different ways at the same time. In a minute, I'll explain how that can happen.

"Now let me remind you of another term you'll remember from introductory sociology. That's the term 'institution.'

'Institutions' are the usual or normal patterns of beliefs, behaviours, and relationships that organize our social life. Again, let me say the same thing in simpler words. An institution is a set of beliefs and behaviours we associate with a particular setting." I put a new slide on the overhead, showing these new definitions.

"With this in mind, we can talk about family institutions, work institutions, educational institutions, and so on. 'Family institutions' are all the roles and expectations Canadians associate with family life in Canada today. 'Work institutions' are all the roles and expectations Canadians associate with work life in Canada today. In different societies, we often find different family and work institutions. Yes, institutions vary from one place to another. They also change over time. But this class will focus on the institutions we find in present-day Canada. Got the idea?"

I looked out over the room and saw lots of heads nodding. The heads that weren't nodding were focused on cell-phone screens. Those heads belonged to students who were checking their social media. I knew I couldn't hold their attention and didn't bother trying.

"Okay, let's take these two ideas, put them together, and see what happens. One thing social scientists know for certain is, you can't apply the rules of one institution to another. If you try, confusion or even conflict will result. That's because of role strain. And role strain occurs because different institutions have different goals. For example, families have what we might call 'expressive goals' while work institutions have 'instrumental or task-oriented goals.'

"Think about families for a moment. Members of a family are tied together by feelings of love and attachment. Without those feelings, a family falls apart. It's just a collection of strangers who live in the same household. Are you still with me?"

Hundreds of students nodded their heads in agreement, while others looked confused. Still on a mental vacation, the lucky dogs.

"Okay, here's a question to consider. If families have expressive goals, what goals do work institutions have?" Anyone who'd been listening at all could easily answer this question.

Dozens of hands shot into the air.

"Okay," I said, picking a student at random. "What's the answer?"

A tall, gawky eighteen-year-old strode to the nearest ground-floor microphone and boomed out his answer. "Work institutions have instrumental goals, Professor," His words echoed off the hundred-foot-high domed ceiling. "But I have a question for you," he said. "Does that mean no one in a work institution feels attached by emotion? Because I'm pretty sure, from my own experience, that isn't correct."

"Thank you for that. You're right," I said. "In every workplace, some people feel emotionally attached to their workmates. At the same time, in every family, some members—especially the parents—have instrumental goals. They have to earn money, do the housework, and care for the children. So, when I talk about the difference between families and workplaces, and between expressive and instrumental goals, I'm talking about *degrees* of difference. Each institution stresses one goal over the other."

Satisfied with my answer, the student smiled and moved self-consciously back to his seat.

"Let me expand on this. A business that pays no attention to bringing in customers and satisfying them will go bankrupt. It will go belly-up even if everyone in the entire company loves everyone else. A business needs customers and profits: that's its supreme goal. Its reason for existing. Its means of survival."

"Now, you may wonder what this has to do with crime and criminology. So, I'll tell you." I paused and looked around the room once again. Students sat poised to write down the answer.

"All organized crime groups—usually called 'gangs' and sometimes called 'crime families'—deal with this problem of role strain. With this clash of rules. In many gangs, the members are related by blood or marriage. This is common in Italian American crime families—so-called Mafia gangs—for example. But here's the problem. Because of these family connections, the leaders are under pressure to apply family rules to criminal business. The question for criminologists is, what happens then? How do gang leaders deal with the resulting role strain—the conflict between business values and family values? Business rules and family rules?"

The room was dead quiet. Most of the students hunched silently over their screens: laptops, iPads, cell phones. I've never stopped marveling at the variety of students: So many different sizes, shapes, and colours, though mostly dressed in jeans and sweatshirts. So many styles of self-presentation, so many facades. And so much engagement in being young.

By now, a few dozen students had started to scratch their heads. Had even started to catch up on social media, or so it appeared. I'd have to turn this around.

"I'll give you an example drawn from a book called *Conkie: A Life in Crime*," I told them. "That book was written by one of my colleagues, Professor Donny Foster. It's about a member of a crime family—originally from New Jersey, now operating in Texas. In case you're wondering, Professor Foster is an expert on smuggling and theft. He wrote the world's best-known textbook on theft and theft prevention and teaches a course on that at our university.

"Now, back to Professor Foster's earlier book about a life in crime. During his teen years, Conkie Rovino had suffered a brain injury in a fight with another neighbourhood gang. He'd been conked on the head with a two-by-four. That put him in a coma for three whole months. When Conkie emerged from the coma, he was a whole new man. Not better, just changed. He couldn't think clearly. He wasn't fast on his feet anymore and had wild mood swings. He also had a violent streak that exploded at unexpected moments.

"Yet the Devlin Crew continued to treat Conkie like a full member of the gang. Of course, they couldn't trust him with complicated business. But the boss kept him around because Conkie could still do a *few* things. After all, Conkie was still a member of Jonny Devlin's family. His biological family. And in this culture, you have to honour family ties whenever you can.

"Here's a quote from the book. The author asks Jonny Devlin, the gang leader, why he keeps Conkie around. Here's what Devlin says: 'Conkie is a great guy, and he can be funny as hell sometimes. We have lots of laughs together. Plus, he's family, and you have to help out family members when you can. Sometimes Conkie is a pain in the butt and I think about getting rid of him. But Conkie is just being Conkie, so I let it go. Of course, I'd never let him get close to anything important. He wouldn't keep his mouth shut and that's a big problem in our business: flapping lips. As long as Conkie doesn't know anything worth repeating, I never worry about Conkie at all.'

"Despite criticisms of the book, *Conkie: A Life in Crime* remains a central work in the study of organized crime. It reminds us of the shadowy line between ordinary lives and criminal lives.

"Now, I'd like you to answer a question in a short essay of about 500 words. We'll discuss the question for fifteen minutes, then you'll write the essay and turn it in online to Questor. We're going to write a lot of short essays in this class, so always remember to bring a pen or your computer. If you forget your laptop, write your essay on paper and hand it to my TA, Altan Asker, as you leave. That's Altan over there, at the side of the hall."

I pointed at Altan and he waved to everyone.

"Here's the question I want you to consider," I said. "'What are two or three ways a gang leader might handle the blurring of family and business roles in his crime family?'"

Pens scratched paper. Keyboards clacked.

"Let's talk for fifteen minutes," I told them. "Then you'll write your essay. Who's first?"

Fifty hands shot up. One especially eager student in the front row was up out of her seat.

"I love the energy," I told them, smiling. "Who would've guessed this topic would get such a reaction?"

At last, I nodded at the keen front-row student. "Okay, you have the floor. Use the mic so everyone can hear."

She stepped to the nearest microphone, stood tall, and spoke loudly. Her voice filled the room. But some students still couldn't hear her clearly, so she spoke even louder. Her words bounced off the high ceiling. After she'd finished, a forest of hands went up again. There were more of them now, eager to challenge or modify what she had said.

The discussion ran hot for fifteen minutes. I let it continue until the room buzzed too loudly, then called time.

"Settle down," I said. "Now write a 500-word answer to the question I posed. As I said, use the Questor app you were told to download. That was in your course syllabus, which, of course, you read carefully this week. Grab a few pieces of paper if you forgot your laptop, or didn't download Questor. When you're done, you can leave. Again, if your essay is on paper, hand it to Altan at the main door."

I pointed to the door I meant, since there were twelve doors in and out of Cudney Hall. And in case you don't know, Questor is a mechanized essay-grading program powered by artificial intelligence. It has done away with the need for human graders, and even teaching assistants. Surprisingly, it does as good as job as a slightly below-average human grader.

"I'll see you again next Tuesday. And please, stay up to date on your assignments. You should read the assigned chapter before my next lecture. See you here on Tuesday."

I walked back to my office thinking about my new book. When I got there, I immediately started making notes and finding references. The next time I looked up, an hour had passed.

Someone was knocking at my office door. The door opened and Altan popped his head in. "Paper essays are at the Grading Lab," he said. "The grading machine broke down—apparently, that happens once a month, on average—but we'll have the results by three. We never did things this way at Istanbul University, you know."

"Yes, and until a few years ago, we didn't do them this way here either. But that's the way Hummingbird wants it," I said. I saw no point discussing this any further. I was stuck with the new arrangement, and so was he.

I haven't mentioned Hummingbird before, have I? The sprawling conglomerate Hummingbird Industries has a 99-year lease on our university. In a new initiative to raise funds, the Premier of Ontario had leased Strachan University to Hummingbird Industries six years ago.

Unfortunately, Hummingbird wasn't interested in academics, only profit. Within mere weeks of completing the deal,

Hummingbird had cut down century-old trees and turned parts of the campus into rental property. They'd cut many of the humanities and social sciences, and trimmed century-old departments. They'd also tripled tuition fees. On the plus side, they'd made new hires in applied research, including criminology. My School got much bigger. On the other hand, tenure wasn't as secure as it used to be. All of this changed my job as boss of the School of Criminology, to be sure.

Today, Strachan's funds came largely from gifts, bequests, and donations. School directors like me had to raise money endlessly. And though I occupied an office in the Hummingbird Strachan School of Criminology, the building's name could change in an instant. The change would only require a donation of $100 million or more.

I'd quickly learned to play the new game: raise money, protect tenure, keep quiet.

4

As I said, Hummingbird had grown our applied science schools dramatically. That's where the money was, they figured. My School of Criminology had grown from twenty-five to seventy-five faculty members in only two years. Likewise, our graduate program had grown from sixty to six hundred students, of whom one hundred were in the doctoral program.

Under my direction, the School had added nearly countless unfamiliar faces and unsocialized minds. And because of our newly swollen size, we had to hold social events in the large dining room of the Faculty Club.

You can probably imagine the noise at one of these huge get-togethers. For most of the two hours, the sound level was deafening. You simply couldn't hold a serious conversation, though maybe that was for the better. Mainly, people came to smile, say hello, shake hands, scope out the newcomers, eat the hors d'oeuvres, and drink the Ontario wine.

As tonight's host, I made sure to circulate and mix. But for my own sanity, I had to slip outside two or three times every hour for a taste of fresh air and quiet. And I was still suffering slight headaches from my head injury two days earlier.

Naturally, Donny—always sociable—was at the event, lecturing a large circle of graduate students. Nearly three times as many female than male graduate students had gathered around him, including two doctoral students I knew well, Maribeth and Lena. Donny was in his element, sipping wine, munching crudités, and telling jokes. He was a ball of fire. When he talked about things he loved, he talked fast, spurting words like machine-gun bullets. With so much fascinating stuff to reveal, he couldn't slow down.

Donny seemed to like our students, and for the most part, they liked him back. I envied his ease and popularity. Although, when Donny put his arm around Maribeth's shoulder, I saw her flinch and pull away. A few minutes later, he did the same to Lena and she also pulled away, visibly uncomfortable. She and Maribeth may have thought he was too handsy. I saw them exchange glances and figured they'd chat about this later, in private. I wished I'd be there to hear what they said.

I moved a little closer to the group, to hear (and watch) what was going on.

My TA, Altan, showed up, said hello, and asked me what he'd missed. He'd been busy finishing a paper. I shouted, "You haven't missed anything. Grab something to eat before the food's gone. Oh, and in case you haven't met them, this is Lena and Maribeth. Lena's in second doctoral year, Maribeth's in third."

Altan smiled and shook their hands.

"You've missed important words of wisdom," Donny said to him. He knew Altan from the research methods course, which had met the day before. "I was telling everyone how to succeed in criminology."

"You're right, Professor, that is important. What do I need to know?"

"It's really simple. Just seize every opportunity. Go to every seminar, visiting lecture, and conference you can. Apply for every grant or scholarship. Most of all, get invited places. Let everyone know you're alive—breathing, thinking, and advancing criminology. That's always been my philosophy."

"Sounds like good advice, Professor. I'll follow it whenever I can."

Maribeth nodded in agreement. "I've been doing that for the last two years, and it isn't easy. But usually—maybe, one time in three—it pays off. And I always learn something when I get out there and try new things." Lena listened carefully, nodding her support.

Other faculty members gathered in knots of three or four, surrounded by only a few graduate students. These colleagues were less confident and perhaps less popular than Donny. But they all felt solidly at home with one another.

Now, try to imagine the next day, when the Faculty of Arts and Sciences held *its* first-of-the-year faculty meet-and-greet. Imagine a much larger setting—the Hummingbird House Main Dining Room—with ten times as many people crowded into it. That vast, high-ceilinged room with heraldry and Old English inscriptions on the walls. Lanterns hung down on twenty-foot wires, the room gleaming with burnished wood panels. Yes, imagine that.

And try to picture the countless unfamiliar faces. The chaotic setting. And the ear-splitting noise, punctuated by short speeches from the President, the Dean of Graduate Studies, and the Director of Fundraising. Plus, jazz in the background, provided by a group from the nearly-defunct School of Music. And the same snacks as those at Criminology's meet-and-greet the day before, but in more lavish quantities.

At the break for speeches, the President reminded us of our illustrious history. He urged us to continue doing great things but to enjoy ourselves today. The Dean cordially welcomed us back for another year of successful teaching and research. The Director of Fundraising reminded us that adding to knowledge was our passion, but fundraising was our responsibility. This year would be Strachan's greatest year ever, if we each did our own little part.

I saw some people who looked familiar. I even knew a few of them by name. I waved to James somebody, from the math department. I had met him at last year's meet-and-greet. Farther away, I could see people I knew from the Athletic Centre, where I usually went to exercise.

At a snack table off to one side, I nearly collided with Jackie Taylor, a colleague from the old English Department, now part of the Department of Languages. She'd been at Strachan far longer than me. "How are you, Jackie?" I shouted over the din, as we put little snacks on little dishes. "Did you have a good summer?"

"It was great, very productive," she may have said. "We went to London for two weeks. The rest of the time, I stayed home and wrote. How about you?"

I tried to tell her about my own summer but saw it would be fruitless, given the noise. This was no place for a conversation. So, we smiled and made 'Phone Me' signs with our hands.

Inching my way back to a knot of criminologists in the

southwest corner, I literally bumped into Alice Turner, Chair of the Classics Department. We knew each other from countless administrative meetings and Christmas parties. Alice was the same age as me and quite a wit. I loved chatting with her. We lunched together once or twice every year, to renew our friendship. But after several futile attempts, we gave up trying to communicate and promised to phone each other next week. Again, with hand signals.

Finally, back in the 'criminology corner,' I found Donny surrounded by a knot of recent hires I hardly knew myself. He was lecturing them about the art of grantsmanship. Specifically, how he had gotten his last big grant to do gang research in Texas.

"The trick there was highlighting the importance of my research for other fields outside criminology. For commerce and economics, for instance. Also, for other countries. You know, countries in the European Union that receive a lot of smuggled cars from North America."

"That's a great idea, Donny," one of the listeners said. "But what if your research doesn't apply so easily across fields, or across societies. I'm studying the criminal behaviour of homeless people in downtown Toronto. How should I refocus my research to get bigger grants?"

"That's a tough one," Donny shouted, sympathetically. "Let's talk about that next week. You may have to build a cross-national comparison into your work. For example, compare a sample of homeless people in Toronto with homeless people in London or Amsterdam or Berlin."

I joined the group, smiled at Donny, and listened to what he was saying. The junior colleagues were following his words with rapt attention. They knew their own success at grant-getting—their own success in academe—would require them to master what he was saying. And Donny made it sound easy. That was just his way of letting them know the process was hard. Certainly, time-consuming.

Shortly after, I excused myself and slipped out for a breath of air. In the gathering darkness, I nearly bumped into the Dean of Arts. She was chatting with the Dean of Medicine, who I knew slightly, and the Dean of Engineering, who I knew a little better from visits to the athletic centre.

"Rachel, do you know everyone?" my own Dean asked. She introduced me to the other Deans, then said, "Excuse me, fellas, I have to talk to Rachel for a moment." She led me to a spot fifteen metres away and started talking.

"What happened to your head?"

"Just a small accident a few days ago," I told her. "Nothing important."

"Did you have a good vacation?"

"Yes, very pleasant. Got out of town for a few weeks, but mainly stayed around and wrote. The kind of vacation I like best," I said. "What about you?"

"Mine was good too. I went to a destination wedding in Sardinia. What a weird place! And I visited family members in Minnesota. Otherwise, I stayed at our cottage in Muskoka and did as little work as possible for two whole weeks. Then, back to the grind. But listen, I have to talk to you about something serious. Can you meet me on Monday at nine? I've already asked your secretary to put it in your datebook."

"Well, if it's in the book, I'll be there, Dean. What's the meeting about?

"It's about your colleague, Donny Foster. I'm going to need your help. Possibly, for an extended period. But I can't go into it now. We'll talk about it on Monday. Okay?"

"You bet. Are you enjoying the party?"

"I'm getting a headache, to tell you the truth. I'll stay for another fifteen minutes, then head home. I desperately need some down time."

"Me too," I said. "In fact, I'm going to take off now." I shook her hand, went back inside for my coat and briefcase, then headed to my car. It was nearly seven-thirty when I got home.

5

The weekend passed quickly, in blessed quiet. My son Josh was out of the house most of the time, visiting his new girlfriend. I did a little work on the new book and prepared for next week's classes. When Monday rolled around, I was ready for that meeting with the Dean, my first of the day.

When I entered the Dean's office, an unfamiliar man stood up. His shoes shone like glass. His suit was charcoal gray and sharply pressed, his tie simple, restrained, expensive. A lawyer, I thought immediately. He had a firm handshake—the handshake of a purposeful, confident man. A guy who played squash on the weekends. Maybe even soccer. In shorts, even on chilly days. It was the handshake of a man who knew the game of life, played it hard, and usually won.

"Rachel," the Dean said. "This is Jason Cook from the university's law firm. He'll sit in with us today, to keep everything on track."

I knew better. Sure, he was the university's lawyer. But he was really Hummingbird's lawyer, with their interests at heart.

"Nice to meet you," I said, smiling. I shook his hand.

The Dean began talking about an end-of-term party I'd thrown last year, the spicy shrimp salad I'd made, how her husband had loved it. The usual niceties. I smiled, as though delighted. "And your kids," she asked. "How are they?"

"They're good," I told her. "My daughter Ellie's got a nice boyfriend and lives downtown, so I don't see her as often as I'd like. My son has a new girlfriend so he's out a lot of the time. Though, he's been stuck on LSAT prep for weeks. Wants to be in the top five percent when he takes the test in January."

The Dean nodded. "I remember when my daughter Vanessa did the same. Wore herself down to a nub worrying about it." She smiled, shaking her head. "But it all worked out in the end."

I nodded. Then, against the Dean's unspoken wish for nothing but cheer, I added, "I'll be soooo glad when it's over." We smiled at each other in silent accord. Parenting teens was no walk in the park. We certainly agreed on that. Happily, Hummingbird Industries had no view on this topic.

With the pleasantries over, the Dean leaned towards me and spoke earnestly. "I need your help with something serious. The Provost is very upset. Very worried about Donny Foster. So that means trouble for you and me."

I sat up straighter. "What about Donny Foster?"

"There's a problem with bringing him back as a full-time faculty member. The Provost is insistent. He says Foster may have broken an ethics agreement. There's talk he may be socially involved with criminals. He may have even brought the university into disrepute. We need to know more before we bring him back to full-time status."

The lawyer spoke next, his voice flat and clear. As though addressing a courtroom. "You probably know Professor Foster was freed of the charges that he had murdered his wife. The jury was deadlocked, and the state decided not to retry the case. That's a matter of public record. True, they could always reopen the case, but that rarely happens. Still, there are questions we have to answer. Foster's been involved with people and activities we don't like. We need to know if he's a risk to the university. A risk to our reputation.

"The Provost thinks Professor Foster may have also violated the terms of an ethics agreement he signed before heading off to Texas. Professor Foster may have been associating with criminals beyond what his research required. As well, there are issues of personal enrichment to consider. And the possibility he brought the university into disrepute.

"We need assurance on all these matters. We need to know Professor Foster won't pose problems for us if he returns to full-time status. That he won't create problems for our students, staff, or faculty. That he hasn't crossed the line in his relations with the gangsters he studies and, especially, with Jonny Devlin. I've heard a few researchers have done that recently, including a researcher who's going to guest lecture at the School of Criminology in October. Janice Dent, isn't that her name?" he asked, looking at me.

"That's Julia Dent, and I don't think she's committed any crimes," I told him. "It's true some criminologists think she's crossed ethical lines. But most of us don't agree. Where to draw the line in ethnographic research is still an open question."

The lawyer nodded, acknowledging my words.

"Most of all, we need to know the university's reputation is safe," he continued, returning to his earlier theme. "That's why we need another look at Professor Foster before ending his probationary status. The Dean and I are meeting Professor Foster today at ten. That will be the first of what may turn into many interviews. We need to feel sure we can defend him in public, if we have to."

By now, the real meeting had begun, and only minutes in, I had to race to keep up.

For the first time that morning, I looked carefully at the Dean. She was in her formal regalia. Unlike me, casually dressed as usual, the Dean was dressed in an expensive, navy-blue suit. Also, in many items of jewelry I guessed were expensive. On one hand, a gold band and a diamond ring, and on the other, a chunky gold and turquoise ring. This was today's chosen costume. Props for performing her role as Dean of Arts at Strachan University.

"You know Professor Foster better than we do, Professor Tile, and that's why the Dean asked you here today," the lawyer said, quite unexpectedly.

"And since you were a member of the Tri-Council Committee on Ethics, we need you to advise us on the ethics of Professor Foster's research. We've been getting questions about research ethics from the Governing Board and the Provost. Yes, Professor Foster's project got approval from the Research Ethics Board over a year ago. But now, even the head of REB wants another look at the project.

"Of course, Professor Foster has tenure. He can't be removed without cause. We can still do it, if push comes to shove. But if we're too aggressive, Professor Foster may bring in his own lawyers, even go to the media. And that's where you come in. As his immediate supervisor, you can tread lightly. You can question him in a collegial way and tell us what you think.

"So, we want you to find out what you can about his recent research. Focus on ethical issues. And if you can, take another look at his possible involvement in Melanie Foster's death. Then, give us the information we need to make the best possible decision."

I listened, my fingers stiffening around the armrests of my chair. I knew this dance. It was always about control—or else money. I was being asked to investigate a colleague I'd worked with for years. The Dean wanted me to gather explosive information and do so without causing an explosion. I was being asked to spy, and that didn't feel right. But I understood the university's concern about safety and reputation.

"I'm confused," I said, looking directly at the lawyer. "If there wasn't enough evidence to convict him, why was Professor Foster brought to trial? And if the jury decided the evidence was inadequate, why isn't that good enough for the university? Why don't we just let him resume his career. On the other hand, if we have serious doubts, why did we let him come back on probation?"

"Those are all good questions, Professor Tile. You'd be right to conclude that the Provost, and Hummingbird Industries, are uncertain about the best course of action. On the one hand, the murder trial cast a dark shadow over Professor Foster and, indirectly, over our university. On the other hand, Professor Foster is an asset, an eminent scholar with tenure. He brings in a lot of grant money and trains many of our top graduate students—or so I've been told. We're caught in a dilemma. So, we need more information, and your advice will be crucial."

The Dean was firm too. "We need you to learn more about what's happened. But keep it casual. You know Professor Foster better than anyone else at Strachan. We need to know if he'll cause any trouble if we bring him back."

I nodded, showing I understood the stakes. If Donny was guilty of criminal violence, the university could be sued for keeping him on. For failing to provide a safe environment for students and staff. But if we tried to get rid of him and he made a fuss, it could cost us lots of money and bad publicity. If he went to the press, there'd be no end of trouble. I was the safe choice to handle this problem. The only one who could tread lightly, ask the right questions, and keep it all under wraps.

I was also expendable, if push came to shove. I was completely aware of that too.

What would happen if I refused, I wondered for a split second. Certainly, I'd lose my easy rapport with the Dean. When budget time rolled around next spring, I wouldn't get all the money my School needed. No, it would be risky to refuse the Dean's request. On the other hand, I couldn't guess how risky it might become if I said yes. Then, the Dean laid it out as clearly as possible.

"You'll have a lot on the line," she reminded me, unnecessarily. "If Professor Foster embarrasses the university, your School will take the hit. Less funding, fewer hires, fewer graduate student applications. You can imagine the effect."

The Dean was right. It was my job to protect the School of Criminology. With seventy-five full-time faculty members, fifteen staff, and two thousand student majors, the School was a multimillion-dollar operation. We'd become huge, one of the largest criminology schools in the world. I didn't want to investigate Donny but couldn't refuse. I didn't know what I was getting into, but knew it wasn't good. I felt a tightness in my chest.

"I'll do it," I blurted out. "I don't believe Donny killed his wife. Or even committed any ethics violations. He's not that kind of person, and I've known him for years. But I'll find out what I can."

The Dean leaned back, relief written on her face. "Good. Now, here's the deal: I'll let you drop a course and a couple of committee assignments. And I'll give you $5,000 for research expenses, in case there are any. I'll want your final report by December 15—much earlier if possible. But this has to stay confidential. And we'll always talk about this in person. No emails or texts. Nothing in writing."

I showed the Dean my serious, no-nonsense look. "Please remember I'm not trained for this kind of thing. But I'll do my best. I'll complete the investigation before December 15 and provide the information you need. If I can." They really should have hired someone trained to investigate other people. But I understood their need to keep all this secret, in-house. And to have someone in-house to blame if this went sideways.

The lawyer handed me a business card. It was heavy, embossed. I could feel the weight of it. The card was a symbol of money, power, connections.

"Get in touch if you need anything," he said. "Don't hesitate to reach out if you have questions."

"Rachel, I'd like you to stay around for our interview with Donny, immediately after this meeting. I've cleared the time with your secretary. So please stay for another hour, okay?"

"Of course, Dean."

She opened the door, and Donny came in from the outer office. He'd obviously been waiting for his own discussion with the Dean. As he entered, the lawyer stood to introduce himself. "I'm one of the university's lawyers," he said. "Don't mind me, I'm just here to listen."

He stuck out a hand. Donny shifted a coffee cup to his left hand, so he could shake the lawyer's right one.

"Professor Foster, thank you for coming in," the Dean said. "Professor Tile is here as the Director of your School, and your colleague. I'll get right to the point. And if you don't mind, I'll call you by your first name. Is that okay?"

Donny nodded and the Dean continued.

"We've been concerned about you. When you went on trial in Texas, the university worried about what might happen. So, we're glad you're here, safe and sound. But before we can put you back on full-time status, we need answers."

Donny nodded again. He'd probably guessed this was going to happen.

The lawyer spoke next, listing concerns and looking mainly at the Dean. "The Provost has reminded me that, on his leave application, Professor Foster agreed to five items that are now in question. They were as follows, paraphrasing the agreement. Professor Foster promised not to endanger members of the university, not to bring the university or its members into disrepute, and not to enrich himself through activities related to his research. As well, he promised to complete a set of research goals named in the application. One item of special interest is a patentable measuring tool named the Foster Score, also known as the D-Algorithm. Earnings from the patented instrument are to go, in part, to the university."

Promises had been made, sure. The university had special concerns about the Foster Score. But what had he completed? What was in progress? That's what the lawyer, the Provost, and the board wanted to know. Show me the money!

The Dean leaned in, wanting to soften the question. "That's right, we need to know how well you fulfilled the promises you made in your ethics agreement. But before that, please tell us a little about yourself. Also, about your work at this university. I know you've been here, doing important work, for many years. But I've only been at Strachan for two years, so please fill me in."

The Dean had spent most of her twenty-year career at the University of Pennsylvania, so she didn't know a lot of our faculty yet. She was also trying to draw Donny out. To see how he presented himself to a relative stranger. How he might present himself in court, if push came to shove.

Donny turned on the charm. "That's a big order, Dean," he said. "But I'll tell you what I can." He paused and loosened his tie. He was preparing himself for a long performance.

6

This wouldn't be hard, I thought. Donny loved talking about himself. He had so much to say. After clearing his throat, he started the monologue.

"I was born in Newark, New Jersey. My old man was an accountant, nothing special. My mother worked as a salesclerk at Saks in Newark. Besides me, they had two daughters. One of them died young. The other vanished from my life a long time ago.

"I went to the local high school, then to City College in New York. My folks never went to college, but I won all the big prizes there. The *real* ones. I went into criminology and decided to continue—to get my PhD at SUNY-Albany. Some say it's the best criminology school in the country. Maybe the world. Am I going on too long with this personal stuff?" he asked the Dean.

Looking up from her desk, she gave him a smile. "No, you're doing fine," she said.

So Donny kept on, full speed ahead.

"As I say, I went to Albany and got my doctorate. I was ready to leave when I met Melanie. She was studying in the English Department. But she was six years behind me, so I had to wait for her. We moved in together in '93. I worked two or three jobs to support us while she wrapped up her doctoral research."

He stopped for a breath. The Dean smiled, the lawyer checked something on his phone and scribbled a few notes. I sat quietly, glad to just listen.

"When Melanie was nearly finished, we started looking for jobs together. After a lot of interviews, I landed a tenure-track position here in criminology and Melanie landed one in English. We never left. I'm still here. Melanie taught here until last year, when she died. I'm heartbroken, of course. You understand that. But life goes on."

He stopped to dab his eyes with a polka-dot handkerchief he'd pulled out of his jacket pocket.

"Thank you, Donny. We're sorry for your loss," the Dean said. "Now, please tell us about your work at this university."

Donny was visibly starting to weary. His shoulders had slumped, and he kept squirming around in the chair. Probably, trying to find a comfortable way to sit in this unfamiliar piece of furniture. One of those hard-backed captain chairs in black-enameled wood the university seemed to possess in vast quantities. The chair had a Hummingbird Industries insignia on the backrest.

Donny smiled at her and shook his head. "It'd take too long to go through all of it. But my first big thing was a book called *Conkie: The Life of a Criminal.* It was about a car thief from New Jersey, part of the Devlin Crew. He got the nickname Conkie after a head injury when he was fifteen."

He paused again to catch his breath. The Dean nodded. The lawyer kept taking notes.

"I've written a lot since then. Articles, books, other things academics write. I've also done lots of high-quality teaching, thesis advising, and committee work. In the last few years, I've been working with AI, building a program to predict the behaviour of smugglers. I want to know where they'll move their stolen cars. If you need a complete resume, I'll give you one.

"But back to the personal side, Melanie and I raised two kids. Now, they're grown up. Our daughter's a second-grade teacher. Her husband's in IT. They've got a two-year-old. Our son, well, he's different. Could've been a doctor or lawyer, he's that smart. Instead, he draws cartoons—graphic novels, he calls them. He also drives for Uber. I don't want to say much more about them."

He patted his chest, then looked up. The Dean was still watching, still patient. The lawyer scribbled something in his daybook.

"Over the years, Melanie and I traveled, made friends. Enjoyed life. If you want more information about our time together, you could talk to Melanie's best friend in the Language Department. Jackie Taylor."

I was surprised to hear Jackie was a close friend of the Fosters. She'd never mentioned Melanie when we'd talked together.

The Dean cleared her throat. "What was Melanie working on during her most recent research leave?"

Donny hesitated. "She was writing a book about a group of writers from New England, early 20th century. They called themselves the 'Furies,' though I don't know why. Radical suffragettes, I think. Feminists, for sure."

He stopped, took a sip of his coffee, and patted his chest again.

"They didn't leave much written work, the Furies. Diaries, letters, that sort of thing. Their material was archived in Texas and that's one reason Melanie wanted to come to Austin. To see the archive."

The Dean nodded, probably writing down 'The Furies,' in case she needed to follow up.

Donny put his coffee down on the floor and stood to remove his jacket, hanging it on the back of his chair. For a moment, his vest chains glinted like comets, reflecting sunlight into the Dean's eyes. She shaded her eyes, then turned away. Looking out the window, she may have seen the huge chestnut tree swaying.

For another five minutes, he returned to talking about his own research. How he'd studied gangs since he was a grad student, before he'd shifted his focus to international car smuggling. The Dean didn't rush him. The lawyer kept noting things down.

"Fifteen years ago, I began studying the Devlin Crew in New Jersey. Then, they moved down to Texas and now they're centred in Houston. Jonny Devlin, their leader, agreed to cooperate with my new research project, so I decided to spend my sabbatical in Houston interviewing his people."

The Dean asked if Donny needed a washroom break or wanted to finish his account another day. He shook his head. A delay wasn't necessary, he said. He didn't want to stop now.

"I presented my research plan to the Research Ethics Board. Everything was fine, they said. They approved my plan. I also got a research grant from SSHRC. Medium-sized, $180,000."

The Dean's attention was starting to drift, but Donny kept talking.

"In July 2023, I moved to Austin. Melanie stayed behind to teach a graduate seminar. Six months later, when she'd finished her teaching, she came down to Austin. A week after that, we drove to Houston. After spending some time there, Melanie was going to drive to New Orleans to meet her friend, Jackie. But she never got there. Two days after she left Houston, I got a call from Jackie. She wondered if Melanie had changed her mind. I hadn't heard from Melanie but wasn't worried. I figured she was busy doing tourist stuff somewhere along the way."

He stopped and took another sip of cold coffee. Coffee that had probably gone cold since he entered the meeting. Waiting for him to resume, the Dean shuffled papers on her desk. The lawyer jotted down more notes in his daybook.

Donny swabbed his face with the polka-dot hanky, seemingly determined to continue.

"After hours of trying Melanie's number, I called the cops. I had to tell them Melanie was missing. I described her and told them about her travel plans. Two days later, they still hadn't found her. They'd searched all along the route Melanie was supposed to take. East along Route I-10—the direct route to New Orleans. Sure, people said it was a boring drive, but safe and fast.

"Instead, and I'll never understand why, she'd taken the I-45. That's the highway running south from Houston to Galveston. An alternate route to New Orleans, the police said. But longer and not so safe. The countryside around I-45 is rough, dangerous. You don't want to be there, that's what people were telling me. But that's where they found Melanie's body. In a place they call the Texas Killing Fields. She shouldn't have taken that route—people warned her against it—but that's what she did. And she got killed there."

I could see Donny was tired but still wanted to finish. His cheeks were sagging, as if all his face muscles had suddenly gone on strike. His eyelids fluttered several times, and he shook his head from side to side, maybe to get more blood into his brain.

"They sent me photos, asking if I could identify her. But the body they'd found was all chewed up. My first reaction was: No, this can't be my wife. There was no face left. Wild dogs, the police said. I didn't want to believe it. I couldn't believe it, so I told them no, it wasn't Melanie. Keep looking. She's got to be alive, on her way to New Orleans. Maybe she's taken a detour. But they kept pressing me. A day later, I broke down and admitted it was her. I knew from the tattoo on her left hip."

The Dean's eyes softened. Was that pity or exhaustion?

"The lie I'd told, about those photos, made the police think I'd had a hand in Melanie's death. So they started investigating me. Then they found out I'd had a visitor in Austin before Melanie got there. Someone I'd known for a long time. And that's when they arrested me for murder. I got the best lawyer in Texas and was out on bail in a few days. A month later, the trial began."

The Dean nodded, waiting for the wind-up. For my part, I'd started thinking about his 'best lawyer' remark. Could he really have paid a top lawyer, someone who might cost hundreds of thousands of dollars?

"Once it got going, the trial was quick. Three weeks—short for a murder trial. But there was no evidence, no motive, nothing. Naturally, the jury found me not guilty."

What Donny had just said was not true. He hadn't been found 'not guilty.' The jury had been deadlocked and no verdict was rendered, either for Donny or against him. I'd be sure to raise this with the Dean in our discussions later.

Meanwhile, Donny had stopped talking and the room was still. Donny let out a breath—whether a sigh of anguish or relief, I couldn't tell. Then he started again.

"For weeks, the prosecutors asked about my marriage. Also, about my relationship to the Devlin Crew and other gangs in the Houston area. They pressed me for information I'd collected about these gangs, but I refused to give them any. I insisted on protecting my research sources. As a researcher I have an ethical duty of confidentiality. I have to protect my information from unauthorized use. All researchers know you have to do that, to build trust with the people you're studying. It's essential. So, I refused, and, in the end, the police stopped asking."

I was familiar with all these ideas, even with the language, having helped draft this policy for the Tri-Council Committee on Research Ethics. Canadian courts hadn't challenged the policy, not yet anyway. I didn't know if they'd challenged it in the US yet. The point is, Donny was treating the policy as law and so, it seemed, were the police.

"After deliberating for three hours, the jury found me not guilty. I was released and came right back to Toronto. Melanie's remains had been buried here. I wanted to start teaching again. And writing. I wanted to start building a new life for myself. That's the whole story, Dean. I'm grateful to you for helping me settle back here."

Again, Donny's claim that he'd been found 'not guilty.' We'd definitely have to discuss this after Donny left. The Dean thanked him and said she'd have more questions later.

The lawyer smiled and nodded. "No questions right now, Dean. I hope that, at our next meeting, we'll return to the issues I raised earlier. The ethics-related issues and what Professor Foster achieved during his sabbatical leave." The Dean nodded her agreement.

Donny stood up, shook our hands, and walked out. The lawyer left moments after.

When they'd both left, I told the Dean, "Donny said several times that he was found 'not guilty.' But that isn't true. No verdict was rendered. Strictly speaking, he was found neither guilty nor innocent."

"I know, Rachel. I picked up on that too. Let it ride for now. We'll ask about it at the next meeting, along with other stuff we didn't get to today."

I smiled, said goodbye to the Dean, and left.

7

It took three days for the trial transcript to arrive. The lawyer had a copy and said he was happy to provide it, so I can't explain why it took so long getting to me. Anyway, I brought the transcript home with plans to read it there.

As usual, Josh was out, and Ellie was downtown. I had a quick dinner—a bit of minestrone soup I'd cooked the previous weekend. Then I sat down in the living room to skim the seven-hundred-page document.

The house was blessedly quiet—just right for reading something dull. I live in peaceful North Toronto, roughly 10 kilometres due north of Strachan University, in one of those detached homes built for low-income workers a century ago. Now only mid-to-high-income professionals can afford them. Three bedrooms, three bathrooms, a small backyard, a small front lawn, a shared driveway, a parking pad. You've probably seen a thousand homes like mine. Maybe a million.

But it's my home and I love it. I've made it my own. It has wood floors, oriental carpets, modern art, a modern, open-concept kitchen, and lots of books. Books everywhere. The best part is, our neighbourhood is safe and quiet, and so is my home. Naturally, I spend as much time at home as I can. And that night, my home would help me get through the dull transcript of Donny Foster's murder trial.

If you've ever seen one, you'll know a trial transcript is nothing but Q&A. The quality of the story it tells depends on the skill of the lawyers involved: on their ability to ask interesting questions and provoke interesting answers.

On that score, the prosecuting attorney was awful while the defense attorney—Donny's lawyer—was great. Very flamboyant, provocative. And he knew how to rile up prosecution witnesses, especially if they were hostile police officers.

Just a few examples. At one point the prosecutor asked Donny, 'Why did your wife run off to New Orleans after just a few days in Houston? Wasn't it because you'd been arguing, and she couldn't take much more?'

To which Donny answered, 'Not at all. She'd always planned to meet her friend in New Orleans the next day.' The defense lawyer later called Jackie Taylor, who corroborated Donny's testimony without hesitating.

As another example, the prosecutor noted Melanie's body had been found in the Killing Fields? Had he, Donny, ever been there himself?

Donny replied, 'Yes, I've been there, once or twice. I'd always wanted to see the place. Every criminologist knows about the Killing Fields and lots have visited it, out of curiosity. It was just a coincidence Melanie's body turned up there. Or maybe the killer planted it there to frame me.' The prosecuting attorney had no way to challenge this answer.

Another instance was even more revealing. The prosecutor asked Donny 'Isn't it true you'd been having affairs with other women—two of them in Texas? And you wanted your wife dead so you could spend more time with these women?' The defense attorney objected, noting that no women had testified to having an affair with Donny, nor had he admitted to doing so.

The defense attorney admitted he'd been unable to produce one of the two women, Gina Wolff. He'd produced a second woman, Hannah Proctor, and she hadn't admitted to having an affair with Donny. 'I'm a graduate student at Briggs College and Professor Foster's research assistant,' she told the court. She admitted to no romantic or sexual connection with him.

Bottom line: the jury couldn't reach a verdict. Ten men and two women just couldn't agree, so the state let Donny go. Even the prosecutor said no one saw him kill his wife. He never confessed to killing her. There was no material evidence showing he'd killed her. No clear motive. The character witnesses, including Jackie Taylor and Donny's daughter Garet, swore he was a good man, that he and Melanie were devoted to each other. Twenty-five years married. These days, almost a record

And still, they had prosecuted him. At first, the police may have thought Donny and Melanie had secrets. Maybe debts. Affairs. Addictions. But they couldn't come up with anything solid. So, in the end, Donny walked out of there, not guilty. Also, not innocent.

By now, I was stretched out on the couch in the living room, half asleep. Boring documents have that effect, don't you find? Plus, my living room couch was so comfy. And I had soft classical music playing in the background—something by Telemann, I think. I'd need a coffee if I was going to spend any more time on that transcript.

But even in my semi-conscious state, I could see things didn't add up. Melanie's body had a distinctive tattoo on it. Yet Donny gave the police false info, then admitted he'd lied. Said it was emotional distress. Said he couldn't admit she was dead. Beyond that, he'd likely had occasional affairs. Just before Melanie went down there, he'd spent two weeks in Austin with another woman, Gina Wolff. She'd lived with him, in his rented house. It sounds like he was guilty of cheating on his wife. Maybe worse. Maybe he'd wanted his wife dead.

But then, why didn't the jury turn against him? I imagined lots of possibilities. Most likely, he'd charmed them. Well-dressed. Big name in criminology. High-priced lawyer. Said all the evidence was circumstantial. Affairs, maybe, but not murder. The lies about the body? Emotional distress. No real proof he did it.

After reading the transcript, I still didn't think Donny had killed his wife. But remember, I ran the School of Criminology. If—and this is a huge if—he *had* killed his wife, I couldn't have him continue teaching at my School. I had to find out for sure, if I could.

I re-read the transcript looking for things that didn't make sense. Gaps in evidence and logic. Points of attack. Most glaringly, I couldn't understand why Melanie had taken route I-45 to New Orleans, then ended up in the Killing Fields.

There were only a few reasons I could think of. One was that Melanie had been misinformed about the best route to New Orleans. I ruled that out almost immediately. Only an idiot would have made taken the wrong route. Any map would have shown Melanie the right way to go.

Another possibility was that she had thought this route would be scenic or interesting. But a short examination of sites around I-45 and Galveston, using Google Earth, ruled that out almost immediately. That whole patch of Texas was ugly and boring.

I could think of two other, more likely explanations. One is that someone kidnapped or ambushed Melanie, killed her, and took her body to the Killing Fields for burial. But who would have done that, and why? The prosecutors hadn't pursued this line of enquiry. Or maybe the police had investigated it without success. Likely, I'd have to contact one of the investigating officers, the prosecutor, or the defense lawyer to find out more. Oh, and I'd have to talk to that woman who'd visited Donny in Austin. Gina Wolff. She might know more about what was going on at the trial, at least from Donny's standpoint.

The other possibility is that Melanie had wanted to see the Killing Fields before heading to New Orleans. But what would she have wanted to see? And why would she have needed to see it before her holiday with Jackie Taylor? Again, the prosecutor had not followed this line of enquiry at the trial. Maybe Jackie knew the answer, so I made a point of asking her.

I might even have to visit Texas and view the Killing Fields myself, I thought. Not that I considered myself a trained investigator. But there was a huge hole in the evidence and I needed a way to fill it.

The next day, I was scheduled to meet my sister for lunch at a new restaurant near my home. But just after I'd arrived, she texted to say she couldn't make it. A business emergency—an old client who required immediate attention, that sort of thing. So I was stuck there all by myself.

Still, it was a pretty nice place to get stuck. The place, named Ferrari Trattoria, had distinctive furnishings. All the walls sported old photos of racing cars—Ferraris, Lamborghinis, Alfa Romeos, and the like. Also, pictures of the mustachioed men who'd driven these cars to victory some fifty or even a hundred years ago.

Like many buildings in North Toronto, this one had a long, checkered history. Part of a commercial block built in 1920, the space had housed first a gravestone maker, then a hardware store, then a clock repair shop. These were followed by a grocery store, a candy store, a convenience store, a Chinese restaurant, a barber shop, another Chinese restaurant, and today, an Italian restaurant. Some of these businesses had lasted only a year or two, others, several decades. But having seen the last four scruffy incarnations, I was delighted with the space's new use.

To my surprise, there were no other customers. Almost immediately, a pretty young server appeared at my table, interrupting my thoughts.

"I love this place. The décor is great," I said to her, smiling lazily. "Do you own it?"

"No, my husband, Paolo, and I run it for the owner who lives in the US. But we plan the menu and take turns with the cooking. It's fun," she said, with a slight New Jersey accent.

"My name's Rachel, and I expect to visit here often."

"I'm Carla. Nice to meet you. What can I get you today?"

I ordered lunch—Caesar salad and pasta dish, plus a half-bottle of Amarone.

As Carla turned to take my order to the kitchen, I called out "One more question, if you don't mind, Carla. The sign outside says you're closed on Wednesday nights. Why is that?"

At first, she hesitated, shy or reluctant to answer. "We have a banquet room upstairs and, well, a men's club meets there on Wednesday nights. We close the downstairs at three on those days."

"What kind of club is it, the one that meets upstairs?"

"It's an auto club. The members talk about vintage cars—racing cars, luxury cars, that sort of thing. Sometimes they even trade cars, I hear. I don't know how the club works, since I've never attended a meeting."

"I have a friend who's a car fan. Could he join the club, if he wanted?" I asked. I meant my boyfriend Farid. I'd been seeing him for the last six months.

"I don't know. My husband and I only do the cooking. Another guy is in charge of the club. I can give you his phone number in Newark, if you want it."

"That's okay. I won't hold you up any longer," I said, smiling.

After Carla had left, I scanned the room again. I bet the upstairs meeting room had an old-fashioned men's club feel. You know, dark lighting, heavy furniture, portraits of rich men on wine-coloured walls. You can probably picture what I mean.

Then my thoughts wandered back to the Foster Problem. I had to get closer to Donny. Find out more about him. Find out why Melanie might have taken that odd route to New Orleans.

Why was I doing this, I wondered again. Investigating a suspected murderer. I wasn't trained for this kind of work. Plus, it didn't feel ethical, spying on Donny, trying to get the goods on him. But you could view this in a much more innocent way. I was merely helping my colleague integrate back into the School after an especially traumatic year in Texas.

No, I wasn't happy about having to do this. But I'd do my best to help the University make a difficult decision. Meanwhile, I'd enjoy lunch and get back to thinking about my regular duties.

Lunch was delightful, and I looked forward to coming back here many times. I strolled home, sozzled by the Amarone, on top of the world. The day was sunny and cool. Everything was fine, but I couldn't stop thinking about Donny's ridiculous trial.

Over the weekend, during breaks from cooking for the week and other chores, I thought about Donny's trial over and over. In fact, I couldn't get it out of my head.

During breaks from thinking about that, I thought about that new book I was writing. I planned to call it *Down Country*, because it was about hidden desires and low behaviour. In the starkest terms, my book-in-progress was about dealing with the Devil. About the reasons many people—even smart, educated people—made foolish deals with the Devil. Political deals, economic deals. And to my way of thinking, the Devil was chaos.

Monday was almost entirely free, so I had plenty of time to think about this newly imagined country of mine—Down Country. And about Donny's trial.

8

By the time Tuesday rolled around, I was ready to lecture my introductory class a third time. Today, I'd talk about 'disinhibition', a cornerstone of my new book-to-be. By that, I meant people's inability to curb inappropriate or unwanted behaviour. Their tendency to act without regard for consequences. To go against the social norms, usually because of poor emotional control.

As usual, I watched my students jostle and straggle into the lecture hall. When everyone was seated, I told them what I planned to discuss and, as usual, that it would be on the final exam. I started by reminding them of what I'd said in the first lecture, about norms, informal rules, and laws. Then I proceeded to examine the reasons people break rules, connecting this to my earlier discussion about institutions.

"How many of you have ever made a music video and posted it on social media. A video in which you're singing?" A few dozen students raised their hands.

"Okay fine. And how many of you have ever punched someone in the nose?" This time, fewer students raised their hands. I also heard what sounded like a wave of jokey comments.

"Finally, how many of you have ever shoplifted—taken something from a store without paying?" This time, only a handful of people raised their hands. Again, I heard some murmured comments, but mostly silence.

"This is my roundabout way of introducing the topic of 'disinhibition.' People avoid doing lots of things they might like to do—may have even thought about doing—because they feel inhibited. They're nervous about breaking the rules, being caught, and suffering consequences. That's true of lots of things we don't do—singing in public, punching people in the nose, and shoplifting, among others. Mind you, singing in public doesn't break any rules, strictly speaking. But it does violate an unspoken norm of public modesty, which Canadians seem to value.

"We feel inhibited because we've learned to follow certain rules. We'd feel guilty and ashamed if we broke those rules. Especially if we were caught and exposed or ridiculed for doing them. On the other hand, sometimes we do feel disinhibited, willing to do things we wouldn't ordinarily do, even willing to break the rules. And disinhibition is an important cause of crime. That's why I'm discussing it at a class in criminology.

"But before moving ahead, I want to make two other important points. First, disinhibition is not the only—perhaps, not even the main—cause of crime. Among other things, people also commit crimes because attractive opportunities arise, friends encourage them, or they've developed skills needed to commit the crime. You need particular skills to embezzle money or break into a house, for example. Admittedly, you need fewer skills to punch someone in the nose or shoplift.

"My second point is that disinhibition is an important cause of political and social upheaval, as well as crime. Many, and perhaps most people need to feel disinhibited before taking part in a political demonstration, especially if taking part meant disobeying the police. And above all, they'll need to feel disinhibited before vandalizing a public institution, as followers of Donald Trump did to the US Capitol Building in Washington on January 6, 2021."

"So the idea of 'disinhibition' provides a useful link between theories about crime and theories about political protest. And I'm especially interested in how people who are enraged— angry enough to commit crimes or attack public institutions— become disinhibited. Disinhibited enough to do these things and not merely think about doing them."

Now, I told them how people could be disinhibited by alcohol, strong emotions, and sexual urges. Sometimes, even by religious or political leaders. I talked about the ways so-called 'charismatic' leaders played on strong emotions to disinhibit their followers and create political turmoil. What the great sociologist, Max Weber, had said about 'charisma' as a force for social change. And how the followers of charismatic leaders create new institutions—new rules and laws—in what Weber had called 'the routinization of charisma.' How the routinization of charisma had stabilized Christianity—especially the Catholic Church—for two thousand years. And how it had worked just as well, and for nearly as long, in the Islamic religion.

That day, I was plenty charismatic myself! I showed them colourful photos, diagrams, and tables of data. I paced around the podium, waving my arms and answering impromptu questions. The high point was a series of film clips of charismatic leaders—Benito Mussolini, Adolf Hitler, Ayatollah Khomeini, and Donald Trump, among others—addressing their followers. We spent a few spirited minutes discussing their body language, speaking style, and stage settings.

I reminded them that new charismatic leaders were always emerging, always using the same tricks to mobilize followers. Always urging them to break traditional norms, rules, and laws. Always trying to disinhibit them—even enrage them—against real and imagined enemies. Always calling for the government to make sweeping changes, and occasionally, even using 'scapegoats' and violence against minorities.

Then, I asked my students to consider the changes President Donald Trump had made since his re-election as President of the United States. How he had canceled military support for Ukraine. Threatened to annex Canada as a 51st state, along with Greenland and perhaps Panama. Suggested turning the Gaza strip into an American-owned Riviera of the Middle East. How all of these, and other actions, had overturned nearly a century of norms, rules, and laws around international trade and cooperation.

After that, I discussed Freudian ideas about disinhibition. About the role of the id, ego, and superego in the human unconscious. I also discussed sociological ideas, applying them to people who committed criminal acts. How some people cut themselves off from groups and institutions that restrained them, then joined groups and institutions that pushed them to act in other ways. Often, in wholly new ways. I cited 'suicide bombers' as particularly extreme examples of this.

Finally, I introduced my question of the day: How useful are theories of disinhibition likely to be in explaining criminal behaviour? For example, in explaining domestic violence? And could we use the same theories to understand revolutionary political behaviour? Or do we need different theories of disinhibition for this purpose?

"Let's spend 15 minutes talking about all this," I said. "Pick a crime and let's consider if it might require disinhibition. Or, conversely, if it is merely a product of learned social behaviour."

Some students looked puzzled. But as usual, other students started waving their hands, then shouting out their answers into the nearest floor mic. Also as usual, they disagreed about the best answers. Today, the discussion got a bit out of hand. The name 'Trump' prompted a lot of outrageous ideas and suggestions. Safe to say, most Canadians—and especially young ones—had strong views about Mr. Trump by this time.

Finally, I halted the discussion and asked everyone to write a 500-word essay applying disinhibition theory to rule-breaking. Students who'd forgotten to bring a laptop were to give Altan a paper copy of their essay as they left the hall.

Today's lecture was a little more complicated than I'd intended. Some students would have trouble with it, and another ten percent of the class might drop the course. But I didn't mind. The students who remained would be serious and capable—dedicated to learning what I had to teach them. Today's lecture was a good way to separate the sheep from the goats.

As I walked back to my office, I continued to think about deviance and the reasons people 'cross the line' from law-abiding to law-breaking behaviour. Or as religious people think of the question, the reasons people sin. Why they turn their backs on goodness and make deals with the Devil.

People have thought about this question, in religious and non-religious ways, for millennia. Countless books and plays had been written about it. I'm still struggling with the question myself. But one thing I'm sure of is that there's such a thing as evil—maybe even a place like Hell. And anyone can cross the boundary into Hell, that country down below. Down Country.

9

Altan showed up at my office a half-hour later, laughing. "The kids loved your lecture today. They understood disinhibition a lot better than I would have imagined. I think you're going to turn out a skilful set of political radicals. Or criminals."

"That's my goal," I said, smiling, then flipped through my desk calendar. "Are you going to the American Criminological Society meetings in Houston next month?" I asked him.

"I hadn't planned on it. No money."

"Maybe I can help with that. But first, I'd like to describe a problem I'm trying to solve. Can you spare the time?"

"Sure. I have an hour before my next class."

"First, I need you to promise everything we discuss will stay between us. No discussing it with anyone else: not your friends or teachers or fellow students. Not even your roommate. Can you promise that?"

"Yes, I promise," he said, a solemn look on his face.

Of course, I'd promised the Dean to keep everything about the Foster case confidential. And I felt conflicted about bringing Altan into the discussion. I didn't know him well and wondered, for a moment, if I could trust him to be discreet. But my intuition told me I could.

"Okay, here's the problem. The wife of a university colleague was murdered last year, in Texas. I don't know who did it. No one at the university knows. And a jury wasn't convinced her husband did it. But the Dean wants me to find out more about the crime. Any thoughts on how I might proceed?"

Sure, Altan would have heard about this murder—it would be the talk of the School by now, especially with Donny back to teaching. I hadn't given Altan much to go on and he looked puzzled. But I wanted to see how his mind worked.

Then, faster than expected, he came up with something smart. "Most times, when a woman is murdered, it's by someone close. A husband, boyfriend, or brother. Someone who feels shamed or threatened. Male relatives can do terrible things. Usually, the murdered woman has shamed them or challenged their authority. So, I would start by thinking about shame and authority. But maybe, these matters are not the same in Texas as they are in Turkey."

I nodded, taking notes in a little notebook I'd pulled out of my pants pocket. I was considering his every word, and Altan seemed to like that. A smile played across his face, and he sat up taller in his chair. He seemed to feel flattered by the respect I was showing his ideas.

"I wonder what was gained from the woman's death. Or what someone would have lost if the woman lived."

"Who would gain and who would lose by this murder? I agree, those are important questions, Madame Professor. But as you know—as even you have written—people who are enraged do not need rational motives to kill someone. Not if they feel dishonoured, and especially not if the person to be killed is a woman. Was this woman's body disfigured by torture or harsh handling, do you know?"

"I know her body had been mauled by dogs, but not if she'd been tortured." I said, scribbling in my notebook again. "I read nothing about that in the trial transcript."

"Had this unfortunate woman been sexually assaulted, Madame Professor?"

"I wish you wouldn't call me 'Madame Professor.' It makes me feel eighty years old. But if you must, do it no more than once a day." I smiled to soften the sting, and he lowered his head, a little embarrassed. "The police found no evidence of sexual assault. The woman had her clothes on when they discovered her body. Anyway, she was a middle-aged woman."

"I can tell you from my own research, Madame—ah, sorry, Professor Tile, that age will not always keep a murderer from raping his victim. Not if the motive is related to rage and dishonour. But perhaps in Texas, men rape only attractive young women."

"I'll try to find out more about that," I said, scribbling more words in my scruffy, two-dollar notepad with a stubby, chewed-on HB pencil.

"I don't know anything at all about the economic motives of criminals in Texas. Do you?"

"Not a thing," I said, ashamed of my ignorance. "Okay, let's put Texas aside. Instead, let's think about the reasons people kill other people—especially, why they kill women."

"Do they have honour killings in Texas? Was this woman a Muslim, do you know?" he offered, looking hopeful.

"No, I don't think so."

"Professor, this may sound odd, but again, I'm going with what I know. Many men I interviewed in Turkey, men who had killed their wives, said their wives were impossible to live with. They sometimes said 'baş belası.' Pardon me, I will translate. As you might say in North America, these women were a pain in the butt. Very irritating. Did people describe the dead woman in Texas that way? As irritating, hard to live with, a pain in the you-know-what? If so, perhaps, we could view this murder as a result of disinhibition."

"I didn't know this woman well. In fact, I only met her a few times. But no, I haven't heard anyone describe her that way. I'll have to look into that too."

I scribbled 'pain in the butt?' in my notebook. An odd expression. What's the opposite, I wondered. A pleasure in the butt? A pain in the neck?

"I'm going to need your help, Altan. To have you listen to my ideas and give me honest reactions. Even, suggest new ways to approach the problem. That's the kind of conversation I need. But again, all of this would have to be confidential. What do you think?"

"How much time might you need, Professor?" he asked carefully.

"I'm not sure. Say a few dozen hours. Here's an offer: I'll pay you an honorarium of $500 and give you a strong letter of recommendation if you do a good job."

"Professor, I'd like to help you. So, let's talk about the investigation some more, really get down to details. Then I can give you a better answer."

I started with a key concern. "I'm wondering if gangs are involved in this woman's murder. The woman's husband studies gangs. She may have gotten tangled up in his research, somehow. But I don't know much about gangs yet. What do you know?"

"I took a course on gangs during my MA studies in Istanbul. If I remember correctly, gangs are like other human groups. They all have a leader, a piece of territory, and a financial goal. Usually, they want to steal money or sell drugs, something like that. To achieve their goal, they have to deal with other gangs and avoid the police. Gang life is like a team sport—like a soccer game where all the players have guns. A very disinhibited soccer game, perhaps."

I liked that comparison. Very apt, and funny too.

I looked at Altan closely. He was a handsome young man—something I hadn't really noticed before. He had a neatly trimmed beard and piercing dark brown eyes. His long hair was carefully styled and I felt certain he used multiple hair products. The kind my style-conscious son Josh used when he went on a date.

More than that, Altan showed all his emotions. You could almost read his thoughts from his facial expressions. He wasn't afraid to show his feelings. And the agility of his face revealed the agility of his mind. I knew when he was laughing at me, even when he made no sound. And now, I could tell from the expression on his face and tilt of his head that he was deep in thought.

"Here's something else I'd need you to do for me, right away," I said. "The university suspects my colleague of violating ethical rules he'd agreed to when he applied for a research leave. I'm expecting the university lawyer to send me information about the relevant ethical rules. But I need you to spend a few hours looking through the human resources literature. To find out the current thinking about breaches of research ethics. In particular, what kinds of violations are serious enough to warrant the removal of a tenured faculty member? What do you say? Will you do these things for me?"

I smiled at him, hoping for a positive answer. Last year, I would have asked my assistant 'Clever Connie' to do this for me. Connie was a marvel. But now she was 110 percent focused on writing her doctoral thesis. I couldn't disturb her with impossible requests anymore. Now I'd have to pass them along to Altan.

He hesitated, then shook his head, looking worried. "Professor, you're asking me to help investigate a member of our own School. Someone I may have to work with. Someone who could affect my academic career. You're asking a lot of me, especially considering I just got here. Will you be able to protect me against any blowback?"

"I will absolutely protect you. Just as important, I will keep your name out of any discussions I have about this investigation. No one will know about your role in it. That is, if you keep it under your hat," I said, touching my hand to my head as though doffing a hat.

"Okay, then," he said. "But if this job interferes with my studies, or threatens to interfere with my career, I'll have to quit. I need good grades to keep my scholarship. Otherwise, shazam, I'm back in Turkey. Do you agree to my terms?"

"Okay, it's a deal."

Altan promised to set up a running record of everything we'd discover.

He kept talking. But by now, I wasn't listening, not one hundred percent. My mind was on darker things. For one thing, on Melanie Foster's chewed body. What kind of woman was she, I wondered? Was she a pain in the butt? Or at least, had Donny thought so?

Then I noticed Altan had paused, waiting for me to chime in.

"I'm going to Houston next month to look for evidence," I told him. "I'll cover your expenses if you want to come along. We could attend the criminology conference, also talk to a few people about this case. Most of all, I want to see the Killing Fields. Something about the place intrigues me. It might help to explain this poor woman's murder."

Altan nodded his agreement, shook my hand, and left my office.

The next day, I was working on my book when a knock interrupted my thoughts. Maribeth and Lena, two graduate students I'd seen at the meet-and-greet, opened the door and stepped in. They looked even more nervous than when I'd seen them a few days ago.

"Professor Tile," Maribeth began, "we don't mean to cause any trouble. But we want to change supervisors. I want a new thesis supervisor, and Lena wants Professor Foster off her exam committee. We don't feel comfortable working with him."

"Have you talked to him about this?" I asked them.

They shook their heads. "We were too nervous," Lena said.

I didn't like what I was hearing. Especially, the potential awkwardness of dealing with Donny. But their requests were justifiable. Awkwardness aside, I saw no reason to refuse them.

"Fill out the forms and I'll sign them," I said. "But please email Professor Foster about the change. Let him know you talked to me first."

They nodded and left. I knew this was just the beginning. Soon, more requests would come in. I felt sorry for Donny but knew I couldn't keep students from leaving his supervision, if they wanted to. Yes, Donny was charming, and many students liked him. But others would be nervous after hearing about the trial in Texas. And others, maybe including Maribeth and Lena, might feel he was just a little too handsy.

10

I was seeing Donny at school every day now. So, the next time I bumped into him in the mailroom, I invited him to lunch at the Faculty Club. Donny was pleased to accept.

At first, none of the ordeal in Texas—the investigation, the whispers—seemed to have touched him. But now, I noticed a few changes. For one thing, he dressed better than he used to. Faculty members at the School were a mixed bag—mainly, they dressed in smart casual or plain slobbery. Unlike them, Donny always wore suits now. Fine suits. Handmade suits, not off the rack.

At the Faculty Club pub, I chose my favourite table, the one near the fireplace. We both started looking through the menu. I wanted to keep it light. Easy. Safe.

"Nice suit," I told him, as I tried to decide between main courses.

Donny looked up, shot his cuffs, and smirked. "Times change. So do suits." He winked.

"Working on anything new?" I asked him.

He lowered his voice. "High-end auto auctions. The rarest cars, the most luxurious ones—they have histories no one talks about. Doubtful origins."

This took me by surprise, and I leaned forward. "From car thieves to auctions? Seems like a leap."

He glanced around the room, checking for eavesdroppers.

Then he leaned in and whispered, "Not really. Stolen cars, you know. Restored. Repainted It's global, Rachel. It's huge." He sat back, watching, waiting for my reaction. Would I look surprised? Would I want more information? Would I approve?

"I've been reading about global auto theft," I said. "You've done great work in that area."

His eyebrow lifted, amused. "Oh? Something catch your eye?"

I took a deep breath, knowing I needed to be careful. "I like the way you interviewed those car thieves in New Jersey—lots of detailed information about what they think and do. How does a scholar like you—successful, respected—come to study something like that up close?"

Donny stared. Then, in a low voice he said, "It just feels natural. Life hands you opportunities. The thrill, the challenge, the money. You have to decide if you're in. Things look grey up close. Not black and white. And people like me, we step into the grey zone for the thrill of it. We're not afraid to bend a few rules." After pausing for effect, he asked "Want to know how deep this rabbit hole goes?"

Suddenly, I found the heat stifling. I was afraid his next words would pull me down into a world far deeper than I'd imagined. I hesitated, my stomach twisting. The fear must have showed on my face.

"Never mind," he said, noticing and waving me off. "You're not ready for this."

Changing the topic, I asked him "Why did they prosecute you for your wife's death? They had absolutely no evidence against you. None of it makes sense to me."

"I know, Rachel, I'm confused about it myself. I think they were fishing for information about the gang I was studying. Trying to pressure me into revealing something."

So maybe that's all it was: an attempt to find out about the Devlin Crew.

For the rest of lunch, we talked about our new graduate students. This and that.

But despite our casual conversation, I felt uneasy. I'd just given one of our doctoral students permission to find another thesis supervisor—almost said something about it but didn't. Didn't want to spoil the mood. Still, I felt guilty and uncomfortable. I was keeping things from him, that's for sure.

I'd even started to think about tailing Donny to one of those auctions he talked about. But I wouldn't know how to tail someone without being seen. The university really should have hired a trained private investigator for this job.

Somehow, we got to the end of what had become an uncomfortable lunch.

Donny returned to the office, and I went home, earlier than usual. I showered, gave myself a manicure and a pedicure, and generally made myself beautiful—well, at least passably attractive. Tonight was a date night. My glamorous boyfriend Farid was taking me to see a new production of Gounod's opera *Faust*.

I wasn't familiar with Faust, the opera. But as an undergraduate I'd read Christopher Marlowe's earlier version of the legend, a play titled *Doctor Faustus*. In the play, an old, lonely scholar makes a deal with Mephistopheles, the devil. He agrees to give up his soul in the afterlife if only he can have the love of beautiful, young Marguerite (also called Gretchen) in this life. In Marlowe's telling, the legend of Faust is a gruesome tale of bad choices. The story has a more pleasant ending in Gounod's opera, based on a version of the legend by Goethe.

Most pleasant of all was my date for the evening. Farid—Dr. Farid Srivastava—was the handsome plastic surgeon I'd been dating for six months. Just thinking about him made me smile.

I'd met Farid one Saturday morning at a nearby gym. Not the place I take martial arts lessons, the other one I go to. I had been on a mat alternating dozens of crunches with dozens of pelvic tilts—kegels, I think they're called. Farid, on a mat next to mine, had been alternating dozens of sit-ups with dozens of push-ups. After finishing twenty sets of each, we'd slumped over panting, bug-eyed, huffing and sweating and staring at each other. Farid smiled, then I smiled, and we'd started talking. Then he had wiped away the sweat on my face before it dripped into my eyes. I'd blinked at him in delight.

The rest of the script wrote itself. We each showered, then went out to dinner. Later that night we went to bed together at my place. That was the beginning of something—a love affair, maybe—that already felt perfect. My oldest friend (and former sister-in-law) Jen said it might be a rebound romance. I'd recently broken up with Daniel after fifteen years of marriage. And Robert, a man I'd actually loved, had just been murdered three months earlier.

But this new thing with Farid felt like much more than that. It might even be the real thing. Time would tell.

Let me tell you all about him. Farid's tall—in fact, tall, dark, and handsome. His skin colour is lighter than mahogany or ebony, but a rich brown. He has the most handsome face, with brown eyes and shiny, wavy black hair. Long black hair I like to run my fingers through. And a beautiful smile. Oh, and he dresses elegantly. No other word can describe how he dresses and carries himself. He looks like a movie star. A Bollywood movie star. Being with him makes me want to be beautiful and elegant myself.

Farid grew up in Baltimore, but he's lived lots of places,

now including Toronto. He said he wanted to see Canada's healthcare system in action. With surprisingly little trouble, he'd gained professional accreditation, then joined the surgical practice of a Toronto doctor he'd met at a conference in Denver. Farid sure liked to move around, though. According to LinkedIn, Farid had received his medical degree from Johns Hopkins University. Then he'd lived in Houston, Chicago, Miami, and Seattle before coming to Toronto to practise medicine here.

Farid was also in Toronto to keep an eye on his young nephew, Billy, and Billy's new wife, Nikki. They'd moved to the GTA a year earlier and, with family backing, opened two businesses. One was a fancy Indian restaurant in Brampton called 'The Brambay.' The other was an exclusive car dealership called 'Brambay Elite Motors.' Billy managed the auto dealership with help from his uncle Krishna. Nikki managed day-to-day operations at the restaurant.

We'd agreed to never talk about ex-spouses, and Farid never mentioned his kids. His ex-wife kept them away from Farid, except for a month each summer. So, he'd moved to Canada for a fresh start, and loved it here. Sure, there was a lot I didn't know about him yet. But what I did know was wonderful. I planned to discuss him more thoroughly with my friend Jen. She was a great judge of character. But so far that hadn't happened. I'd have to get her and Farid together, at the right time.

Still, I was sure Farid was a good man. I wasn't ready for long-term plans, but I was crazy about him. And I couldn't help laughing when I thought of the jokes he'd made about his patients. "I've inspected more female boobs and butts than 99 percent of the male Canadian population," he'd told me once. He liked mine best, he told me flatly. Yes, that's what he'd said.

I wasn't going to rush into anything. But Farid seemed perfect.

That night, he arrived at my home wearing a tuxedo. Right away, he fastened a beautiful orchid corsage to my evening dress. Very old fashioned, you know. Yes, I'd dressed up, and a good thing I had. As I'd discover, most people came to the opera in formal dress clothes. There were no slobs at the opera house tonight.

I won't bore you with details, but the opera was a lavish, glorious experience. Something I'll never forget. Back home around midnight, I tried to remember all of the opera, but couldn't get the Texas murder out of my mind. Then, inexplicably, I started thinking about Thanksgiving and couldn't get that out of my mind either.

11

Thanksgiving was coming up quickly and I needed to plan a dinner menu. This wasn't going to be easy, I thought. I looked through my weekly schedule: Tuesday and Thursday teaching, a graduate seminar on Wednesday, monthly faculty meetings, a book in progress, an upcoming conference in Texas, a deadline to file my report on Donny—how was I going to squeeze in a Thanksgiving dinner, I wondered. Did I have enough time to plan it? And who am I going to invite? My brain threatened to fracture with all these questions.

Still, I had to do it. Just yesterday, my daughter Ellie had called to ask about Thanksgiving. Was I was making dinner? Should she keep the date open? She'd been invited to visit her boyfriend's family that night, would go there for dinner if I wasn't planning anything.

Without thinking, I'd said, "Of course, I'm making Thanksgiving dinner. I do it every year." So now, I had to do it.

And for over ten years, I'd been promising my family a turkey-free Thanksgiving. In fact, almost everyone I knew felt the same way about turkey, these days. So, this year, I'd make good on the promise. This year, we'd eat anything but turkey: roast beef, salmon steaks, and mushroom risotto, for instance. Add a green salad, mashed potatoes, roasted root vegetables and Bob's your uncle. Pecan pie, pumpkin pie, and ice cream. Plus wine. Lots of wine.

The next morning, I phoned a fancy grocery store nearby. I was almost too late, they told me. They were nearly booked up for Thanksgiving dinners. But, they'd deliver everything I wanted. Their premium service included servers to set the table and clean up afterward. I'd cook the risotto myself, just for fun.

I can do this, I thought. Thanksgiving won't be so hard, after all. And the planned dinner would impress Farid, my gorgeous (and slightly mysterious) boyfriend. I wondered how he usually celebrated Thanksgiving.

When I phoned Roxy to invite her, I told her all about Farid and she laughed. "It sounds like you've won the jackpot. You'd better keep that guy." One of my earliest criminology students, Roxy Duncan was now a friend—also, a detective in the Toronto Police Department. She always wanted to hear about my private life. It was somewhat more eventful than hers.

"Of course, he's the perfect man," I said, smiling to myself. "He likes mine best," I repeated, and we broke down laughing again. What a punchline.

"Farid is curious about everything I do, and I mean everything. He asked if he could sit in on one of my lectures, and when I said okay, he actually came. He did, Roxy. He also read my book on theories of rage—the book that won a few prizes.

He even wants to know all the gossip about my colleagues, their peculiarities and rivalries. Stuff that bores me to death fascinates him."

Eventually, the conversation turned to other things, but I'd already decided. Thanksgiving dinner would be fine. I'd even invite Donny Foster. Poor Donny needed company, I thought, feeling very charitable. Having nailed down Thanksgiving, I got back to work on my book.

First thing the next morning, I had to endure the monthly meeting of 'PDADC'—the committee of executive officers of all the major units at Strachan University (that's the Principals, Deans, Academic Directors, and Chairs).

Cudney Hall was not only where I lectured my intro class twice a week; because of its size and grandeur, it was also the Provost's favourite venue. He took the first Friday of each month to highlight 'pressing problems and current concerns,' and today was the first Friday in October. More often than not, he stressed the need to make sure faculty members 'comported themselves in a professional manner.' Also, he reminded us to prod our faculty members to raise dollars. To apply for as many, and as big, grants as they could. Also, to make sure the grants they applied for yielded funds for 'university overhead.'

By ten-fifteen, our monthly meeting was over, and I was back in my office.

The theme at PDADC today had been 'Large Research Grants' and Donny was famous for getting large grants. But did he merit them? What did experts in the field think about his recent work? After making a suitable list, I reached out to six other criminologists who studied smuggling. I couldn't reach one of them—away on sabbatical. Two others praised Donny. Three didn't. Envy, maybe? One, Professor Jacobs from Manchester, was cagey. "He's been seen at auctions," Jacobs said. "Not just watching. Buying. Selling. With the wrong kind of people."

I felt my stomach start to knot. "Do you think he's involved in something shady?"

"I wouldn't say without proof," Jacobs replied, still furtive. "But it's possible. Some researchers forget where to draw the line."

Again, the problem of rules: who followed them, who didn't. And what disinhibited the rule-breakers, the people who didn't follow rules, I wondered.

Gradually, I was starting to piece things together. Donny's suits. His travels. The auctions he attended. Maybe he was an actor in the smuggling world he studied. But I still couldn't believe it. On the other hand, if he was involved, how deeply entrenched was he?

My phone rang. "Rachel Tile here," I answered.

"Professor, this is Garet Foster. Donny's daughter."

I was startled. For reasons I couldn't explain, I'd never met Garet, though Donny and I had been colleagues for over a decade.

"How can I help you?"

"I'm worried about my father. He's been nervous about his return to teaching. Afraid people will think he killed my mother. But he didn't. He couldn't have."

"I'm sure you're right, Garet," I said, calmingly. "But what makes you so certain he couldn't have done what he was accused of doing?" I asked, as politely as I could.

"He's not that kind of person, and I know him. I've watched him and thought about him all my life. I probably know him better than anyone else, except for my mother, of course."

"It's good to hear from you, Garet. What led you to call me out of the blue—a stranger you've never met?"

"I know we haven't met, Professor Tile, but my mother's friend Jackie Taylor always spoke positively about you, whenever your name came up. And frankly, I'm worried about my father. I'm the only person looking out for him now. I'm hoping you'll help me keep tabs on him. Just a little, anyway."

This was a perfect opportunity to grill Garet about the case, her parents, and what had happened. I might not get a better chance, so I plunged in.

"I'm guessing you were at the trial in Texas, right?" I asked her.

"Yes, I was there for the whole thing, start to finish. I had to take three weeks off teaching to do it. My school principal was very understanding."

"Did people say anything that shook your faith in your father? For instance, did any of the evidence or accusations seem valid to you?"

"Not really, Professor. I thought there were huge gaps in the prosecution's case. People who should have been called as witnesses were never called. Evidence I would have classified as hearsay was treated as believable. Claims were made that I thought were unfounded, even wild."

"So, if there wasn't enough evidence to convict your father, why do you think they brought him to trial?"

"I don't know. My father said it was to pressure him into revealing information about the Devlin Crew. Maybe that was the reason. Otherwise, I have no idea."

"Do you have any idea why your mother was killed? Or by whom?"

"Again, I don't know the answer. Maybe she picked up hitchhikers on the way to New Orleans and they killed her. That's possible. But they never followed up that line of reasoning at the trial. And for that matter, the police almost never catch killers who leave bodies in the Killing Fields. At least, that's what I've heard."

It felt odd, having this conversation with a complete stranger who seemed to know more about me than I knew about her. And probably knew more about the Foster Case than I did. Also, I couldn't get a fix on the girl. Sometimes it felt like I was speaking to an earnest teenager—someone who loved her daddy very much and wouldn't say a bad word about him. Other times, Garet sounded more like who she actually was: a woman in her thirties, I guessed. And, as I knew from that first meeting in the Dean's office, a wife, a mother, a schoolteacher. A genuine grown-up.

"Where are you calling from, anyway?" I asked her.

"I'm at home, in Markham. Did you want to get together and talk some more?"

"Not right now. But I wouldn't mind meeting you, so I can put a face to a name."

"That would be great, Professor. Just name the time and place, and I'll be there."

Garet sounded sweet. Kind. A little shy, not like her father at all.

I told her I'd keep an eye on her father and promised to call if anything went wrong. She gave me her contact info.

After hanging up, I felt a moment of doubt. What if the caller wasn't Garet after all? What if she was a reporter? Or a woman Donny had charmed, someone checking up on him? The thought lingered, then evaporated. It was too unlikely.

Coincidentally, the next day, the Dean asked me to drop in for another chat about the Foster Problem.

"Have you made any progress in your investigation?" she asked me, right off the bat.

"I've read the trial transcript and started trying to put the facts together. Oh yes, and I had a chat with Donny Foster's daughter yesterday. She phoned me, very concerned about her father. But so far, there's nothing to report. Is there anything new I should know?" I asked her.

The Dean hesitated, tilting her head to one side. "Just rumours. About a secret group called 'The Workshop.' Connected to Donny Foster's research somehow. We don't know anything about it yet. Oh, and related to that, do you know anything about a group of American writers who lived a century ago? Called themselves the 'Furies.' Donny mentioned them at his interview last week. Maybe you remember him saying that."

Yes, I remembered, but didn't have anything to say on the topic. "Never heard of them," I said. "Why?"

"Donny said Melanie had been working on a book about the group, so I want to learn more about it. Never mind for now. Remember, moving forward, be careful in everything you do. So, tread softly. Don't take unreasonable risks. And watch out for leaks. The university can't afford a scandal. Meanwhile, let me know if you hear anything about the Workshop or the Furies."

I nodded and left the Dean's office. I didn't plan to tell her about the help I was getting from Altan. She wouldn't want to know, and so far, he was keeping everything nice and quiet.

I thought about Donny and his sweet young daughter. Then I wondered, what if everyone was wrong and Donny was the victim of circumstances? Maybe he hadn't killed his wife. It would be so unfair to badger him if he hadn't. And even if he *had* killed his wife, would that make him a danger to anyone else? He'd never shown signs of violence before—or had he?

12

I didn't know the answer to that simple, important question. Had Donny ever committed any acts of violence? If he had, that wouldn't prove he'd killed his wife. But if he hadn't hurt anyone else, killing his wife would have been very unlikely.

Back in my office, I called Roxy.

"Detective Duncan," Roxy said. "What can I do for you?"

"It's Rachel. I need a favour. Do you have a minute?"

"For you, always. By the way, I'm looking forward to your Thanksgiving dinner next week. What's up?"

"I'm collecting information about one of our faculty members, Donny Foster. He was tried for murdering his wife in Texas, but the jury couldn't agree on a verdict. The Dean wants me to make sure he's not a risk to the university."

"I remember that case. What do you need?"

"Anything about his history. Violence, criminal behaviour, whatever. I need it fast, and it has to stay quiet. I don't want the press hearing about this."

"I'll get back to you today," Roxy said. Her voice then dropped to a whisper. "But keep my name out of it. The folks here know we're friends, but they mustn't know I've given you information."

"Don't worry. I won't mention your name."

I hung up, feeling uneasy. Was I putting my life in danger? My chest tightened. As my therapist Anita had taught me last year, I pulled a paper bag out of the top desk drawer, breathed in, held the air, and let it out slowly. My pulse steadied, but the questions didn't go away.

An hour later, Roxy called back. "Donny has a sealed juvenile record," she whispered. "When he was fifteen, there was a violent incident at his high school. He hurt another student. I don't have the details, but it was serious. I also checked the national and international databases. Except for speeding tickets, his record is clean. No adult offenses."

"However, and this is a big however, Rachel, the local cops are talking about Donny. They've spotted him at an underground fight club and an illegal gambling house. He's hanging out with bad people. I thought you'd want to know."

"That could hurt his career. And if he's spending his free time with criminals, he could also be a danger to the School," I said.

I thanked Roxy and hung up. Then, I thought about Donny: what I knew about him and what I didn't know. For sure, I needed to know a lot more. So, after considering all this, I walked down to Donny's office.

I knocked on his door and he welcomed me in. As I looked around the room, I saw blank spaces outlined on the walls. Pictures had hung there, maybe for a long time. On the floor, two framed paintings leaned against his desk. One was the portrait of a woman I recognized as Melanie. The other showed an empty field, scrubby and dull, with a purple bush in the foreground. An azalea, I thought, remembering an undergraduate botany course from decades earlier. A 'beautiful and resource-

ful plant', the lecturer had called it.

Donny saw I was interested in the pictures. "A friend painted Melanie's portrait," he said. "Melanie painted the other picture herself. Frankly, I never liked either of them. What's up?"

Melanie's picture looked

stern to me: serious, determined. She looked like the kind of woman who could, indeed, be a 'pain in the butt' if something irritated her. I'd have to recall everything Altan had said about this during our first meeting on the topic.

"Is there anything I can do for you? To smooth your return to teaching?"

Donny's eyes narrowed. "Nothing special, thanks for asking. But you know, I expect fair treatment from the university. If they violate my rights, I'll bring in a lawyer and make some noise."

"I hear you," I said. "I'm on your side, Donny. So let's get through this. And on a more sociable note, I'm hoping you can come to dinner at my house on Thanksgiving. It will be fun. You'll meet nice people."

He smiled. "Thank you. I'd like to come. Please send me the details." He held out his hand to me. We shook, and I went back to my office.

On my desk, I found a flyer advertising the School's lecture series for 2024–2025. My secretary had put it there, as a gentle reminder. I had to make sure everything was ready for our first guest lecturer. Celebratory events, security arrangements, things like that.

The first lecture was scheduled for October 23rd, a week after Canadian Thanksgiving. And the year's first guest was esteemed American sociologist, Julia Dent. Her most famous work examined the effect of policing on low-income African American communities. Dent's prize-winning book, *Hiding in Plain Sight*, painted an intimate portrait of young black criminals in a poor urban neighborhood.

Young men in the community Dent studied played hide-and-seek with the police, every hour of every day. To study them, Dent had spent six years immersed in this community. Her research strategy had been intensely personal. She'd even made close friends with a few of the young criminals. By building relations with them, she'd learned a lot about how they lived, thought, and acted.

However, her research also raised ethical questions. Some critics—including a few of my colleagues—even suggested Dent had involved herself in illegal activities. "What she did is absurd," one colleague told me last month. "Maybe you remember how Dent accompanied Jevon when he went after Dudley Moss, who'd cheated him out of money. Thank goodness Moss wasn't home, so nothing happened. As a professional, Dent should have intervened or reported Jevon's plans to the police. Or, she should have stayed away when Jevon headed out to kill Moss."

"Dent couldn't do either of those things," I told him. "If she had, they'd never talk to her again," I'd responded.

A few of my older colleagues thought Dent had gotten too involved, that this had biased her findings. And I understood why. The close relations with criminals had also exposed her to harm, a risk she seemed far too willing to take. That wasn't something I thought we ought to encourage our students to do.

On the other hand, ethnographers needed to develop strong connections with the people they studied. That was why many of the younger criminologists defended Dent. Another colleague, a recent addition to the School, praised Dent's 'dedication to understanding the lived experiences of poor people.' Many other colleagues and students felt the same. So, they'd voted to make Professor Dent their first visiting scholar of the 2024-2025 academic year.

I signed off on the arrangements. Everything was ready to go.

When I got home that evening, the streetlights were on and my house, empty. Josh was probably visiting his new girlfriend, so I was on my own again. Today had been… difficult. Worse still, I hadn't eaten since breakfast. No time. Finally able to grab a sandwich, I switched on the TV for company.

A local show came on, *Your Toronto*. I was surprised to see Donny, waving his arms and joking about car theft. Next to him sat Roxy Duncan, looking confident and composed. And next to her was someone called Kim Cressy—a sharp contrast to the others. Polished, magnetic, Kim talked fluent lawyer-speak about 'bespoke older vehicles' and 'time-tested tax strategies.'

Now I remembered: Roxy had told me about this show. *'Be sure to watch me on TV tonight,'* she had texted that morning. But of course, I'd forgotten. And it turned out Kim was an international expert on the management of risk in new businesses. Especially, car businesses.

I watched, fascinated, as Kim talked about her new venture, 'Bespoke Classics,' a luxury car business. Donny chimed in now and then, cocky, as if he knew Kim well. Maybe he did.

I wondered why Kim said everything in lawyer-speak. Was she trying to hide what she was doing—probably helping rich businesspeople evade taxes? Or was I just imagining that? I couldn't tell. Lawyer-speak aside, Kim impressed me. She was beautiful and charming. She had a voice men would find attractive and women, reassuring. I imagined becoming friends with Kim, even eating lunches together. Kim probably had that effect on people; her voice suggested a confident friendliness that even I, cautious around strangers, found appealing.

At the end of the show, I turned off the TV, but my thoughts stayed with cars. Bespoke cars. Custom-made cars. Smuggled cars. Ports where smuggled cars left the country. The highways that led to and from these ports.

I Googled American ports, my fingers dancing over the keyboard. Among the many seaports in North America, the Port of Houston stood out in sheer size. It sprawled from downtown Houston to Galveston on the Gulf of Mexico. The vast port was second, in tonnage shipped, to only one other port in the US. With a little help from crooked customs officers, stolen cars could easily sail out of Houston to anywhere in South America, Europe, or West Africa.

Then I studied a map of Texas. Highway I-45, the main route from Houston to Galveston, cut right through the Texas Killing Fields. Where Melanie Foster's body had been found. Was there a connection between Melanie's murder and the shipping routes smugglers used? I wondered. The question gnawed at me.

To get some fresh input, I phoned Altan. Not noticing it was nearly midnight.

"What do you need, Professor?" he asked, sounding slightly put out.

"Did you know over thirty bodies have been found in the Killing Fields since the 1970s? Teenaged females, mostly. Many raped, all murdered. But Melanie wasn't raped. Also, she wasn't a sex worker, and it wasn't robbery."

I could imagine Altan, on the other end of the line, crossing his arms and wanting to get back to whatever he was doing before.

"What are you saying?" he asked, sounding impatient.

"You've probably figured out we're looking into the death of Professor Foster's wife, Melanie. I'm wondering if there's a connection between the death of Melanie Foster, Donny Foster's research on smuggling, and the Killing Fields. After all, stolen cars are smuggled out of the Port of Houston and the Killing Fields are near the Port. That can't be a coincidence.

Either Melanie, or her killer, had a reason to be in that location."

These things were connected, I was sure of it.

"Professor, I can think of three reasons to leave a body somewhere as remote as the Killing Fields: convenience, familiarity, or to send a message."

"If it's a message, who's it for? Professor Foster?"

Altan wasn't going to bite. "Maybe it's just a matter of convenience, then. Don't get carried away." He was trying to calm me down, I thought. And get me off the phone.

"Fine. Okay. Now, before I go, on a related topic, would you look into a group of writers called the Furies? Early 1900s, New England. I think they may be important for this case."

"Sure thing," he said. He said goodbye, and hung up the phone. That was one of our shorter, less congenial conversations, I thought. I must have caught him at a bad time. I keep forgetting other people have lives.

<h1 style="text-align:center">13</h1>

The next morning over breakfast, I was startled by a ringing phone. It was Gene Tretnikoff, calling from London, England. I'd come to know him last year, when he'd briefly lived in Toronto. When he'd been a friend and employer of Robert, the man I loved. Important factoid: Gene was also enormously wealthy. He dabbled in many businesses, with varying degrees of legality.

Gene's a unique person, to be sure. As I learned last year, he was born into a desperately poor family in some Russian backwater. It was a dangerous time and place for Gene. In fact, ruffians had raped and killed his beloved sister, Irina. So, Gene did what any upstanding Russian older brother might have done under the circumstances. He grabbed a long iron rod, found the three offending boys, and beat them to death. In revenge, you understand.

You'd never guess any of that, meeting Gene today. He wears stylish but understated, expensive clothing. Speaks confidently and sometimes loudly, but always politely. Owns a great deal of property around the world, including Picton, Ontario—the home of his popular Calypso Casino. And will do anything for his family and friends. Including me, as I've found out.

Gene and I were still friendly, though we rarely spoke. So I was both delighted and surprised to hear from him.

Gene's voice boomed, "HELLO, Rachel. How ARE you today?"

"Fine, Gene. What can I do for you?"

"I'm coming over to visit IRINA at Thanksgiving. Can you meet me for lunch?"

"Why not come to Thanksgiving dinner at my house? Bring Irina. You'll meet my family and a few other people you might find interesting."

"If you're SURE we won't intrude, I'm pleased to accept," Gene said. "By the way, Irina's studying criminology now and she's especially interested in learning about theft. Any courses you can recommend?"

I hesitated, then said, "Donny Foster teaches a course on theft. It started a few weeks ago, but I'll put in a good word if Irina's interested."

"Thank you. That would be WONDERFUL. I'll pass along this information and let you know if Irina needs your SUP-PORT."

"While we're on the topic, can you tell me something about auto theft? For example, if stolen cars were smuggled out of the United States for delivery in Europe, where would they likely leave the country? And where would they unload?"

"I'm sure your colleague Professor Foster could answer these questions. But since we're talking, Baltimore and Houston are the key American seaports on the east coast. For purposes of international smuggling, at least," he told me. "As for Europe? The cars would likely unload in Greece or Spain."

"And this would be profitable, I suppose?" I asked, already knowing the answer.

"Oh yes, very profitable. A good-quality car will bring three or even four times its North American price in many parts of Europe and Asia. Of course, the smugglers ALSO profit from contraband on the return trips. They own the containers and never bring them back empty. They pack the containers with guns, heroin, stolen art, even refugees—anything that will bring a profit."

"Even people?" I asked, my voice rising, my stomach turning.

Gene's voice hardened. "Yes. Desperate people will pay for this OPPORTUNITY. Of course, people die on the trip. But millions are desperate to escape wherever they've been living. And there's a ready market for sex workers in North America. But if you plan to study this line of activity, please be careful. Curiosity is dangerous. Remember that."

After ending our chat, I thought about smuggling for a few minutes, then put aside my research on seaports. I needed information about that writing group the Dean had mentioned—the Furies. But how to proceed? I hadn't heard from Altan or found much online. I needed other people—smart people, experts—to help me.

So I phoned my friend Alice Turner, Chair of the Classics Department (now called the History and Classics Department). As I mentioned earlier, we knew each other from innumerable PDADC meetings, Christmas parties, and chats at the Athletic Centre. And not so long ago, we'd bumped into each other at the Faculty meet-and-greet.

It was early for nighttime, just eleven-thirty. And I guessed Alice would be up working. Another night owl.

"Alice, it's Rachel Tile. I need to pick your brain. Can you spare a few minutes?"

"Of course. I'm dying to find out what someone in criminology might need from a classicist," she said, laughing softly.

"I need to find out about a group of early 20th century fiction writers who nicknamed themselves the Furies. This has to do with a crime I'm studying. And I think there's a classical basis to that group. What can you tell me?"

"It's funny you should ask. I answered a similar question from a colleague in the Language Department four or five years ago. Was it Jackie Taylor who asked? No, Melanie Foster. Poor Melanie, I miss her. Anyway, she asked the same question, also without giving me any background or reasons."

"I'm sorry I can't go into details. What can you tell me about the Furies?"

"I don't know anything about a 20th century group of that name, but I can tell you about the discussion of Furies in classical writing. As I told Melanie, you can learn a lot from Aeschylus' classic tragedy, *The Oresteia*. I taught that work for years, so I know it pretty well. Do you want a brief account or a long, detailed one?"

"Maybe something in between," I said politely.

"Okay, an in-between account, as requested. Let me know if I go on too long. The Greek author Aeschylus—I can give you his birth and death dates, if you like—wrote three connected plays scholars call *The Oresteia*. At the start of the trilogy, Orestes avenges his father, King Agamemnon, by killing his mother

Clytemnestra and her lover Aegisthus. This invokes the wrath of the Furies, who follow Orestes with plans to punish him. You have to understand, matricide was considered an atrocious crime in ancient Greece. The Furies—imagine a cross between gods and witches—had committed themselves to punishing such acts. Even when those acts were a response to infidelity or murder, as in this case."

"Were there particular sanctions against killing women in ancient Greece?" I asked her.

"Women were legally protected from murder, just like men. But their deaths were not punished as severely as those of men, especially free male citizens. Women, especially those of lower status like slaves or courtesans, had few rights. And sometimes the murder of a woman was seen as a personal or family matter, not a public crime. A husband who killed an adulterous wife, for instance, might not face severe legal consequences. But one thing is certain: the Furies didn't like the murder of mothers. They thought it was especially heinous.

"Now, according to classical scholarship, the Furies represent ancient, savage laws of blood vengeance. They're agents of revenge, particularly for crimes against family members. Protectors of society's oldest, most basic values.

"As Aeschylus tells us, the Furies chase Orestes across Greece, driving him to madness. Orestes seeks refuge at the temple of Apollo in Delphi. There, the goddess Athena takes pity on him. She sets up a court in Athens to try him, and the trial pits the Furies (as prosecutors) against Orestes (as defendant), with Apollo as the defense attorney. The Furies, as you would expect, argue for the sanctity of family bonds and the need to punish matricide. That's the only way to preserve cosmic order, they claim. On the other side, Apollo argues the murders Orestes committed were justified—acts of revenge that Apollo himself had sanctioned.

"Athena casts the deciding vote, acquitting Orestes. However, she sees the value of the old ideas too. So, she offers the Furies a place of honour in her new justice system. Now, they are to be protectors of the city and upholders of lawful order.

"Scholars have argued about these plays for centuries, Rachel. But they agree the plays describe a shift in Greek society from chaotic vengeance to structured legality. From primitive justice to rational decision-making. And in these plays, the Furies personify an ancient approach to justice through violent revenge."

"Wow, that's heavy stuff" was all I could say. I saw no reason for Melanie to be interested in ancient Furies. But the key ideas—rage, vengeance, bloodshed—swirled around in my mind. They were somehow connected to Melanie's death. I just couldn't figure out how.

"Alice," I asked, "why might a group of 20th century women writers call themselves the Furies? Off the top of your head?"

"Again, this is something I discussed with Melanie. But then, I was the one asking that question. So, I'll tell you what she told me. Not her exact words, but the gist. She said that, to judge from their writing, these women wanted revenge against men—all men. They wanted to punish men for their bad treatment of women over the ages. They particularly wanted to punish men who used violence to subdue and dominate women. Especially, though not only, their wives and girlfriends."

"Thank you, Alice. You've told me what I need to know. I'll get back to you if I have any more questions about the ancient Furies and the Oresteia. And sorry for phoning so late."

"I was working anyway, so not a problem. All the best, Rachel," Alice said and hung up.

By now, I knew enough about the Furies to connect the

dots. And twelve hours later, that afternoon, I got a call from Altan confirming what Alice had told me. He'd found an out-of-print book on the history of women's writing in the United States. It contained a brief but detailed entry on the writers who called themselves the Furies.

"Let me give you a short version of this, Professor," he said. I could hear him pause to unfold a page of notes. Then he started reading. "Founded in Boston in 1890, the Furies were women writers centred in Boston. Between 1890 and 1915, they were famous—maybe, infamous—for their work on female suffrage and other causes of interest to women. Especially, prostitution, drunkenness, public education, and women's property rights. These writers called themselves the Furies to connect with ancient deities in Greek mythology.

"Group members were committed to punishing men who had committed atrocious crimes against women. Drawings and cartoons from the period portray the Furies, and especially their leaders, as hags with snakes in their hair, blood dripping from their fangs, and wings or dark robes.

"Leaders of the group encouraged this reputation, nicknaming themselves after the original Greek Furies. Writer Alexis Bissell Wright often referred to herself as Alecto ('The Unceasing') and claimed to represent relentless anger. Meghan Carter Jones referred to herself as Megaera ('The Jealous') and claimed to symbolize envy and resentment. Tessie Bernard Williams claimed an affinity with the Greek deity Tisiphone ('The Avenger') who personified punishment for murder.

"The scant fictional work of this group is mostly unread today," Altan said, continuing to read aloud. "The heroines of their published stories enforce cosmic justice and uphold moral order. All of their stories highlight the idea of divine retribution. They also stress the idea that all males—even kings and gods— will be held to account for their actions."

I thanked Altan for his hard work and told him I'd ponder this information later. It had some bearing on the Donny Foster case—I knew it did—but couldn't see exactly how.

14

Just after midnight, I still couldn't put Melanie and the Furies out of my mind. So, I phoned Jackie Taylor to arrange a meeting. I knew she'd be up working, yet another night owl.

"Jackie, I need to ask you a few questions about Melanie Foster. How about meeting this afternoon, say around two? I'll bring the coffee. How do you take it?"

"One cream, one sugar. You'll find me in the Blugerman Building, room 1149. See you at two."

After hanging up, I thought about the Furies and lost track of time. Eventually, I woke up with my head on the computer keyboard. I dragged myself out of the desk chair and into bed, where I slept dreamlessly until eight in the morning.

Last night's research on the Furies had left me with a lot to think about. Both the Faust story and the Furies' story concerned disinhibition, or what Freud might have called 'id-work'. In Faust's case, the disinhibition of sexual desires. The pursuit of pleasure. In the Furies' case, the disinhibition of aggressive or violent impulses. The pursuit of death.

Not a surprise, I thought. For some people, nothing was more riveting than the satisfaction of sexual urges. And for others, nothing was more satisfying than violence, especially through acts of revenge. Especially, in the pursuit of death.

But I'd have to turn off that part of my brain and think about other things for a while. First of all, I had a date to talk to Jackie about Melanie Foster. Around noon, I showered, dressed, ate a sandwich, and headed down to the University.

"Come on in. Let's get comfortable," she said when I arrived. Her small, pleasantly appointed office was almost stiflingly warm and stuffed with knick-knacks from foreign travel. As I handed Jackie the coffee I'd brought, I spied a silver ring on her right hand.

"The ring's unusual, isn't it?" she said, noticing my interest. "It's like a traditional Claddagh ring—two hands clasping a heart for love—but different. Over the heart is a ruby. It's said to represent freedom, freedom from captivity. I've heard people call it the 'Secret Circle.'"

I leaned in to see it better. "A beautiful name for a beautiful ring."

Settling into a small sofa, I told Jackie the Dean had asked me to keep an eye on Donny Foster. At least while he got back into the swing of teaching and research.

"How long did you know Melanie?" I asked her.

"Almost thirty years," she said. "We started at Strachan around the same time and met at a party. Became fast friends and eventually brought our husbands together. Lots of group activities followed: vacations, theater, picnics, you name it."

"So, you knew Donny and Melanie well?"

"Oh yes, very well." Jackie's voice softened. "Melanie's death was horrible for all of us."

"Do you still see Donny?"

Jackie sighed, dabbing at her eyes with a pale blue handkerchief. "Not anymore. Melanie was the link between us."

"What was Melanie like?" I asked, leaning forward.

Jackie smiled at the memory of her friend. "Kind, loyal, a devoted teacher, a good neighbor. She had a great sense of humor. But she wasn't perfect. Far from it. She spoke her mind and sometimes made enemies that way. Toward the end, she was nervous—cautious, always looking over her shoulder."

"Did she say why?"

Jackie hesitated. "It usually had something to do with Donny."

"Were they close?"

Jackie nodded. "Yes. Melanie was his anchor. Donny could be brilliant, but he was unpredictable. Melanie kept him steady. She'd have done anything for him. Well, almost anything."

"What do you mean?"

"Melanie was committed to telling the truth. She'd never lie, not for anyone or for any reason. That's the one thing she wouldn't have done for Donny, if the issue had arisen."

"Did you follow his trial?" I asked.

"Of course. My husband and I were called as character witnesses."

"And you weren't convinced by any of the prosecutor's evidence? The evidence that he'd lied about Melanie's tattoo? Or that he'd had an affair shortly before Melanie arrived in Texas?"

"None of that amounted to anything. I accepted Donny's explanations at face value."

"Did he have many flings with other women while he and Melanie were married?"

"Gosh, I don't know. Melanie tolerated no end of silliness when it came to Donny. He loves women—loves looking at them, talking to them, and making them smile. He needs to win the approval of every pretty woman on the planet. It's like an addiction for him. His head was on a swivel whenever they left the house. Melanie just saw it as one of his weaknesses. None of that came to anything."

"And what about the Workshop? What can you tell me about that?"

The blood drained out of Jackie's face. "Why do you ask?"

"The Dean mentioned that name the other day. But we don't know anything about the group. Only that it has a connection with Donny."

Jackie hesitated, then said, "Melanie was working with a group of students. She said they did important work—dangerous work—but wouldn't say more."

Not wanting to impose any further on Jackie's hospitality, I stood to leave, thanking Jackie for her time. As I left her office, I wondered if Jackie had told me the whole, unvarnished truth about the Workshop.

15

Winter was earlier than usual this year. The sky was dark. A strong wind buffeted the trees and snowflakes flew into my face, making it hard to see. Leaving Jackie's office for the parking garage, I buttoned the collar on my winter coat. Hunching my shoulders, I lowered my head and pushed into the wind.

Stepping through the cold, I spotted a manila envelope on my windshield. I glanced around, took the envelope, and slid into the car. Immediately, I locked the doors.

A note inside the envelope read: 'You're getting close to the truth, Professor Tile. But many secrets are best left buried. Stop digging.'

My hands tightened on the steering wheel. I looked for the person who'd left the note and, finding no one, started the car. And as I drove away, my mind flooded with new questions. Who'd put the note on my windshield? Why did they leave it here, outside Jackie Taylor's office? And what secret were they so eager to hide?

I wasn't just trying to please the Dean anymore. I was trying to find out the truth, and I'd never turn my back on that challenge.

Not surprisingly, I had trouble falling asleep that night. I dreamed of Furies, of Faust and Mephistopheles, of secret notes with mysterious meanings.

The next morning, my phone rang as I got ready to leave for the office. "Professor Tile? This is Garet Foster."

"Hi, Garet. What's up?"

"It's my father. He says he's hearing voices. His mother's, my mother's, other voices he can't identify. They're all criticizing him. He's depressed, and I don't know what to do for him. Has he seemed any different to you?"

I pictured Garet in my imagination: frail and delicate, slight, in need of gentle handling.

"No," I said. "He's his usual self—full of energy and stories. But I'll keep an eye out and let you know if anything changes."

"Thank you," she whispered, her voice still heavy with worry.

After hanging up, I wondered why Garet was reaching out so often, while her brother Dylan stayed silent.

I started thinking about my new book again and an hour rushed by.

Then, during a break from writing, I looked for more information about the Texas Killing Fields. I had little success so, after two hours of frustration, I phoned Altan.

"Do you have time to talk about the Killing Fields?"

"Sure," he said. Three minutes later, he was in my office.

I laid out the grim details again—thirty bodies found in the Killing Fields, few convictions.

He listened, frowning. "Sounds like bad police work," he said.

"Maybe," I said. "Or something worse. Bribery, corruption.

There's also a theory those killings are tied to the oil and shipping industries—to transient workers and rootless men. Those guys make good suspects."

He nodded. "I get that. And it's hard to track drifters. It gives the police an excuse not to try."

Before I could answer, I heard a knock at the door. Almost immediately, the door opened, and a man stepped inside. Gray suit, gray skin, bloodshot eyes. Even at a distance, he smelled of tobacco.

"Professor Tile?" he asked.

"Yes. How can I help you?"

"I'm Agent Craig Harrison, FBI," he said, fishing a badge out of his pocket and flashing it. "Can we talk for a few minutes? Alone?"

Altan excused himself and left the office.

"I didn't know the FBI operates in Canada."

"I'm here unofficially," he said. "Talking with people at CSIS. Off the record."

"How can I help you?"

"I'm looking for information about Donny Foster. He knows something about the Killing Fields—something Melanie Foster may have uncovered before her death. We think it may be something big. Someone wanted her dead because of what she'd discovered. And we think her husband knows what it was, so I need your help finding out what he knows."

"Sure, but I have one or two questions for you too."

Harrison nodded his head and smiled. "Shoot. I'll answer them if I can."

He fumbled for cigarettes in his jacket pocket and pulled one out but didn't light it. He jiggled it in his hand while he waited for me to ask my first question.

"The Devlin Crew that works in the Houston area. It's the

same gang that operated in New Jersey a few decades ago, right?"

"Yes, pretty much the same. Jonny Devlin is still the boss, though they've added new people since coming to Texas."

"Why did the Crew leave New Jersey?"

"I don't know all the reasons, but I can tell you a few. The Crew was being squeezed for control of the waterfront by a New York gang. Jonny knew it would be easier to gain control of the Houston waterfront than regain the docks in New Jersey, Brooklyn, and Manhattan. It was obvious even in the '90s that Houston was just as good a place to centre a smuggling operation as New Jersey or even Baltimore."

"Was it hard for the Crew to change its location?"

"Oh sure, very hard. The local gangs shed a lot of blood fighting it out with Jonny Devlin. The largest, the Smith Brothers gang, lost dozens of people. Bloodshed aside, the Devlins hated leaving New Jersey. Their roots were there. Lots and lots of family. That's a huge thing with those northern gangs. They feel lonely with fewer than a hundred relatives in the neighbourhood."

"So, if Jonny Devlin had to choose between his family and his business, which do you think he'd choose?"

"We already know the answer: he'd choose business every time. He made that choice when he moved to Houston. Now, I'm not saying family is unimportant to Jonny. Look, he keeps Conkie Rovino around, one of his million cousins, yet Conkie is as close to a vegetable as you'll find in the American underworld—and that's saying a lot. So yes, family is important to Jonny and his Crew. But in the end, everything in organized crime is about business. It's about making a profit. End of sentence. Exclamation mark."

I felt a chill.

"And you want to find out what Donny knows about the Killing Fields?"

Harrison smiled, yellow teeth showing. "In a nutshell, that's it. So, keep an eye on him. Let me know if you hear anything useful."

"Fine. But I'll have to clear it with my Dean. If she agrees, how do I reach you?"

Harrison handed me a card. A telephone number, nothing else.

"Call me," he said. "Leave a message if I don't answer. I'll call you back."

He turned to leave, coughing into his sleeve. His laugh came low and bitter. "Damn smoking. It'll kill you every time."

My office was starting to stink of tobacco, sweat, and cheap aftershave. I stared at the card in my hand, thoughts already racing. As Harrison left, I held my breath, finally relieved when he was out of the room. In the hallway, he coughed again. Then I heard the flick of a lighter.

Something about Harrison bothered me. He didn't seem trustworthy, not one hundred percent. I couldn't say why, but I felt it. Maybe it was the way he talked about the case, like the Texas Killing Fields mattered more than Melanie Foster. Maybe Melanie had stumbled into something Harrison cared about more than her murder. He made me uneasy.

My phone rang, cutting into my thoughts again. It was Farid.

"Hiya," I said, trying to sound cheerful. "What's up?"

"I was thinking about our last date. It was perfect, Rachel. When can I see you again?"

I sighed audibly. "I'm buried in work. And this Foster business is turning into a headache. An FBI agent showed up today, asking questions about Donny. I'll call you later when I can think straight, okay?"

"Of course," Farid whispered. "You know how I feel."

"Me too," I said, and hung up. I winced. Why did I say that? But Farid would understand. He always did.

Seeing a spare hour, I returned to the Foster problem. I searched for Donny's published papers on Google Scholar, then read a few. His interviews with car thieves in New Jersey were impressive. He'd gained their trust, but how? Had he crossed ethical lines, like Julia Dent was accused of doing? I shot him a quick message praising the articles and asking if he'd collected the same kinds of data in Texas.

He answered right away. 'Thanks for reading. Same kinds of data as in New Jersey, but I got even more in Texas. The New Jersey work made them trust me.'

'How did you get those guys to open up?'

'Vanity,' he replied. 'They wanted me to see them as businessmen, not crooks. Maybe they lied a little, but most of it was true.'

'Do you think you crossed any lines?' I asked, pressing him on the issue.

'Some people might say so. I don't think I did. I'm in Chicago right now. Let's talk when I'm back in Toronto on Friday.'

16

Overnight, the snow had stopped. Today, Toronto had one of those clear, bright, sunny skies that raised my spirits. Well, made me as glad as I could be with below-zero temperatures. Everything looked white and Christmassy, two months ahead of time. The roads had been cleared, so I had no trouble getting down to work. And the million other drivers heading down Avenue Road also had smiles on their faces.

Finally in my office with a hot cup of what passed for coffee, I was reviewing a Master's thesis when I heard a knock at the door. A tall man with broad shoulders stood there, holding a badge.

"Professor Tile? I'm Officer Raymond Decker, CSIS. Can I come in?"

I waved him in, wary. He sat down.

"We're investigating car thefts in Canada," he said. "We think Donny Foster may be doing more than research. His connections to the underworld are troubling. Maybe you can help us with information on that."

"I was approached about Donny just yesterday, by the FBI. But you probably know that already."

Decker nodded his head to signal that he did indeed know. "Yeah, Craig Harrison told me he might drop by."

"The Dean's watching me. So I'm limited in what I can do. And so far, I haven't found out very much."

"Do what you can and let us know if you learn anything interesting." Decker nodded again, handed me a card and left. I stared at the card, my mind racing.

Why this sudden flood of attention from law enforcement? I wondered if they'd been monitoring my email or phone calls. Then I considered looking for a more secure way to communicate—maybe, a new internet address or a burner phone. But in the end, I decided to stay with my current technology. I wasn't doing anything a court would consider wrong.

Later that day, two new messages rattled my nerves. The first was anonymous: 'We know you're looking into car smuggling. Stop, or you'll regret it.'

The second, from a Texas lawyer, warned me to back off or face legal action.

The Texas Stock Exchange
Suite 1289, Marriott Tower
Houston, TX 77007

Dear Professor Tile,

Your activities are continuing to threaten the business interests of Lone Star Entertainments, a leading member of the new Texas Stock Exchange (TXX). As well, members of the TXX Board are concerned that your interference will delay the launch of the new Texas Stock Exchange on January 1, 2026.

The Board is asking you to cease and desist from your investigations at once. If you fail to heed this warning, the Board will take legal action. Such action may force you to engage in unwanted legal proceedings, interfering with your academic activities and coming at notable cost.

To avoid this, please have your lawyer discuss the matter with our staff at Crombie, Finch, Melber, Harden, and Feldman in Houston. Please direct your responses to Albert Harden at 713-222-1111 during regular business hours. Meanwhile, we urge you to suspend your interference with the activities of Lone Star Entertainment.

Yours truly,
Benjamin Melber, LL.B

I had no idea why this lawyer was telling me to 'cease and desist.' Did TXX want me to stop investigating Donny Foster, and if so, why? What did Donny have to do with TXX, or even Lone Star Entertainments? I didn't want to get trapped in a legal case and made a note to contact a lawyer. But right now, I was far too busy.

Despite the danger signs, I still couldn't see Donny as a criminal. He was a colleague who did academic research, and it was good research. Although, maybe he'd overreached himself, like some academics tended to do.

I went back over the evidence I'd collected. Maybe Melanie had stumbled onto something she shouldn't have known. Secret knowledge of criminal activity, let's say. Maybe a discovery that had sealed her fate, something Donny hadn't wanted her to know. Maybe even something he didn't know. But what Melanie knew was something I still couldn't guess.

Altan had continued looking into the Killing Fields and, later that day, he sent me his findings. 'Six bodies in five years,' he'd written. 'Three teenagers from small towns on I-45, a sex worker, a homeless woman, and Lana Bond—a known associate of the Devlin Crew. A woman named Kim Cressy reported Lana missing after they'd gone barhopping.'

He'd attached photos of Lana and Kim to his report. The two women were both beautiful, though Kim was blonde and Lana, a brunette. Kim was as lovely in the photograph as she'd been on television a few nights earlier. An attached article said Lana had studied accounting before starting to manage a Houston club, the Bells N' Whistle. The article described BNW as 'upscale.' A place where businessmen closed million-dollar deals while women 'strutted their stuff.' I didn't know what that meant, having never been to such a place.

'Lana was executed,' the article declared. Two bullets to the head.

According to the article, Lana may have been a member, or at least associate, of the Devlin Crew. And the Devlin Crew had been under increasing pressure from another gang based in Maryland. It was challenging the Devlin Crew for control over docking rights at Valencia and Piraeus. Recent murders in Spain and Greece were probably part of this gang war, and so was Lana's death, though no reason was given in the article.

'This may be tied to a gang war between the Devlin Crew and the Smith Brothers,' Altan suggested. 'Recent murders in Spain and Greece are part of that, and Melanie's death may connect, somehow. Some reports say those murders may involve the Smith Brothers. It's also possible that Melanie and Lana both messed with the same people and got killed for their trouble.'

I looked for more information about Kim Cressy but found only a few brief entries on the internet. One identified her as a self-employed 'Financial Consultant.' Checking LinkedIn, I found a brief listing there too. But again, no background information. No personal history, no list of degrees and qualifications, no organizational affiliations. Maybe she'd changed her name. Maybe she'd married and taken her husband's name. Or she'd been born with an unpronounceable surname she was happy to exchange for 'Cressy'.

Still, so little online presence was odd for a self-employed consultant. I wrote the names of Lana and Kim in my notebook, resolving to find out more about them later.

Coincidentally, a ringing phone interrupted my thoughts. Jackie Taylor was on the line.

"I contacted a few members of the Workshop and told them about your interest in Melanie's death. What did you want to know?"

"For one thing, I'm curious about a woman named Kim Cressy. She reported a missing friend two years ago, a friend whose body then turned up in the Texas Killing Fields. She's in the car business, and I've just seen her on a local TV show. I don't believe in coincidences, Jackie. So I'm trying to find out if she's connected to Melanie's death in any way. Do you think the Workshop can find out anything about her?"

"I don't know, but I'll pass your query along. If they find out anything, I'll get back to you."

"One more thing: how did they get the name the Workshop? Do you know?"

"I hear they modelled themselves on the ancient Furies but didn't want to call themselves that. Maybe the name sounded too old-fashioned. So, they called themselves the Workshop instead. The name's more up to date—more ironic and business-like, I guess," Jackie said.

"Thanks for your help with this," I told her.

"No worries. I'm glad to help." Jackie hung up and I went back to working.

Then I asked Altan to find out what he could about Donny Foster's Austin visitor, Gina Wolff. I hadn't seen much about her in the trial transcript, since she hadn't been called as a witness.

I also emailed Roxy to ask if she knew anything about international smuggling gangs that worked out of the US. In less than an hour, she'd found one reference to an FBI investigation into smuggling gangs in the southern US—a gang war in Texas over contested landing rights. The FBI had asked CSIS to supply information about clashes between these same gangs in Montreal, Toronto, and Calgary.

Shortly after midnight, Altan emailed to tell me Gina Wolff, a woman of about 35, lived in Ottawa and owned a business called Gina's Custom Travel. He provided a phone number and email address for the travel agency. I emailed Ms. Wolff, asking her to contact me, saying I hoped we could talk about 'matters of common interest.'

To my surprise, she was still awake and replied within half an hour. We agreed to meet in Ottawa later that day at the

Metropolitain Brasserie, a lunch place in Byward Market. I made the necessary online reservations: a plane ticket for 10 a.m. and a lunch table at 12:30.

Feeling a bit refreshed, I worked on my book until 4 a.m. Then, almost comatose, I collapsed into bed. I slept deeply for three hours, until my alarm went off.

Waking up foggy-headed, I showered, dressed, and caught the 10:00 a.m. plane out of Billy Bishop, the waterfront airport. Almost before I'd finished reading the newspaper, the plane had put down in Ottawa's Macdonald-Cartier Airport. I grabbed a cab to the ByWard Market and with time to spare, killed the better part of an hour looking into gift shops and antique stores that dotted the neighbourhood. Around 12:30, I entered Metropolitain Brasserie and sat down at a corner table where no one would hear us. Just after I'd made myself comfortable, Gina Wolff arrived. I recognized her right away. She was my former student, Gina Gropner.

Gina still had that long, black wavy hair I remembered from nearly fifteen years earlier. Also, the big, dimpled cheeks and beautiful smile. She exuded lively enthusiasm, just as she had when she sat in my class and argued about … whatever. Gina loved arguing, though always in a pleasant, humorous way. She'd never left anyone with hurt feelings.

"Not Gina Gropner anymore, I take it," I said, embracing her, a broad smile pasted to my face. Gina, though older, was still youthful and attractive. I also noticed she was wearing a silver ring on her right hand, just like the one Jackie Taylor had worn. The "secret circle" ring, as Jackie had called it.

"I traded in Gropner when I married Billy Wolff eight years ago. We're divorced now but I've kept his name, since it's on several of my diplomas. Besides, I was never keen about the name Gropner."

"So you see yourself as a Wolff instead, eh? A Wolff in sheep's clothing?"

"Yes, all of that. But please, Professor Tile, I *have* heard that joke once or twice before."

"Why didn't you mention you were—had been—Gina Gropner when I emailed you?"

"I thought it would be fun to see your reaction when I walked in here," Gina replied, laughing. "And it was."

"Well, call me Rachel, and thanks for meeting me on such short notice. Let's order lunch and then talk. I'm starving."

We ordered lunch—scallops for me and a bouillabaisse for Gina, plus green salad for both. While we waited for the food, I turned our conversation to the topic of Donny Foster.

"You spent a few weeks with Foster in Austin before his wife Melanie arrived, right? I'd like to know about your connection with him. Understand, this is not out of pure nosiness. The Dean needs me to reintegrate Donny into our faculty. But some people feel uneasy having him around, because of the accusation that he killed his wife. What can you tell me about him?"

"I'm glad you're asking, because the Houston police sure didn't spend much time on this. They made unfounded assumptions instead. Not that those assumptions made any difference to the outcome of the trial."

Gina paused for a sip of water, her eyes staring into the distance. For a minute, I thought she wouldn't continue. Then she drew a deep breath and met my gaze full on.

"First, let me tell you I work for CSIS. My travel agency is just a cover. It gives me plenty of freedom to travel, meet people, and gather intel without drawing attention. And recently, I've spent a lot of time studying the Devlin Crew."

That bit of information rocked me back on my heels. This girl was full of surprises.

"Donny and I were friends with benefits," she continued. "It was no more than an escape for both of us. I was getting over my divorce, and he felt trapped in his marriage. Not trapped exactly, just bored. He never criticized Melanie. Was he frustrated with her? Yes, sometimes. But he never would have killed her."

"It came out in the trial that he'd had a huge fight with Melanie the night before she disappeared," I said.

Gina nodded. "That's right. Donny phoned to tell me all about it. We talked for hours. That's how I know that, if Melanie died on the day she disappeared, he couldn't have killed her. For a large part of that day, he was on the phone with me. Melanie had given him a lot of grief about his work in Texas and the people he was interviewing. Also, about his research assistant, Hannah Proctor. Melanie didn't like her at all."

We stopped talking while a server put dishes of food on the table. Gina started talking again and I started to eat. She paused now and then for a spoonful of soup.

"I offered to testify. But his lawyer said it would look bad if the defense was based on an affair. He thought it would be more damaging than helpful. So I kept my mouth shut."

If what Gina said was true, then Donny had something like an alibi for the time of Melanie's death. Not perfect, but better than nothing.

"Did you think of telling the media about this?"

Gina hesitated. "I couldn't. If I'd come forward, it would have tipped off the Devlin Crew. All the work I'd done for CSIS would've been wasted. It might have also undermined my other investigations."

My whole view of the case was turning on a dime.

"I also had to think of my own reputation, and my travel business," she admitted "Maybe I was being selfish. But the media would have torn me apart and I was trying to rebuild my life after the divorce."

I thought about this while chewing a tasty, delicate, scallop.

"So, you must think Donny is innocent?" I mumbled, my mouth half full.

Gina looked directly at me, her eyes full of conviction. "I don't think he killed Melanie, if that's what you mean."

Should I tell any of this to Garet Foster, I wondered. It might set her mind at ease, knowing her father had an alibi for the time her mother was killed. But hearing more about his affair wouldn't make her feel any better. For reasons I couldn't understand, I found myself identifying with Garet. And worrying about her.

17

"Tell me more about your connection with Donny," I said to Gina. "Start at the beginning, would you?"

"Sure. More than a dozen years ago, I was his student in a third-year research methods course. Then, in fourth year, I did a project on car smuggling under his supervision. That summer, after graduating, Donny and I met for drinks a few times, then we slept together. But I had a boyfriend and he was married, so it didn't turn into anything. He was infatuated with a younger woman, I with an older man. End of story."

"I don't get it. You were a smart young woman with a brilliant future. What did you see in Donny that made you want to sleep with him?"

"You have to see him through my eyes—at least, the way he looked to me then. He was famous, and smart, and often funny. More than that, he was so determined. He may have been the only person I knew who had dedicated his whole life to research and discovery. That made him very special, even unique. Many of the more intellectually-minded girls in our class felt the same way."

"Okay, I get that. He's a smart guy who's achieved a lot of fame in the field."

"Anyway, I went off to graduate school in the US and we weren't in touch for about five years. When I came back to Canada, I joined CSIS, settled in Ottawa, and started my travel agency. Around that time, I contacted Donny again and we started exchanging emails. After arranging to spend his sabbatical year in Texas, he invited me to visit him there for a week or two. I'd just divorced my husband and was up for a change, so I said okay. I went down to Texas and spent two weeks with him in Austin. It was fun. Then I returned to Ottawa."

"Weren't you afraid Melanie would find out what you were doing?"

Gina snorted, spraying red wine across the lunch table. Then she laughed raucously.

"Gosh, no. She knew all about it. Melanie and I were close friends, though Donny didn't have a clue about that. I'd met her around the same time I started taking his third-year course. She headed up a small group that worked to end the abuse of women. I helped her for years. Donny had no idea any of that was going on."

"So, Melanie knew you were going to spend time with Donny in Austin while she was teaching in Toronto?"

Gina started laughing again. "Rachel, she asked me to do it. She wanted me close to him, so I could monitor his activities. She suspected the Devlin Crew of using women as sex slaves in their clubs."

"Then Melanie didn't care you were having sex with her husband?"

"Not a bit. After all, they'd been together for thirty years. Besides, his sex drive is pretty low these days, compared with younger men I've known. So, if occasional sex could help me get info on the Devlin Crew, Melanie was all for it. Oh, and if you're wondering, my boss at CSIS was fine with it too."

"It sounds like something out of a spy movie," I said, only half-joking.

Gina gave an ironic smile, "Sometimes, life is stranger than fiction." Then she made a DUH-DUH-DUH sound, mimicking the dramatic music of a suspense movie.

I pretended to look shocked, eyes bulging, mouth gaping open. We both had a good laugh.

"Was Donny involved in the Devlin Crew's criminal activities? Or was he just an observer?" I asked her.

Gina's eyes darkened. "I don't think he committed any crimes. But they might have liked having him around. The Devlin Crew operated a legitimate business under the name of Lone Star Investments. Donny may have played a part in that business, though I don't know for sure."

"So what now?"

"Now? Donny is free and the Devlin Crew is still smuggling cars. The FBI and CSIS have beefed up their surveillance. But they need more solid evidence before they can make arrests. Melanie must have stumbled on something important, and that's why she was killed. If you're up for it, I'd like you to help me find out what Melanie discovered."

This frightened me but I knew I'd plunge ahead anyway.

"Is Donny in danger of being killed himself?"

"I don't know what Melanie's killers may or may not do. But the fact he's back at work, still collecting data and writing articles, suggests the smuggling community doesn't view Donny as a threat."

"One more question, Gina, and I'll let you go," I said, lowering my voice to make extra sure no one could hear us. "Do you know anything about Lana Bond? Police found her body in the Killing Fields a year or two before Melanie's death. I hear she was an associate of the Devlin Crew."

"I met Lana once, about five years ago, though I didn't get to know her well. The FBI had planted her in Houston, to get close to the Crew. Jonny must have figured out what Lana was up to, so he had her killed."

"If that's true, both Melanie and Lana may have been killed trying to expose the Devlin Crew's activities. But the authorities treated their deaths as isolated incidents. They never connected the dots."

Gina sipped her water, a hint of sadness—also, tiredness—creeping into her face. "The Devlin Crew is good at covering their tracks. They also have a lot of pull in Texas. Local authorities may have thought it was easier to ignore the deaths. I don't know if you've heard about this, but Jonny Devlin is behind a new push to create a Texas Stock Exchange. The political bigwigs like that a lot."

"What's in it for them?"

"For the VIPs, another chance to show off Texas and thumb their noses at New York City, or as they sometimes call it, Jew York City. For Jonny, a chance to launder money, do a little insider trading, and get himself a Key to the City."

The idea that people in authority had ignored these deaths made me sick with anger. "It sounds like the Devlin Crew has eyes and ears everywhere," I may have snarled slightly more loudly and harshly than I'd intended.

Gina nodded. "That's why I hesitated to email this information. We're not only protecting our own safety. We're protecting everyone close to us. One wrong move could kill your children or my parents."

"But we can't let it slide. We owe it to Melanie, to Lana, and other women those killers might harm in the future."

Gina sighed, her shoulders drooping under the weight of this responsibility. "Yes, and we'll have to be smart. To bypass the usual channels to avoid leaks."

"I'm with you. How do we start?"

Gina leaned forward, her eyes intense. "First, we gather any information Melanie left behind. Notes, journals, correspondence, anything we can find. Then, we retrace her steps. This may help us find out what Melanie discovered that made her a target. And don't underestimate Donny. He could do a lot of harm if he puts his mind to it. He acts like a goof sometimes, but he's a dangerous goof with a brilliant mind."

I felt a rush of resolve for the first time in weeks.

"You're right. If the Devlin Crew figures out what we're doing, we'll be their next targets. And if Donny figures out what we're doing…. well, that's another problem."

Gina reached across the table and grabbed my hand. "We're in this together. For Melanie. For Lana. For justice." Then, she made her DUH-DUH-DUH sound again.

I laughed again. "Gina, you always were a bit of an ass," I told her, softly.

Gina grinned, nodding her head in hearty agreement.

This would be a daunting task, but I saw a glimmer of light in the distance. No matter what, the Devlin Crew would have to pay for their actions, and so would Donny. Though I was still having trouble imagining he'd done anything seriously illegal.

I got up and hugged Gina, hoping we'd see each other again soon.

Three hours later, I was back in my Toronto living room. I couldn't stop thinking about the Killing Fields, about Lana and Melanie. But as I thought of all the bodies that had piled up there, I started to panic. I took deep breaths and blew into a paper bag, and after a few minutes, my heart rate slowed back down to normal again.

I desperately needed time off work, some down time. But there'd be no time for a break, not now. For one thing, Garet Foster had left me another message. "Call me when you can, Professor Tile," the message said. "It's an emergency."

I poured myself a glass of club soda and dialed Garet's number.

"What's up, Garet? You said it's an emergency."

"It is. My father took a handful of sleeping pills last night and phoned to say goodbye forever. I called Emergency Services, and they rushed him to the hospital, pumped his stomach out. The doctor says he should be okay in twenty-four hours. But he may need counseling. Do you have any advice? I'm so frightened for my father's safety."

"That's awful, Garet. But I'm sure your father didn't want to kill himself. If he had, he wouldn't have phoned you. That was a cry for help, and you have to hear him. He's had terrible experiences in the past year, what with your mother's death and then his trial. Push him to get professional help."

"Thank you, Professor. I'm already doing that, and I'll tell him you suggest the same thing."

"No. Please don't tell him you talked to me. That would make him feel worse. Just push him to get counseling. Even if this supposed suicide attempt was just an effort to get your attention, spend more time with him. Maybe get your brother involved too."

"Okay, I'll try that. Thanks again," Garet said and rang off.

18

The next morning brought me yet another official-looking letter from the Texas Stock Exchange.

The first half of the letter described the advantages of the Texas Stock Exchange (TXX) versus the more famous New York Stock Exchange (NYSE). The second half invited me to take part in discussions around establishing this new exchange. Or, as the letter said, more pompously, to 'lend my expertise in helping to establish the foundational principles for an emerging stock exchange.'

I emailed Altan, gave him a short version of what Gina Wolff had said, and told him about the letter from TXX. We met in my office two hours later and I launched into a rant even before he sat down.

"I can't figure out why they wrote me, of all people. How did they get my name, and what do they think I can bring to their discussions? I don't know anything about stock exchanges. Or how people might set up new ones."

"We'll get this sorted, Professor," he murmured, comfortingly. "I went online and discovered two interesting facts. First, the organizers expect TXX to draw in more conservative business organizations that prefer 'less woke' and 'less regulated' business activities. This suggests the TXX has a political goal, though I don't know what it is."

As he said all this, he used scary-fingers to highlight the odd goals TXX had stated.

"The other is that a few big organizations have provided the money for this start-up. Lone Star Entertainments (LSE), a lead donor, put in $50 million. Interestingly, Lone Star Entertainments is a subsidiary of Lone Star Investments. It owns about fifty restaurants, casinos, and 'gentlemen's clubs' throughout the southern United States. Until now, LSE has been in private hands. But it plans to go public when the TXX opens. And here's the most interesting part: the Chairman of the Board of Lone Star Investments is Jonny Devlin. He's the guy we know about through Donny Foster."

"That's very useful," I mumbled. Then, having calmed a bit, I switched topics. I'd just remembered my coming dinner party. "On a more pleasant topic, are you free Monday night? Friends are coming over for Thanksgiving dinner. I'd like you and your roommate to come, if you can."

"I'll ask him if we have other plans. But if we're free, we'll certainly come. Please let me know the details: where, when, and so on."

I promised to email the details and Altan left. I used the next few hours to work on my new book. All this stopping and starting wasn't good for my creative juices, but I soldiered on.

Later that afternoon, when I was about to leave for home, I noticed the cleaning person had left the door to Donny's office unlatched. I didn't know if she was coming back any time soon but wanted a quick look around. So, after listening for footsteps, I slipped into the office, shut the door, and turned on the light.

There, as before, were the two paintings Donny had taken down. Looking closely, I noted the signatures. Jackie Taylor had painted the portrait of Melanie. Melanie had painted the haunting picture of an empty field. Turning them over, I found nothing on the back of Melanie's portrait. The other picture showed a pencilled inscription: 'Killing Fields, Texas, June 2016.' This told me Melanie had been aware of—even fascinated by—the Killing Fields, many years before her death and burial there.

A closer inspection revealed a black rectangle in the distance with what looked like tiny windows on it. Melanie must have thought this black blob was a trailer home. But who'd live in such a bleak, deserted area?

Then I heard someone singing softly in the hall. Fearing the cleaner was headed back, I turned off the light and slipped out the door. I walked briskly, to look like I was going home after another normal day at work. But what I'd seen in Donny's office was anything but normal.

My drive home was also far from relaxed. What I'd seen in Donny's office, and then imagined, had distressed me. I wondered what the Killing Fields really looked like. And what *was* that black rectangular blob in the distance—the one that had fascinated Melanie? Was it important? Had Melanie gone in for a closer look? Did she know what it was, and if so, had she recorded her observations anywhere? For example, in another picture? Maybe I'd find another picture if I investigated the basement of the Language Arts building.

Back home, I kept thinking about what I'd seen in Donny's office. But I had other things to worry about now. Thanksgiving weekend was only a few days off.

I sketched an action plan on a scrap of paper. I'd pick up champagne and wine at the LCBO on Saturday and prepare the risotto on Sunday. All the other food—roast beef, salmon, root vegetables, salads and salad dressings, and desserts— would arrive at 4 p.m. on Monday, Thanksgiving Day. The bartender and serving staff would arrive at 5 p.m. Guests would start arriving between 5:30 and 6 p.m. Before all that, I'd need to do a laundry and make sure the house was clean. I phoned Molly Maid and arranged for two of my favourite cleaners to spend the day at my house.

This dinner will be fun, I thought, smiling to myself. But I knew when Thanksgiving arrived, I'd have to deal with Donny carefully. He'd be sensitive to questions about his wife's death, his trial in Texas, and the illicit car trade.

19

As expected, Thanksgiving Day was busy from morning to night. In the morning, I did my laundry while 'maids' cleaned the house, top to bottom. Josh, home for once (it seemed), made sure we had all the glassware we needed. Some had to go into the dishwasher.

By four in the afternoon, I'd showered and dressed. As usual, in smart, casual clothing.

Ellie was the first to arrive, looking beautiful in a new, tight-fitting emerald-green cashmere sweater. Thrilled to see her, I hugged her close. We hadn't spent any time together in the past month. Whenever I suggested meeting up, Ellie was always busy. That's the way it is with college students. I'd probably been just as unavailable when I was her age. But I missed my daughter. I vowed to find ways, and times, to get us together more often.

Roxy showed up ten minutes later in black pants and a green silk blouse, a good bottle of red wine in her right hand. Arriving just behind her were Connie and her roommate, both in their best tailored shirts and corduroy pants. Connie—my old assistant, Clever Connie—handed me a small but heavy box of homemade mince tarts. Minutes later, Altan and his roommate arrived, each in a dress shirt and tie. Altan handed me a box of rose-scented Turkish delight—a 'small gift to Madame Professor.' A minute later, my oldest friend arrived. Jen always remembered my Thanksgiving dinners and always came alone.

At ten to six, Gene Tretnikoff showed up with his beautiful

daughter, Irina. He, in a black silk tuxedo and she, in a stylish black cashmere dress that ended above her knees. They'd brought a special bottle of brandy for after dinner.

Then finally, Farid arrived. Wearing a white dinner jacket, he carried the largest bouquet of red roses I'd ever seen. I put them on a side table and we kissed slowly, tenderly. How embarrassing, I thought suddenly, blushing and separating from him.

I had a server put the flowers into three different vases. They couldn't all fit into one, not even my largest.

I was nuts about Farid. I couldn't help it. That's how I always fell in love—how I'd fallen in love with Michael (my first husband), Robert Delamont (last year's crush), and now Farid. True, my first marriage had ended terribly, with desertion and divorce, and much later, Michael's murder. My crush on Robert had also ended badly, with death by gunshot. And interestingly, my best friend Jen was tied to the first two of these love affairs: as Michael's sister and Robert's honorary 'godmother'. What would she become to Farid, I wondered.

But I wasn't going to think about a pattern, not tonight anyway.

As they arrived, I seated my guests in the just-large-enough living room. A fire was burning in the fireplace, soft music was playing, and everyone looked comfortable. Soon, Farid was handing everyone glasses of champagne. My new fella sure knew how to please me.

When everyone else had arrived, Donny made a grand entrance. He wore a double-breasted grey suit and red bowtie with white polka dots. Before taking off his overcoat, he handed me two elegant gold boxes. "Let's not open these until after dinner, okay?" he said.

To get us used to one another, I asked everyone to reveal

how they'd spent the day. Connie started. "We slept in, then went out for breakfast—something we don't do very often. We went to a nice place nearby, had pancakes, then came home, read the newspapers, watched TV, took a shower, and went for a walk. All pretty relaxed."

Connie's roommate nodded his head energetically in agreement. "That's right," he said. "Very relaxed. Even romantic." He smirked when he said that. Connie gave him a severe look, then laughed.

"We slept in late this morning," Altan said, next. "I cooked us a magnificent brunch, many dishes from my homeland, then we tidied up the flat. After brunch, we went down to the Beaches and strolled on the boardwalk. We saw many magnificent dogs. Then we came back home, showered, and came over here."

Ellie was next. "I had coffee and went to the gym. Had breakfast at a friend's place, then came home and did a wash. After not washing my clothes for over a week, I was running out of things to wear. Did the reading for this week's classes, took a shower, then came over here. BORING."

Josh, sitting to Ellie's left, was next. "I slept until noon, listened to music, had breakfast, then did the reading for my classes too. Oh yes, and played a videogame with a friend in Calgary."

Josh's girlfriend followed. "I helped Mom clean the house, did laundry, then homework for my statistics class. It was a busy day, not relaxing at all, until I came over here to hang out." She smiled at Josh and squeezed his hand.

Jen was up next. "I went to Seaton House and helped serve the homeless men. Porridge, toast, coffee, and one apple each. Then I went to the Royal York Hotel. I photographed guests eating *their* holiday brunch—bacon, sausages, pancakes, grilled fish, fresh fruit, croissants, coffee, and mimosas. You can imagine what that buffet looks like. It's huge. Back home, I downloaded the photos and printed a few. I'll show them to you, if you like. The contrast is amusing," she said, aware that we'd soon be eating something like a Royal York dinner.

Irina was next. "Vera made breakfast for Daddy and me—the usual: cereal, muffins, fruit, and yogurt. Then, Daddy talked business on the phone, took a shower, and got dressed. I read for tomorrow's classes, went for a run, showered, and dressed for dinner."

"That's all CORRECT," Gene said, jumping in. "I got in from London around SEVEN this morning, took a cab from the airport, and waited for SLEEPYHEAD here to wake up. We ate breakfast together, I showered, changed, and did a little WORK. Then I walked around Forest Hill, to see if anything had changed there. It HADN'T. It NEVER does."

Roxy went next. "I got up, fed the dog, fed the kids, then went to the gym while my neighbour watched the brats. I got back, gave the kids lunch, did three loads of laundry, cleaned the house, then took the kids to the corner store for Thanksgiving treats. Brought them home, waited for the babysitter, then came over here. It was all very relaxing, as you can imagine."

Farid was up next. "I went to the gym, came home, ate breakfast, then read surgical journals for a few hours. Took a nap, showered, and came over here. Also BORING. But I can tell you that last night, I had the most spectacular dreams. I won't go into detail, but they involved a certain person I'm crazy about. I dreamed about vacationing with her in a romantic spot—someplace warm, where we could swim in the ocean and snorkel. Oh yes, and stare into each other's eyes. Alas, it was a dream—just a dream *so far*."

Farid sure knew how to push my buttons. I found myself

imagining a faraway beach. The day was sunny, and white sand burned the soles of my feet. Just a few other couples were on the beach. Like Farid and me, they were holding hands and staring into each other's eyes. One pair of lovers held each other tight. They were kissing and rubbing against each other slowly, quietly, rhythmically. It was going to get downright embarrassing in a minute or two, I thought, turning away from them.

In a blink, I was back in my own dining room, hosting Thanksgiving dinner. Farid smiled. I tilted my head and sent him a telepathic message: 'Farid, sometimes you're impossible.' But I loved it, and he knew it, and I knew he knew it.

The dinner was turning out great so far!

Donny, not seeing the foreplay between me and Farid, jumped into the conversation. "No dreams about a vacation for me. I spent most of the day looking at D-scores from Valencia."

"Does that refer to a digestive problem in SPAIN?" Gene asked, smiling.

"No, D-scores measure the fitness of different locations for car smuggling. It's an artificial intelligence program I've developed. I wrote the algorithms myself, so 'D' stands for Donny. Anyway, that's all I've done today. Checked my D-scores."

An opening had presented itself and I seized it. Eager to draw him out, I asked "Can you tell us about these D-scores, how they work?"

"I don't want to bore everyone, so I'll keep it brief," he said. "I've developed a computer program that predicts where car smugglers will move the cars they've brought into a country. Suppose they've smuggled cars into Spain through the port of Valencia. Where will they move the cars from there? That's the question I'm trying to answer."

His willingness to talk about this so freely surprised me.

After all, it was the illicit car trade he was discussing. But then I realized he wanted, above all, to impress us.

"I've modeled my theory on the work of Ernst Georg Ravenstein, a 19th century British-German geographer. He laid the groundwork with his so-called 'Laws of Migration.' By analyzing English migration statistics, Ravenstein noted long-distance migration typically occurs in steps or stages, not in one long move.

"I've added elements from network research to show how social factors also influence the flow of people and goods. My own theory predicts the smuggler will move cars to a secondary distribution site no more than 500 kilometers away from the landing site. Ideally, a place with high population density and a high average income. Also, a place accessible to tertiary distribution."

Donny scanned the room to make sure everyone was listening, then continued. "Now, if you look at a map of Spain, you can guess the best secondary site will be Barcelona. It's near Valencia. Plus, it's prosperous and handy to the French border. The best secondary site will *not* be Seville or Granada or Lisbon, or an even smaller place. Those are all geographic dead-ends, according to my theory.

"But will the tertiary distribution site be Lyon or Marseille? They're both near Barcelona, and both are good destinations, though in different ways. Marseille is better for moving cars into Italy, while Lyon is better for moving cars to Paris. They're both good for moving cars into Milan. So, which of the two is better for linking to a fourth distribution site? Those are the kinds of questions I'm trying to answer. I have one doctoral student looking at cars that land in Valencia and another doing the same for cars landing in Piraeus, Greece."

From the corner of my eye, I could see Altan recording

everything on his phone. Not quite legal, of course. But I knew this material would end up in our files by noon tomorrow.

20

I felt like the already-small living room was shrinking—that we were somehow pulling together. Maybe this was a result of getting to know one another. Thankfully, the effect was communal, not claustrophobic. Even the lighting had seemed to dim slightly. People's faces had taken on a warm glow. I liked this feeling—it was friendly, cozy.

Yet, dangers remained. Many in the room would have known about the death of Donny's wife, and he would know—or at least suspect—that they knew. Some would be afraid of hurting him with an insensitive question. Others who thought he was guilty wouldn't want to come out and say it. With everyone being ever so polite, conversation might be a bit awkward. It was hard to predict who'd respond to his theory, and how.

Yet somehow, right now, everything was flowing smoothly.

Finally, Irina couldn't restrain herself. "That's an amazing theory, Professor Foster."

Gene, ever the skeptic, cocked an eyebrow. "Yes, it is VERY interesting. But impressive as it sounds, Donny, how PRAC-TICAL is it? Could the police use your model to prevent or shut down SMUGGLING routes?"

Donny looked pensive. "I've approached the FBI with preliminary findings. But they haven't shown much interest. Plus, I'm still refining the model to increase its accuracy. I hope that, one day, police forces around the world will use my program."

Throughout the presentation, Roxy had been unusually

attentive. Not the usual 'Sure, I'm interested,' but a 'This could be useful' kind of interested.

"Donny, how safe are your findings? Given what you're doing, you'll draw the attention of criminals," she warned.

Donny smirked, brushing away her concern. "Remember, this is still a theoretical model. At this point, who'd be interested, outside the academic world?"

Everyone except Donny could see this work was potentially dangerous. A model that predicted and, therefore, could disrupt car smuggling would put him at risk. Meanwhile, he acted like he was doing something completely harmless.

Gene jumped in with another question. "I understand what you're GETTING at. And why this might interest a geographer or car smuggler. By why does it interest a CRIMINOLOGIST? Are you trying to revise the proverbial notion that 'crime doesn't pay'?"

Donny wasted no time answering. "I'm developing a model that predicts criminal behaviour. The D-Algorithm I've created is far too simple to use just yet. But the work of my doctoral students will refine it, adding variables that make the model more accurate. In the end, I'll have a model that accurately predicts smuggling behaviour. This will be a first for criminology. So far, we don't have any strong theories of criminal behaviour. None that accurately predict what criminals will do. And good prediction is the first step in explaining something. So, when I finish, I'll have created a theory of auto smuggling."

As he said this, Donny held out both hands. As if he was handing everyone—maybe all humanity—a precious gift.

I have to admit, I was impressed. Donny had set himself a tough goal. He was reaching for greatness, no doubt about it, and I admired his ambition. Now I remembered why I'd always respected him and his exploits.

"What variables are you adding to the theory?" Altan asked, his forehead wrinkled in concentration.

"At least three kinds. First, we're adding topographic variables, like the terrain. Travel over flat ground will appeal to smugglers far more than travel through mountains. And smugglers will prefer travel on good highways versus travel on poor highways. Second, we're adding variables related to policing. For example, travel into regions with weak or dishonest policing will appeal to smugglers far more than travel into regions with strong, honest policing. Third and perhaps most important, we're considering the availability of storage and repair facilities."

All these assumptions were valid and important. As with any good theory, the factors Donny had identified were obvious, once someone pointed them out. But until now, no one had put the pieces together.

"What are your doctoral students doing for you?" Connie asked, as any doctoral student would.

"They're collecting data in regions with high D-values, looking for higher- or lower-than-expected levels of smuggling. For example, looking for evidence of new storage facilities. Where they find more smuggling activity than expected, they're looking to see whether new storage facilities explain the variation. They're also looking for unusual topographic and policing features, then feeding these variables into the algorithm. As they do this, our predictions improve. So, this is a continuing process of prediction, validation, and revision."

"How will your students know when it's time to stop collecting new data?" Connie's partner asked. He, like Altan and Connie, was also a doctoral student.

"That was the first thing they asked when I gave them their assignment," Donny said, laughing. "In the end, my students agreed to examine three secondary locations and two tertiary locations with high D-values. It should take them about a year and a half to collect the data. Then, another year or two to publish articles using the data. So, they should finish their doctoral work in about three years."

"Couldn't this be dangerous?" Altan asked him. "After all, you have doctoral students poking around in police business. Also, watching—and perhaps disturbing—the activities of smugglers."

"Any research can be dangerous, if you're collecting real data from real people," Donny said. "I've told my assistants to back off if they sense any danger. I'm in contact with them every week, to make sure they're okay."

"But the danger increases when you're dealing with organized crime, doesn't it?" Roxy chimed in. "We're talking about large networks of criminals with lots of power. It's like your students are exploring the jungle with no more than guidebooks to keep them safe."

Gene added, "And professional smugglers are sure to push back. If they feel THREATENED, they'll track your students, maybe even lash out at them."

Donny looked uncomfortable now. The weight of opinion was starting to press down on him. "I've trained my students to be discreet, to watch everything from a distance. Still, you raise good points."

Connie leaned in, her analytical mind hard at work. "Isn't there a way to collect the same data without sending your students into the field? Maybe, coordinate with police agencies for access to their intel? Or partner with tech companies for satellite surveillance?"

"I've looked for cooperation from local law enforcers," Donny admitted, "but they're wary of academic research.

Afraid I might leak sensitive information. As for tech partnerships, that's a route I hadn't considered. Maybe I'll try it, using drones and satellites. What do you think?"

Connie signaled her approval with two thumbs up.

"Maybe I can help," Roxy said. "I have contacts in a big tech firm that specializes in satellite surveillance. They might be willing to collaborate."

His eyes brightened, "That would be great, Roxy."

"Aren't you afraid your research will irritate the wrong people and they'll turn violent?" Altan asked.

"People know my interest in criminals is just academic, Altan. I've promised not to reveal my findings to the police. And the people I study know I can't be forced to."

I felt my phone buzz and looked down at the screen. A text message from Garet Foster read, 'My dad's not answering. I wonder if he's okay. I never know what to expect these days.'

'Your father's fine. He's at my house talking about his research. Relax. Happy Thanksgiving,' I texted back.

When I looked up from my phone, Roxy seemed to be lecturing Donny. "Isn't this a rebranding exercise for the criminals you study? They hope you'll change the way people think about their activities."

"Maybe so," he replied. "And many criminals are proud of their business smarts. In a different world, they might have been successful CEOs. To these guys, everything's about supply and demand. They supply a demand and manage their risk, just like other businesspeople."

Gene sipped his drink and said, "But this is a double-edged SWORD, Donny. You're glamorizing a dangerous, illegal trade. Won't this attract bright young people to CAREERS IN CRIME?"

I knew Gene couldn't have cared less about Donny's answer

and reflected on the weirdness of this for a minute. A glamorous master criminal telling someone not to glamorize crime and criminals. The world is crazy, I thought briefly.

Undaunted, Donny forged ahead. "That's a fair question," he said. "But understanding those people is a first step in controlling them. We need to understand their motives and show them respect."

Josh seemed skeptical. "Still, it's one thing to study their minds and another to risk people's lives. What if someone doesn't think your work is just academic? Or a new gang leader decides you know too much?"

"I admit it's a risk," Donny replied, rubbing the back of his neck. "But that's the nature of research. Every field comes with its own challenges."

"What makes you think this research will produce useful results?" Connie asked in the most courteous way she could.

"Well, two years ago, I ran a small-scale version of the project in Ontario, studying the flow of stolen cars from the United States. With only six predictor variables, I achieved 80 percent accuracy in predicting secondary sites, 72 percent accuracy predicting tertiary sites, and 65 percent accuracy predicting fourth-degree sites. That impressed the reviewers enough to get me funding for a large-scale version of the project in Europe."

The room went quiet. Donny's findings were impressive, even remarkable. Everyone could see his work was important, though dangerous too.

Roxy broke the silence, "You need to be careful. This is your life we're talking about."

Looking around the room, Donny saw genuine concern on everyone's face. He gave us a relaxed smile. "I promise, I'll be careful. If anything smells bad, I'll back off. My research is important but not at the cost of my life."

A serving person leaned down and whispered in my ear.

"Dinner is served, everyone," I announced, more loudly than I'd intended. "Sit wherever you like."

21

We left the living room and filed, slowly, courteously, into the brightly-lit dining room. The room looked magnificent, if I don't say so myself. The wall sconces were adorned with holly and mistletoe—yes, it was a little early for Christmas decoration, but what the heck! The table was glowing with candles, my heaviest silverware, and a lovely crimson tablecloth from India. I dimmed the overhead lights, to make the setting more romantic.

With only a little confusion, we arranged ourselves at the round table. Servers filled all the wine glasses, then brought everyone salad. When the salad plates had been cleared away, three main courses appeared almost magically. Beautiful trays of roast beef in a wine sauce, salmon in a lemon and dill sauce, and my own mushroom risotto. Elegant mounds of sweet potato, turnip, asparagus, Brussels sprouts, and horse radish and other condiments accompanied the main courses.

After people had loaded their plates with first helpings, Gene stood to propose a toast. "Let's drink to our hostess RACHEL and her marvelous family. May we ALWAYS enjoy the good food and company we are enjoying tonight." Everyone sipped their wine and servers leaned in to top up the glasses.

Then Jen stood to offer another toast. "Let's drink to the joys of learning. Knowledge is as necessary to a healthy soul as good food to a healthy body." Everyone took another sip of wine and the servers refilled our glasses a second time.

Next, I stood to propose a toast. "Let's drink to our wonderful children. Maybe we can even get them to talk about the great things they've done this week."

As the older guests raised their glasses for another sip, Ellie shook her head and covered her mouth. Josh put his hands forward in a 'STOP' sign and his girlfriend's eye's bugged out in horror. Irina just laughed. The youngsters weren't going to boast about their activities—not today or any other day. Meanwhile, the grownups chuckled and took small sips of wine. Gradually, people started to feel the effects of earlier sips.

Now Farid stood up to make a toast. "Let's drink to people who change the world. Also, to people who know when changes aren't needed. And I say that as a plastic surgeon."

Everyone laughed, as Farid had planned.

"Please don't let your food get cold," I urged them. "There will be time for more toasts after the main course." I smiled at Farid and lifted my glass, toasting him silently.

People ate quietly, occasionally murmuring with pleasure. Remarking to neighbours on one or another dish. In the background, bits of my favourite playlist—Billie Holiday, Freddy Cole, Diana Krall, Stacey Kent, Miles Davis—filled the air with music. First, the guests talked to people on their right, with Donny chatting up Jen. After Jen excused herself to take photos, he started chatting up Ellie, on his left. Asked about her studies, how she liked her profs, and so on. Meanwhile, Jen circled the room, snapping candid photos.

Soon, everyone was feeling mellow. Servers began to take away the dinner plates, then poured champagne. In short order, desserts began to appear—a pumpkin pie, an apple pie, Connie's mince tarts, and Altan's Turkish delight. There was even vanilla ice cream for people who shunned any but the simplest pleasures.

Now Irina stood up, glass in hand, her voice steady and clear. "Professor Foster," she said, "your work challenges and excites us. Today you've given us a lot to ponder. So let's all toast important research." She raised her glass and all of us followed, glasses clinking.

I was astonished. The girl was young—not even out of her teens—but carried herself with confidence. A natural, I thought. Her father's daughter.

Donny rose to answer her toast, smiling. "Irina, it's been a pleasure meeting you. Meeting everyone here. It means a lot to hear you say my work is interesting. For me, that's one of the highest compliments. I'll join you in a toast to research—it improves the world and keeps life exciting."

Suddenly, the room buzzed with laughter and conversation, everyone talking at once.

Just as suddenly, we heard three sharp knocks at the door, then the ringing of a doorbell. Instantly, the mood chilled. A server answered, and moments later, a tall man stepped into the dining room.

His head was shaved to a shine and his shoes squeaked. Scanning the table, his eyes locked on Donny.

"Professor Foster?" he asked firmly.

Donny hesitated. "Yes. Can I help you?"

The man pulled out a badge. "Detective Leon Mills, Toronto Police Department. I need a word. In private."

Then he turned to me. "Sorry to intrude, Professor Tile, but this is urgent. I got your address from Beth Coale."

"Of course," I said, nervously. "I'll show you to the study."

The table buzzed with speculation. Irina looked pale, on the verge of tears. Altan squeezed his wine glass, steadying for bad news.

The door to the study closed behind them, then we heard

the cadence of muffled voices. Minutes passed, long and uneasy.

Finally, the door opened, and the men returned. Mills' face was unreadable, Donny's, flushed.

"Thank you, Professor," Mills said, nodding at me. "Sorry for the interruption. Enjoy your dinner." The policeman left as suddenly as he had arrived, footsteps echoing in the silence.

Donny cleared his throat. "One of my research assistants, Pam Riley, was injured in Greece. The detective wanted to let me know and get a few details."

Altan leaned forward. "Is she alright?"

He nodded. "She's in a Greek hospital and will be back here in a few days, they think."

I smiled uneasily at my guests. "Well, let's continue our dinner as happily as we can. We need to celebrate this time together. And give thanks for the health and safety of our loved ones."

We tried to rekindle conversation, but the occasion had cooled. Exchanges were brief and muted. Guests picked at their desserts in silence, their thoughts elsewhere. Desperate to break the tension, I fetched the bottle of brandy Gene had brought.

"Gene, why don't you tell us about this?"

Gene stood, bottle in hand. "This brandy is forty-five years old. And like our CHILDREN, it's either wonderful or terrible, depending on how it's aged. Let's drink it and find out."

I heard a light chuckle. Then Donny seized the moment. "Let's also open the boxes I brought along."

I carried his two gold-wrapped packages to the table and Donny unwrapped them with great delicacy.

"Chocolate truffles," he said. "I had them specially made by Oberschlager and Brothers, master chocolatiers in Lucerne, Switzerland. Vincent Oberschlager produces only one hundred of these boxes each year. When you see them, you'll understand why they appeal to me."

He showed the first open box around the table, allowing us to see twelve beautifully wrapped chocolate truffles.

"Each is a miniature version of a car likely to be stolen and smuggled," Donny explained. "Here's a Honda CR-V," he said, pointing to one near the centre of the box. "The most-often stolen car in North America. It has a plum brandy filling, I think," he said, scanning a French-language 'map' that identified the contents of each candy.

This change of pace was silly, but it worked. The mood eased. Everyone agreed these masterful candies were unique and delicious. The two gold boxes were soon emptied. And the brandy was sumptuous. Each sip was an occasion, an education.

Excusing myself, I went upstairs for a moment alone. I was tired and woozy. Also, a little bothered. I'd begun to notice that, as the evening wore on, Donny's behaviour had shifted. At first, he'd been charming, complimenting my home and engaging the other guests. But after a while, he'd gotten louder, his comments bolder. He'd steered every conversation back to criminology and car smuggling, eager to show off his expertise. It seemed like he was trying to hog the event, and I didn't like it.

Back downstairs, I found the younger guests growing restless. Soon, most of them— Irina, Josh's girlfriend, Altan and his partner, and Connie and her partner went up to Josh's room. To listen to music, Josh said—and maybe smoke some weed. Meanwhile, Donny zeroed in on Ellie, asking personal but harmless questions, his smile familiar and ingratiating.

In a corner, I chatted quietly with Gene, Roxy, and Farid. "Does the Devlin Crew understand what he's doing?" Gene wondered aloud. "I doubt it. Because if they did, they wouldn't LIKE it."

"Agreed," Roxy said. "His research is dangerous."

"Very dangerous," Farid muttered, shaking his head. "And strange. It isn't the kind of academic work I expected to hear about tonight."

The evening slowly wound down. One by one, guests thanked me for the evening and left. After saying goodnight to the last guest, I leaned against the wall, exhausted. Thanksgiving dinner had been a success. It had also revealed more of Donny's flaws than I'd bargained for.

22

The next morning, I woke late, my head heavy and hung-over. I sent Farid home, then showered and dressed. The weather was sunny and crisp. No one was on the street, though I could hear a dog barking in the distance. Probably, the dog that lives with that new family on the corner. They leave her outside for hours at a time, whether it's hot or cold, day or night. I'd treat a dog better, I thought. If I still had one.

At twelve-thirty, I met Jen at Ferrari, as planned. After ordering food, she handed me a stack of glossy black-and-white photos. "Shots from yesterday," she said, grinning. "You'll get a laugh out of them."

I flipped through the pictures. One showed me looking every bit the hostess. Another, Farid gazing at me like I was Venus herself. Another, Connie gesturing wildly while her partner stared, wide-eyed, like she was Einstein. Another, Altan and his partner holding hands under the table, silent, contented. I'd never seen Altan in repose before and liked the look. I had suspected he and his roommate were lovers, and was pleased to see this confirmed.

One photo caught Gene watching Irina toast Donny, fatherly pride written all over his face. Another showed Josh staring across the table at Irina like she was a fertility goddess, while his girlfriend blazed with irritation. Another showed Roxy listening to Donny talk about his D-scores, head tilted, skeptical. The last photo showed Donny leaning toward Josh's girlfriend like she was either a love interest or a breakthrough in his data.

"What do these tell you?" I asked her, chuckling.

Jen smirked. "That Farid, Josh, and Donny are world-class pussy-hounds. Also, Connie and her partner will be married for eighty-five years."

"And Gene's the proudest father in the world."

"With good reason," Jen said. "Irina's going places. Whether to heaven or hell is harder to say."

"What'd you think of my guests?"

"Ellie, Josh? Solid. Connie's a gem. Altan's sharp. Gene is exactly who you think he is. I like Roxy—salt of the earth. Farid's a dreamboat, and I bet he's funny as hell."

"And Donny?"

Jen paused, narrowing her eyes. "He's something else. A genius, but also an ass," she said after pausing briefly. "Somewhere on the spectrum, I think. No social skills, no empathy, no tact. Desperate for attention."

"You figured him out fast," I said.

"He's not the first Donny-like person I've met. My brother Michael—your first husband, right?—wasn't too far off."

I had to laugh at Jen's coy reference to Michael, her brother and my husband. But that was Jen all over. Meanwhile, I had other fish to fry. "Could you see Donny killing his wife?"

Jen smirked. "I don't think so. If he had, he would have bragged about it at dinner and waited for applause. So no,

I don't think he did it. Melanie probably wasn't even on his radar. Once upon a time, he may have loved her, but now he *really* loves his D-scores."

"Sure," I said, laughing, "he loved Melanie the way he loves his old bathrobe. But you said it yourself—he's a pussy-hound. Maybe he wanted to ditch Melanie and build a bachelor pad."

"Maybe. He drooled over every woman at your party—Connie, Roxy, Irina, Ellie, even you and me. But it's the D-scores that get him going."

"Get out of here," I exclaimed, a little too loudly.

"I'm serious. I keep an eye on those things, and trust me, he got stiff talking about his research. D-scores are his religion. his ecstasy. His orgasm."

I laughed so hard I almost fell out of my chair. "You're insane."

"Maybe, but I'm right. He's even more turned on by his D-scores—his 'algorithms'—than by pretty women. Meanwhile, Pam Riley's in a hospital bed, could be for a long time, thanks to his D-scores." Then Jen leaned forward. "Tell me, Director Tile, are you going to let him send more students to Greece?"

"No," I said, shaking my head. "and the Ethics Board won't allow it, either. They might even recall his other student from Spain."

"So the project's dead, right?"

"Unless he finds a safer way to collect data."

Jen smiled, lifting her fork. "On that happy note, let's eat. All this talk of sex, murder, and D-scores has made me hungry."

I was about to dig in when my phone buzzed. It was Garet again. I excused myself and read the message: 'Dad seemed much cheerier today. Thought you'd like to know. Oh, and I've asked Dylan to contact you too.'

I sent Garet a thumbs-up emoji and put the phone away.

The girl lingered in my mind. Such a caring young woman, such a difficult father.

Meanwhile, Jen shook her head. She wondered what mess I'd gotten myself into this time. And when it would start to cost me too much.

Back home after lunch, I began to prepare a report for the Dean that summarized my current thoughts. But first, I looked up the Lithwick Narcissism Checklist, ran the twenty-item list with Donny in mind, and concluded he was a certifiable narcissist. And I knew that narcissism and psychopathy were related. But did that make him a dangerous psychopath? He *might* be a narcissistic psychopath, a danger to the faculty and students at Strachan. But so far, I had no real evidence to support this conclusion.

The Thanksgiving dinner had changed my view of Donny. Sure, I'd known him for more than a decade. I'd even gone through the restructuring of our School with him. But now I see things I'd never seen before.

Now I could see how driven Donny was, how preoccupied by his need for success and approval. The dinner had also exposed Donny to objective viewers—well, to my friends and family. And they had seen the same flaws I did. Thanksgiving dinner had exposed the real Donny. He was a man who could harm other people without hesitation or feelings of guilt.

But I still didn't know who'd killed Melanie, and why. Deep down, I still didn't think Donny could have done it.

I found lots of emails waiting for me after lunch, including the latest edition of *Inklings*, the School's monthly newsletter. Altan had offered to write an advice column for *Inklings* and today, belatedly, the first issue of the new semester had appeared. Altan's column was on page 3. He'd chosen to call it "Ask the Asker." Witty, I thought.

Ask The Asker
By Altan Asker
Doctoral Candidate
School of Criminology
Strachan University

I've received a lot of queries from people who plan to attend Julia Dent's guest lecture on October 20. Many are puzzled—even, worried—about the ethical issues some have said her book, *Hiding In Plain Sight*, raises. Below, I have answered a few of the more common questions you have asked me.

From Confused and Troubled, September 28:
Dear Asker,
Could you advise me on proper etiquette for people who plan to attend Julia Dent's coming lecture at the School? For example, would it be proper to ask if she thinks she has violated professional ethics by going on drive-by shootings with her research informants?

Dear Confused and Troubled,
Many others have asked me a similar question in the past four weeks. I would say, go right ahead. But if you intend to ask Professor Dent this, preface your question by asking if she is licensed to carry a firearm, and if so, whether she's brought it with her today.

From Now You're Talkin', September 18:
Dear Asker,
I can hardly wait for Julia Dent's lecture! This will be an exciting moment in Strachan's academic life, which is

otherwise pretty ho-hum. Would it be okay to ask whether she thinks the behaviour of her criminal informants is a result of 'intergenerational trauma?'

Dear Now You're Talkin',
I see where you're going with this. You're referencing the intergenerational trauma of Indigenous people in Canada. Are you asking if Canadian criminologists should build similarly close relationships with Indigenous criminals they are studying? The answer is definitely yes. But any criminologist who goes on drive-by shootings with Indigenous respondents should avoid doing anything worse than what their informants are doing. Otherwise, they'll be guilty of bad ethics and, worse still, bad manners.

From Clear and Present Danger, September 25:
Dear Asker,
I gather from her book, *Hiding in Plain Sight*, that Julia Dent amassed a lot of information about likely criminal activity, even including planned murders. Should she be obliged by law to provide this information to the police, to save lives and prevent future violence?

Dear Clear and Present Danger,
I am in favour of saving lives and preventing violence, and perhaps you are, too. However, if you have taken any of the School's required courses on research methods, you will have learned that protecting the sanctity of your data comes first. Don't ever disclose any research information you have collected, unless threatened with a jail term of more than two years.

That's all the space I have, dear reader. This is The Asker saying TTFN. Remember, I'll be back with more advice in the next edition of *Inklings*. Meanwhile, send me your questions at TheAsker@gmail.com and I'll answer as many as I can.

23

All too soon, Thursday morning rolled around. With another busy day on my schedule, I showered, ate breakfast, and drove downtown at the usual snail's pace. Today, like yesterday, was cool and crisp. The leaves—yellow, orange, and red—were falling off the trees at an ever-increasing pace. Within a few days, the trees would be bare. We'd see nothing but blue sky above us. Until the snow started, of course.

I parked the car, speed-walked to my office, and made myself comfortable. While trying to stay detached, I completed an interim report on Donny. And against the Dean's stated wishes, I put it in writing. To prevent any chance of confusion.

After the morning lecture and a quick lunch, I hand-delivered my report to the Dean's office. In it, I'd written, 'I doubt Professor Foster played an active role in the death of his wife. However, he has taken unreasonable risks with his graduate students, as I learned on Monday evening. Going forward, we must monitor all the research proposals he presents for approval by the Research Ethics Board. Let me know if you need other information right now.'

News of Pam Riley's injury upset the Dean. Quite a bit more than I had expected, actually. After reading my report, she summoned Donny for another interview the next morning. The university lawyer and I were to be present as well.

By nine, when Donny showed up, we were all present, lying in wait. The Dean was in a foul mood, and she got straight to the point as soon as Donny was seated.

"I hear one of your graduate students, Pam Riley, was attacked in Greece while collecting data for her thesis. What can you tell me about that?"

Donny squirmed as he answered. "I didn't expect any trouble. But sometimes things get out of control. I'll make sure it doesn't happen again."

The Dean pressed on. "What steps had you taken to protect your students?"

"I'd given them the names of local people to contact if they needed help. Pam didn't follow up with all of them, so part of the fault lies with her. I also shared risk-assessment information from the Peace Corps and urged my students to rely on interpreters for help."

The Dean made notes as Donny answered, though she was also taping the interview. "I also hear some of your students here in Toronto have requested new supervisors?"

Donny scowled at me, then answered. "They may have been led to think I'm dangerous. But I can't control what people think."

The Dean shifted gears. "Was any of Pam Riley's research related to your wife's death?"

"Not at all," he replied. "Pam Riley was in Greece collecting data to test my D-score theory. Melanie had nothing to do with that research." He mopped his brow, clearly uneasy.

The Dean hadn't been pleased by his last answer. It may have sounded evasive to her. She looked over a list of questions I'd helped to prepare, then shifted the topic to keep him off balance.

"Last winter, you were down in Texas questioning members

of the Devlin Crew, a gang of car smugglers. Could Melanie have overheard these discussions and gathered information that endangered her safety?"

Donny answered this question slowly and carefully. But first he mopped his face, hands, and neck with a huge polka dotted handkerchief.

"I always took pains to keep Melanie from knowing much about my research. I hadn't even invited her to join me in Houston. It was her idea to come to Texas during my research leave, not mine. I'd told her I'd be busy collecting data, but she insisted on coming anyway. And while she was there, I stopped working so we could see the sights together. But Melanie never met any of the people I was interviewing. Nor did I tell her about them." He said all this in a slightly whiny tone. As though he felt mistreated.

"Dean, I did everything possible to keep Melanie out of my research. If she looked at the notes I'd taken during interviews with the Devlin Crew, it would have been without my knowledge or permission. And whenever I spoke on the phone with members of the Devlin Crew, I always talked in another room. Nothing suggested Melanie had seen or heard anything of importance. If I thought I was at fault here, I'd say so. I'd hold myself responsible for her death."

I watched his face as he made these solemn declarations. Yes, he spoke with conviction. But then I saw a few of his tell-tale mannerisms.

At meetings and social events, Donny always looked down and away when he was agitated. He'd done that several times in the last few minutes. He also patted his chest when he was nervous. This made me think of a little boy getting pats on the chest from an adoring mother. 'Good boy, Donny. Good boy.' And there had been a lot of chest-patting at today's meeting too.

The Dean read the next question right off the list on her desk. "Do you know if Melanie's interest in violence against women posed a problem for the Devlin Crew?"

Donny looked puzzled, then formed an answer. "Melanie and I didn't discuss that topic during her visit to Houston. In fact, she never showed any interest in the way the Devlin Crew treated women—not around me, anyway. And here's the most important thing. When I started my Texas research, I promised Jonny Devlin I'd limit my attention to car smuggling. So I know nothing of his gang's activities outside car smuggling. Nothing about the Crew's treatment of women."

Again, he mopped his face, hands, and neck with that huge polka dotted handkerchief. Again, he patted his chest, perhaps a little self-consciously.

"Shall we continue?" the Dean asked gruffly.

He nodded. "Sure, go ahead."

"Your research has always concerned auto thieves and auto smugglers. Is it possible your written articles have served to justify or 'whitewash' criminal activity?"

Donny started to squirm in his seat. "I've never justified or whitewashed crimes of any kind. And I've never knowingly witnessed, let alone joined in criminal activity. I've only interviewed car smugglers to find out how they view their work. But whenever the police have asked me to share my information, I've always refused. It is my ethical duty as a research scientist to do so."

The Dean came back with a puzzling, new question. "Let me ask you about car auctions—a topic that's come up in connection with car smuggling. Have you ever attended the auction of expensive automobiles? If so, what did you learn at these auctions? For example, did you learn if these automobiles had been stolen?"

Donny thought for a minute, then said "I've attended car auctions at various locations in North America and Europe. Even a few in Toronto. I knew members of the smuggling community would be present. Also, anonymous buyers. I wanted to learn how people behaved in these situations. What prices the different cars were able to fetch. I suspect many of these expensive cars had been stolen, but no one confirmed that."

"Speaking of expensive items, can you tell us how much your trial lawyer in Houston cost, and how you managed to pay that amount?"

This change of topic surprised him, but he didn't hesitate. "My lawyer cost me $300,000 US. Normally, I couldn't have paid it without mortgaging my house. But a wealthy aunt had died recently, leaving me a large inheritance—a vacation home, which I sold in 2022. That more than covered the cost of the lawyer."

The Dean began her next question almost right away. "Did you ever discuss the practical value of your research findings with the gangs you studied? Here, I have in mind the Devlin Crew in Houston and local gangs in Spain and Greece?"

"I discussed my D-score research with Jonny Devlin," Donny said. "I also hired people to translate descriptions of my research into Spanish and Greek and told my students to offer write-ups to anyone who was interested. The piece I wrote said my students were gathering data for an academic project. But looking back, I should have treated the issue more carefully. That might have kept Pam Riley safe from harm."

I was still on the fence about Donny's guilt or innocence. But I didn't like his self-serving evasiveness.

After a brief pause, the Dean continued.

"How accurate and trustworthy was the information you received from members of the Devlin Crew? Did you have any way to verify the information they gave you? And if you did, how reliable did the information turn out to be?"

"Dean, I did three things to verify the data. First, I cross-checked it with other gang members. If three or more people told me the same thing, I treated it as credible. Second, I applied my own knowledge to what people told me. I asked myself if a piece of information fit what I already knew. Third, I ran the information by Jonny Devlin whenever I got a chance. He had the final say on what I could and couldn't publish. If the information passed these three tests, I felt confident about its accuracy."

The Dean nodded and went back to her handwritten notes. Then, I saw her shoulders hunch slightly. Her body language suggested she was about to put more pressure on Donny.

"Melanie's body was found in the so-called Killing Fields. The body of an associate of the Devlin Crew, Lana Bond, had been found there two years earlier. No more than 200 yards away from where Melanie's body was found. What do you make of that coincidence?"

24

Okay, now we were getting down to business, I thought. Even the university lawyer was on the edge of his chair, eyes momentarily averted from his cellphone and day planner. The room was suddenly silent—a sharp contrast from moments earlier Student noise on the street suddenly filled the otherwise silent room.

"Dean, I'd heard about the discovery of Lana Bond's body a while back. I'd even met Lana years earlier, while interviewing members of the Devlin Crew. People told me Lana had gotten herself into trouble with another group in the area—the Smith Brothers. Lana had been giving information about the Smiths to her boyfriend in the Devlin Crew. It turns out, she'd also been giving information about the Devlin Crew to the Smith Brothers. But in the end, the police never charged anyone with her murder.

"As to the connection, I don't know why Melanie's body was buried 200 yards from where Lana's body was found. Melanie didn't know Lana and I don't think she knew much about the Devlin Crew or the Smith Brothers," he said.

He was starting to perspire even more heavily. Out came the polka dot hanky.

"After your wife was murdered in Texas, did you think you might be at risk of murder yourself? Maybe by the same people who'd killed your wife? And is it possible your wife's murder was intended to frighten you away? To make you stop studying the Devlin Crew, or collecting D-scores?"

Now, that's a good question, I thought. I was eager to hear his answer.

"Dean, I was never afraid for my life. Jonny had promised that no member of his gang would ever harm me. He'd also told the Smith Brothers I wasn't a gang member, just an academic researcher. He'd warned them that harming me would get media attention. That harming me would increase the police pressure on all Houston gangs, the Smith Brothers included. No one wanted that. So, Jonny put my fears to rest on that score."

"Have you found any notes Melanie may have written about the Devlin Crew, or any other gang, in the year before her death? If so, can you let us see those notes, or copies of those notes?"

"Funny you should mention that, Dean. Just the other

day I found two notes she may have written. One was in her home office and the other, in her computer mailbox. The police who looked into Melanie's murder didn't find these messages, though they took away all the written material they found in Houston or on Melanie's person. But the two notes are in a code I can't understand. Maybe you can figure out what they're saying."

"Please turn those over to us by the end of the day," the Dean said. Then she continued, "In the months since your trial, have you come to any conclusions about who may have killed your wife, and for what reason?"

"Dean, I think my wife was killed by members of the Kirilov gang. I told that to the police but, so far as I know, they've failed to investigate this possibility. The Kirilovs have political influence in Texas. That may be why the police refused to take my idea seriously."

"Who are the Kirilovs and why might they have wanted Melanie dead?" the Dean asked.

"The Kirilovs are a Russian mob based in Manhattan. They've been making inroads into car smuggling on the Eastern Seaboard. In 2022, they approached me for information about the Devlin Crew and, of course, I refused. They threatened my life, and still I refused. Then they killed Melanie, as a way to put even more pressure on me. But I still haven't told them anything they want to know." Donny was trying to make himself sound heroic, I thought.

"And you told all of this to the police?" the Dean asked.

"Of course. But I didn't have written evidence to back me up. All of the Kirilov communications were verbal. So, they treated this as no more than hearsay. They ignored me."

"Do you have any evidence the Kirilovs killed Melanie?" I asked, jumping into the discussion.

"Only that they said they might do it. And they've done similar things to people in New York, people they were pressing for information. At least, that's what I've heard."

Suddenly, the Dean slammed her fist down on the desk, leapt out of her chair, and began shouting. I was stunned and so was Donny.

"Professor Foster, you're failing to tell me something important. Not about the Kirilovs. I don't believe that nonsense for a moment. You're not telling me something about your relationship with Jonny Devlin. Why he's been so willing to encourage research that couldn't help his bottom line. And why he's supported research that would strain his relations with European smugglers, people with whom he has business dealings. What do you have on Jonny Devlin that's made him cooperate?"

"I don't have anything on Jonny Devlin," Donny muttered, squirming in his chair.

Now, the lawyer jumped out of his chair too. "What are you doing for Devlin? Do you have friends Jonny Devlin wants to please? I'm with the Dean on this. I don't see why he's cooperating."

This felt like a turning point in our discussion. I held my breath, waiting for Donny to answer.

Instead, he went back to wiping his forehead with that big polka-dotted handkerchief. A silence hung over the room as he finished the cleanup. Meanwhile, the Dean and lawyer sat back down in their chairs.

Arms crossed, we all waited for his answer.

Donny may have thought about continuing to lie. But then he realized it wouldn't work. He might as well come clean—or at least, appear to come clean—about his connection with the Devlin Crew. He hesitated for several seconds, then broke down.

"Okay, okay, I'll tell you *why* I got so much cooperation from Jonny Devlin," he said, exasperated. "Jonny's my uncle, my mother's younger brother. He was born John Ghirardelli and changed his name to Jonny Devlin in his twenties. We were close when I grew up in Newark and I've remained close to him since moving to Toronto. However—and I want to stress this—I have never taken part in Jonny's criminal activities. Nor has he ever asked me to."

I was flabbergasted to hear about this blood connection between Donny Foster and Jonny Devlin. Minutes earlier, I wouldn't have imagined it.

"Now we're getting somewhere," the Dean declared softly, ready for the next attack. "So, your family engages in crime and you, Professor Foster, spend time in Houston studying their activities as a criminologist. Using grant money from the Social Sciences and Humanities Research Council. Do you see an ethical problem with this?"

"Dean, I've never done anything wrong. I don't take part in other people's crimes, even if they're family members."

"Did you reveal this family connection on your application for a research leave? Or on your application to the Research Ethics Board, when you applied for clearance of the project?"

"No," Donny stammered, "I didn't reveal it. But where does it say a researcher can't study a group that contains family members?"

"Family ties always pose a conflict of interest in our rules about research leaves, research grants, and ethical approval for faculty projects," the university lawyer said, firmly. "Human Resources is very strict about such things. And I have a note in my files that you asked Human Resources about this matter more than twelve years ago. They told you then that you were not permitted to include family members in any funded research. Their insistence on that rule has never wavered."

"Professor Tile, do you have any questions? Or comments you want to make?" the Dean asked me.

"No, thank you. No questions or comments at this time," I said quietly.

"Mr. Cook, any questions you want to ask?" she asked the lawyer.

"No, Dean, thank you."

"Then I assume I can leave. Is that right, Dean?" Donny asked, in a hurry to get away.

"Of course. But keep yourself available. Please understand, your position at this university is precarious. I will discuss all of this with the Provost and see what he advises."

"Thank you, Dean. When I get back to my office, I'll email you the two coded messages I found. Maybe you'll have better luck with them than I've had."

Donny nodded silently to me and the lawyer, then left the Dean's office.

"I'm out of here, Dean," the lawyer said, getting up to leave. "Another meeting, I'm afraid. But at last, we got the information we needed about his link to the Devlin Crew. We may be able to revoke Professor Foster's tenure on ethical grounds now. But I'll need to verify that with the Provost."

"Phew, that was a long one, wasn't it?" I said to the Dean, after the lawyer had gone.

"Can you stay for a coffee?" she asked me.

"I should get back to my office and think about what we heard today. I may have to find out something about the Kirilovs too. Are you going to transcribe the audio recording of this interview? Or should I arrange it?"

"I'll have someone here do it and send you a copy. Meanwhile, take a look at those two coded messages. I'll send them over as soon as I get them. Maybe one of your people can crack the code. If not, I'll get someone here to give it a try. And let me know what you find out about the Kirilovs."

"Okay, Dean. Let's talk again in a few days. What Donny said today was shocking. Now, I'm starting to think he poses a real threat to our university."

The Dean perked up her ears. "I know you wouldn't suggest that without good reason."

"Well, I'm basing my opinion on things I've noticed over the years. Also, things repeated in the last two interviews. Donny has often shown a lack of empathy and I think he's indifferent to the suffering of others. For example, I've never seen him grieve for his dead wife. And as we've seen with Pam Riley, he refuses to take responsibility for his actions. He blames others when things go wrong.

"He's a liar and sticks to false stories even when confronted with evidence that he's lying. We've both seen evidence of that. Beyond that, he has an inflated sense of importance and often talks about how exceptional he is. Maybe that's why he shows no respect for authority and doesn't like to follow the rules. More often than not, he appears to base his decisions on personal gain, not concerns about right and wrong."

"I agree. We've seen evidence of all those things in our recent meetings. Where does that leave us?"

"It may be dangerous to keep him around. I hate to say that, because Donny is a valuable faculty member. He's famous, but now I see he's also radioactive."

"I'm inclined to strip Donny of tenure right away," the Dean said, after a moment. "But the Provost may move him off to the side for a while. The Board of Hummingbird Industries has warned the Provost to avoid bad press at any cost. So we'll have to wait to see what the Big Guy proposes."

25

I nodded, said goodbye, and left the Dean's office. I still didn't know who'd killed Melanie, but now I was very suspicious of Donny's behaviour. Trudging back to my office, I felt the clear sunny sky was mocking me. It was pretending the world was clear and simple, when as we'd just heard, the world is dim and duplicitous. What should I believe, I wondered? My eyes or my ears?

I was inclined to trust my ears. And to make sure, I phoned my friend Gene in London.

"Gene, do you know a Kirilov Gang?" I asked him. "Supposedly, they operate in the Houston area?"

Gene took a moment to answer. "I'm not sure. I do know a businessman named Yuri Kirilov. He used to engage in criminal activity. But in the past decade or so, he's mainly been buying and developing real estate. In Charleston, Savannah, Biloxi, Houston, other southern locations. Why do you ASK?"

"I heard the name Kirilov mentioned in connection with the murder of Melanie Foster. Do you think he or his gang might be involved? Would they have had any beef with Melanie or Donny Foster?"

"I doubt it. These days, Yuri is making himself wealthy through real estate deals, not crime."

"So you don't think he's involved in car smuggling at present?"

"No, not the guy I know. He's gone straight and made a LOT of money doing that. At least that's what I've HEARD," Gene said, decisively.

After hanging up, I found a brief message from Garet's brother, Dylan Foster.

'Hello, Professor Tile,' the message read. 'My sister Garet

insisted I thank you for efforts you've made on our father's behalf. As someone who's stayed out of my father's business for the last twelve years, I hesitated to contact you. But Garet, as I'm sure you have discovered, is a worrier. By now, you've discovered what my father is. Yours, Dylan Foster.'

Short and mysterious. Dylan had done the minimum required to satisfy his needy sister.

Then I checked my email. It contained the coded messages Melanie had written. At first glance, they were utterly unreadable. Here's what I saw:

2024.01.04dvjtvjcyjllwjctwjdbyyjzjrgryjzjpxjndxjcvjtwjsvjc yjntxjnzjxjngxjmmxjgrvjtxjyjnyjfswjxwyjrkwjrsfryjm Tzjrkwjy,Rzjssxjvj,Myjldyjvvj,Syrxjvj,vjndszjbSvjhvjrvj nVJfrxjcvj,wjntwjrxjngCvjnvjdvjvjtbyjrdwjrwxjthVwjrmyjnt. RwjswjvjrchnyjtwjsbyPvjckwjrrwjvwjvjlthwjyvjrwjcyjmxjng xjnwjmptycvjrgyjshxjpbyjxwjsfxjrstzjswjdtyjtrvjnspyjrtsmzj gglwjdvjzjtyjstyjWJzjryjpwjvxjvjSpvjxjnvjndGrwjwjcw j.ThwjJyjhnsyjncrwjwrwjcwjxjvwjsthwjwyjmwjnvjtthwjp yjrtyjfHyjzjstyjn,thwjndrxjvwjsthwjmnyjrthxjnpvjnwjltrzjc ks.Dwjtvjxjlwjdxjnfyjrmvjtxjyjnhvjsbwjwjnpryjvxjdwjdtyj Bvjdgwjs1vjnd2.GryjzjplwjvjdwjrwxjllvxjsxjtHyjzjstyjnxjn Mvjrchtyjgvjxjnmyjrwjxjnfyjrmvjtxjyjnvjbyjzjtthwjxjmpyjrt wjrs,vjndwxjllrwjpyjrtbvjckthwjn.

2.2024.01.25YJvwjrhwjvjrdryjnnxjwjdxjsczjssxjyjnwxjthj yjhnsyjntyjdvjyvjbyjzjtthwjzjswjyjfwjmptycyjntvjxjnwjrsyj nrwjtzjrnvyjyvjgwjfryjmWJzjryjpwj.Ryjnnxjwjvjskwjdxjfj yjhnsyjnbryjzjghtvjnycvjrgyjbvjckfryjmWJzjryjpwjvjssyj mwjpwjyjplwj(hwjmwjvjntmwj)swjwjmwjdtyjthxjnk.Jyjhn syjnsvjxjdhwjvjlwvjysbryjzjghtstzjffbvjckxjnthwjcvjrgyjbyjx wjs,xjnclzjdxjngdrzjgs,styjlwjnvjrtwyjrkyjrjwjwwjlry,vjndh zjmvjn'wyjrkxjngwyjmwjn.'Ryjnnxjwjsvjxjdhwjhvjdthyj zjghtthvjtmxjghtbwjthwjcvjswjvjnddxjdn'tswjwjkfzjrthwjr xjnfyjrmvjtxjyjn.Jyjhnsyjnsvjxjdnvjtzjrvjlly,thxjswvjsbwjtw wjwjnthwjmvjndshyjzjldnyjtbwjshvjrwjdwxjthvjnyyjnwj,xj nclzjdxjngmwj.

What was Melanie trying to say in these weird, unintelligible messages? It might take days to decode them, and I couldn't afford the time. So I walked down to the student offices and asked Altan to take a crack at them.

He said he'd give it a try but wasn't willing to make any promises. "This may take me a while, so please be patient."

"Do the best you can," I told him, sympathetically.

At home that evening, I was hard at work on my new rage book when I heard a banging on the front door. The noise was hard and angry.

Through a small window in the door, I could see Donny's face pressed against the glass, his breath fogging the diamond-shaped opening. When he stepped back, I could see his clothes were rumpled. He swayed like someone who'd had too much to drink.

"What do you want? You look like hell. Go home and sleep it off," I shouted.

He muttered something I couldn't make out, then raised his voice. "Let me in. You're trying to ruin my career. You need to treat me better." Then he slumped down against my door.

"Don't pass out on the porch, Donny. Go home."

He didn't move.

I thought about bringing him inside and calling a cab. But the idea of dealing with a drunk, angry Donny soured my stomach. I grabbed the phone and dialed his daughter.

"Garet, this is Rachel. Your dad's drunk, passed out on my

porch. Can you pick him up and take him home? He needs to sleep this off."

Garet's voice was panicky. "I'm so sorry, Professor Tile. I'll be there right away."

I turned off the porch light and covered Donny with a blanket. The night air wasn't cold enough to hurt him.

Fifteen minutes later, Garet showed up with her husband. She was small and lively, her frantic energy contrasting sharply with her father's limp form. We looked at each other for a moment, and I hugged her on impulse. Then she and her husband hefted Donny down the sidewalk, into their car.

"Thanks, Rachel," Garet called out. "I'm really sorry about this."

"It's fine. We'll talk another time."

I closed the front door, turned off the lights, and drank a few glasses of club soda to calm my nerves. Eventually, I went upstairs and fell off to sleep.

The next morning, Altan came to see me with the decoded messages. He was smiling, proud of the accomplishment. "Actually, my partner cracked the code. A simple substitution cipher. Melanie had replaced all the vowels with pairs of consonants. In this case, a=vj, e=wj, i=xj, o=yj, and u=zj. That's all!"

I read the translated messages, and they were damning. Decoded, they read:

1.   2024.01.04 Data collected by our group indicates continuing immigration of sex workers from Turkey, Russia, Moldova, Syria, and sub-Saharan Africa. Research notes by Foster reveal they're coming in empty cargo ship boxes first used to transport smuggled autos to Europe via Spain and Greece. The Devlin Crew receives the women at the port of Houston, then drives

them north in panel trucks. Detailed information has been provided to Badges 1 and 2. Group leader will visit Houston in March to gain more information about the importers and will report back then.

2.   2024.01.25 Overheard Donny discussion with Devlin today about the use of empty containers on return voyage from Europe. Donny asked if Devlin brought any cargo back from Europe as some people (he meant me) seemed to think. Devlin said he always brought stuff back in the cargo boxes, including drugs, stolen artwork or jewelry, and human 'working women.' Donny said he had thought that might be the case and didn't seek further information. Devlin said naturally, this was between them and should not be shared with anyone, including me.

I photocopied the translations, sealed them in an envelope, and had my assistant hand-deliver them to the Dean. A cover letter said simply, 'These messages change everything, Dean. Let's talk soon.'

Evidently, the Devlin Crew had been bringing refugee women to Texas in cargo containers, then forcing them into prostitution. The decoded notes showed Donny had known all about this. What's more, Melanie Foster had known too, and she knew her husband knew. Donny and Jonny Devlin had even discussed Melanie's interest in this topic.

The second note confirmed Donny had lied to the Dean when he said he knew nothing about the Devlin Crew's other criminal activity. He'd turned a blind eye to human trafficking so he could continue to collect data on car smuggling. Now, I knew we couldn't believe anything he'd told us. Including what he'd said about Melanie's death.

Why had Melanie stayed with Donny, I wondered? To peer over his shoulder, so she could take actions of her own against the Devlin Crew? As I pondered this, the phone rang.

"Hi Rachel, it's Garet again. Thanks for helping out last night. My father told me he's been quizzed by the Dean about my mother's death. That's awful hard for him. Is he holding up okay at work?"

"Yes. Your dad is holding up fine. But I can't talk about this right now."

"Please call if my father needs help. He doesn't always ask for help when he needs it. Thanks again, and goodbye."

I wondered how Donny and Melanie had kept Garet in the dark about their activities and, especially, about Donny's lies. Then, I wondered what Dylan may have known about his father. Maybe he'd known everything and that was why he'd severed connections with his father.

And what about the Kirilov gang? Had they murdered Melanie Foster? Had they set up Donny to look like the killer? Had they staged the murder so the police would investigate his links with the Devlin Crew and, specifically, with Johnny Devlin? All of that seemed doubtful, but I was open to new evidence.

26

Life was getting busy, but I knew I had to visit Pam Riley, Donny's injured student. It was the least I could do. She'd gotten back to Canada three days earlier and was recovering at a local hospital. After filling my briefcase with stuff I'd need at home, I hopped in the car and drove across town to Sunnybrook Health Centre.

In the last twenty years, the original hospital—built specifically to treat war veterans—had grown into a small town. I wondered what it might be like to be a patient there. I'd soon find out. After navigating the underground parking, a huge map of the facilities, and half a dozen hallways, I found Pam's room. She was in bed in her designated room. Her leg was suspended in a gigantic cast, but she smiled to see me. Painkillers had dulled her edges.

"Don't mind the mess," she mumbled, pointing at a pile of gifts her parents had brought.

I handed her a box of chocolates. "Every piece is different," I said, grinning.

Pam chuckled softly and set the box on the table. The room was cold and bright, all hard surfaces and sterile light. It also smelled like antiseptic, sharp and sour. I didn't like the place and couldn't help shivering.

"How do you feel?" I asked her, almost whispering.

"Not great, but better. Glad to be back in Canada." She slowly opened the box and offered it to me. I picked a cherry-filled truffle. Pam chose a square candy, bit into it, and winced. "This one has a nut inside, I think." She put it down on the night table.

"Has Professor Foster visited you?"

Pam frowned. "Not yet."

"Tell me what happened in Greece."

Pam recounted the attack, her voice calm, her eyes distant. The men, the bat, the pain. She spoke like it had happened to someone else.

I leaned back in my chair. My stomach was churning, but I kept my face steady.

"How long will they keep you here?"

"I'm not sure," said Pam. "Less than a week, I hope. My

folks have set up a recovery room for me at home. It's got a hospital bed, a TV, anything else I might need."

"How are they taking this?"

"That's something I want to tell you, though maybe I shouldn't. My dad's a lawyer with Greenspan Fogel and he says he's going to sue the university for $10 million."

"Maybe I shouldn't hear about this from you, but I'm glad you told me. How'd he come up with that number?"

"It's $5 million for the pain and suffering—a result of negligence by the Research Ethics Board. And another $5 million for punitive damages. My father is mad as hell. He'd run Professor Foster out of town on a rail if he could arrange it." She stopped for a sip of water, exhausted by the long sentence.

"Why didn't he sue Professor Foster, then?"

"Professor Foster wouldn't be good for $10 million. Besides, my dad wants to teach the university a lesson," she said.

"What are your own plans?"

"I don't know yet. I may enter a criminology program in the US. Or give up criminology and apply to law school. But I won't continue in Strachan's doctoral program. I'll lose a few years, but it's the safest thing to do. Don't you agree?"

"I don't know," I said, honestly. "We're going to make sure nothing like this ever happens again. You'll be safe if you come back to our program."

Pam made a wry face. "Naw, I've had it with Strachan. No offense, but it hasn't worked out for me. Besides, my parents wouldn't let me. They'd say I was nuts, and I guess, at this point, I'd have to agree."

After a few minutes of casual banter, I said goodbye and headed home. Donny didn't seem to care about Pam Riley—not enough to even visit her in the hospital. Maybe he'd felt the same way about his wife.

It was time to inventory what I knew about Melanie's death, what I merely suspected, and what I didn't know at all. So I asked Altan to meet me and warned the meeting might take a few hours. He suggested we meet the next day at "the break of dawn," since, he reminded me, he did his best fighting at that hour. I thanked him for his delightful Turkish zeal but suggested we wait until at least nine in the morning.

Then I recalled something odd and wondered about it. Leaving my office this afternoon, I'd bumped into Irina Tretnikoff. I was seeing her just about every day at the School of Criminology. She was headed towards Donny Foster's office, carrying two paper cups of coffee. I made a mental note to find out what was bringing Irina to our School so often.

The next morning, Altan arrived at our meeting with a thick printout of all our evidence for easy reference. I asked him to review everything we knew so far.

"Okay, Professor. Here's what we know. That's according to our evidence file, which I'd like to think is complete." He gave me a probing stare.

"Yes, I've put everything into it—at least, everything I can share with you."

"Here it is, then. Melanie Foster was murdered in or around Houston. Donny may have expected the murder to happen. He may have even been involved, but there's no evidence he arranged for her killing."

"I agree. He may not have known when or how it would happen, or who would do it. That means we still don't know the identity of the killer," I interjected. It felt funny, now thinking Donny might bear responsibility for his wife's death. But there it was.

"Okay, consider the motive," he continued. "There's no evidence the killing had anything to do with sexual desire or jealousy. Nothing to do with money issues. Nothing to do with debt or insurance or gambling, for example. It probably had something to do with information about the crimes the Devlin Crew was committing. And it was probably aimed at silencing Melanie, though it's just made us look more closely at whatever information she may have had."

"Do you think someone murdered Melanie to throw a scare into Donny? He told the Dean the Kirilov gang did it to get information out of him about the Devlin Crew."

"Professor, I've made every effort to find out about the Kirilovs. All I could discover is that they exist. They are very big in the London underworld. Also, in Manhattan. But that's all I could find out from a search of the internet. Maybe your contacts in the police can tell you more, if they're willing to tell you anything."

"I talked to Gene Tretnikoff and he doesn't think any of this sounds like the Kirilov gang. They're too busy buying up the Southern United States to mess with crime. At least, not in Texas. So, let's put the Kirilov Gang off to the side for now. And if Melanie knew anything the Devlin Crew and Smith Brothers didn't want revealed, it probably didn't have to do with automobile smuggling. It may have had something to do with human trafficking."

"You could be right, Professor. The Devlin Crew has the most to lose, since they may be the biggest traffickers in Texas. Or at least, I've seen that suggested somewhere."

"Yes, and as the next biggest, the Smith Brothers have a lot to lose too," I said, as Altan closed his notes.

"But I don't think the Smith Brothers would have murdered Melanie without Jonny's permission. After all, she was a member of Jonny Devlin's extended family."

"No, they wouldn't have wanted a gang war," I put in.

"So," he continued, "either the Devlin Crew murdered Melanie, or they gave the Smith Brothers permission to do it. Or they did it together. But Professor, would competing gangs work together like that?"

"I've come across examples of it in the research literature. Now and then, gangs work together to deal with a common danger. When the danger passes, they return to business as usual."

"If that's what happened here, we may be looking for a pair of killers—one from the Devlin Crew and another from the Smith Brothers," he said, with an air of satisfaction. "But why would the two gangs cooperate, Professor?"

"It's elementary, my dear Altan. Cooperation would give the gangs joint authority and joint responsibility. Also, joint deniability."

"So, if we can identify one murderer, we may be able to identify the other. But how do we identify the first killer?"

"We'll have to look for more clues. Also, more information about the Kirilov gang. We haven't eliminated them, not yet. But we're making progress," I said, decisively.

I have to admit, this sleuthing was making me suspicious of just about everyone. Well, not members of my own family or people I'd known for a long time like Jen and Roxy, or even Gina and Jackie. But what did I actually know about Farid, I wondered. Isn't he just too good to be true? Then I snapped out of this mode of thinking. It wouldn't get me anywhere, but might lose me a boyfriend.

After Altan left, I phoned the Dean and told her about the Riley lawsuit. Shocked by the news, the Dean said she'd pass it on to the Provost. He wouldn't be happy about it either.

"What are your next steps?" she asked.

"I still want to find out who killed Melanie Foster. There's a criminology conference in Houston next week. I'm planning to talk to a few people about the Foster case while I'm down there. Is that okay with you?"

"Do what you think is best," the Dean said. "But remember, no unnecessary risks and no media attention. Keep all this under wraps until we have a better idea of what to do with Donny."

I phoned Gina in Ottawa. "Do you have police contacts in Houston I could talk to? I need to find out more about Melanie's death."

"I've been dealing with Craig Harrison at the FBI office there," she said. "You've already met him, in Toronto. He's reliable, though I've had doubts about him, now and then. He's sure not telling me everything he knows."

"Okay, I have his phone number. I'll set up a meeting with him in Houston. I also want to look at the Killing Fields. There's something I want to check out there. Could you make the travel and hotel arrangements for me and my assistant, Altan Asker? And keep the expense down—I'm on a budget." I provided the necessary credit card and passport details.

"Will do," Gina said cheerily.

"Great. Email the details when you're ready." I hung up and told my admin assistant about the travel plans for next week.

The weekend passed slowly. I used the time to think over what I'd do in Houston, besides talk to Harrison and visit the Killing Fields. Oh yes, and attend a few sessions of the conference.

On Saturday afternoon, I got a text from Farid. "I haven't heard from you today. What are you up to?"

"I'm getting ready for a conference in Houston, but I'll be back next Friday," I texted. "Let's get together then. I'll tell you all about it."

Against my will, I found myself ending the message with two heart emojis. I was glad to know Farid cared about me. That he even worried about my safety when I travelled.

27

Was I taking too many risks, I wondered. Risks no one in their right mind would take? My heart rate sped up again and I panicked. I took deep breaths and blew into a paper bag. Minute by minute, my heart rate slowed, and I started to feel better again. Despite the stresses of the past two months, I hadn't returned to binge-drinking.

But I couldn't stop thinking about the Fosters, and Donny's possible role in Melanie's death. Donny had surrounded himself with evil people, I knew that. Maybe, he's even been taking part in criminal activities.

Suppose he's made a deal with the Devil, I thought metaphorically. Is there anyone in his life to pull him back from the brink of disaster. Obviously, Melanie can't do it; she's dead. Dylan won't do it; he's cut himself out of Donny's life. Only Garet can save Donny, and I think she wants to. But Donny seems to ignore everything Garet says. It's as though Garet doesn't exist in Donny's moral universe.

Then I thought about the opera I'd seen with Farid weeks earlier. If the Faust legend taught me anything at all, it's that Donny will lose his soul to the Devil. And maybe that's already happened. Maybe Melanie's death was the first installment of Donny's descent into hell.

All these new ideas were confusing, and I promised myself I'd think about them further. But first, I'd chance another, not altogether legal, venture onto university property. I'd been wondering what Melanie may have left behind at the Department of Language Arts, which had absorbed the former Department of English.

Around 5:30, I left Criminology and strolled over to what had, earlier, been the University Drill Hall. Built during World War One to drill male students in military formations, the building had later been used as a massive examination hall. Then, with the erection of a larger, newer examination hall on the south end of the campus, the Drill Hall had been retrofitted. It was now home to the new Language Arts Department and contained four dozen miniature offices, each the size of two or three phone booths.

Seeing no sign of other people, I tried the front door. It was unlocked. Security staff locked the university buildings at 6 p.m. if they weren't in use for night classes. That gave me half an hour to look around before I got locked in for the night. So I entered quietly, searched the faculty directory, and found Melanie's office number: 108-C. Flashlight in hand, I looked at a wall map of the building and oriented myself to the layout. Down one long hall to the left, then another to the right, I found Office 108, and within 108, the door to office 108-C.

Melanie Foster's name was still on the door. Fortunately, the door was unlocked.

Entering the nearly empty office, I saw her desk had been cleared and all the bookshelves, emptied. Against one wall, I saw a stack of cardboard boxes and looked in several of the most accessible ones. The first contained old, much-used textbooks and monographs. The second contained knick-knacks, pens, pads of paper, and a folder containing correspondence. Also, what looked like a soft-covered graphic novel by Dylan Foster.

Suddenly I heard a voice in the hall and saw a flashlight

shine through the window of Office 108. "Anyone in there?" the voice asked. There was a slight tremble in the voice.

To be on the safe side, I hid under Melanie's old desk. God, it was dusty down there. I felt certain I'd sneeze and give myself away. Whoever had called out came into the office and shone his flashlight around the boxes. It was too dark to see him clearly.

After scanning the room for five seconds, the security person left. I stayed in a crouch until I heard footsteps recede down the hallway. Then I stood up and shook the dust balls off my clothing. Using the light from my phone, I took another quick look at what I'd found. The correspondence was dated from January 2016 to February 2024, shortly before Melanie went down to Texas. I'd take a closer look when I got home.

Unclaimed odds and ends were stored in the basement, and I considered looking down there. But that was too big a risk. The campus police wouldn't like to find me rifling through people's belongings, and neither would the Dean. Besides, I wasn't likely to find much more than I'd already found in Melanie's old office. So I tucked Dylan's book and the folder of correspondence into my briefcase, looked around the office one last time, and hastily exited the Drill Hall. By now, I was shivering with anxiety, aware of the danger I'd just faced. But the risk had been worth it.

When I got home, I looked through the folder of correspondence. It contained messages to and from people with code-names: Twerp, Blister, Fang, and the like. The messages dealt mainly with the doings of Donny Foster. I ended up spending three hours sifting through this rich record the Workshop had created. It showed me how members of the Workshop thought, spoke, and acted.

Melanie must have been their leader, and judging from the

messages, all the group members respected her. On the other hand, they all held harshly negative views of Donny Foster. None of them seemed to think he was only studying car smugglers. However, they disagreed about what his other activities might include.

'Twerp' thought Donny was a paid member of the Devlin Crew. That he supervised the Canadian branch of their smuggling ring. 'Blister' contested this notion. She thought he had a hand in organizing the archives and personnel files of Devlin Crew in Houston. 'Fang' produced evidence Donny was engaged in auctioning stolen vehicles in New York and New Jersey. Finally, and most shockingly, 'Cherry' suggested he played a part in selecting and 'recruiting' women for prostitution. That he occasionally even traveled to Greece and Spain for this purpose.

Obviously, Melanie was at the centre of a group effort to record—and maybe undermine—Donny's activities. I hoped to learn more about this during my coming trip to Houston, though I didn't know how.

Soon, I was drowsy, and my eyes were getting sore. I stepped outside, figuring a dose of cold air on the back porch would wake me up. It did. Then I stopped in the kitchen for a glass of ice water, expecting it would help me to stay awake for another few hours. It did. Oh yes, and two oatmeal cookies helped too.

I went upstairs to my home office. Finally, I'd have a chance to look through Dylan's graphic novel. It was inscribed 'To Mom, with love.' I read the novel quickly and may not have picked up on all the subtleties. But roughly speaking, the story line was clear. It was about a life-and-death struggle between two road racers, Flashin' Jack and Quinnie Quinn.

Here's an outline: For years, the two racers have travelled up and down the Eastern Seaboard, vying for the national road racing championship. When the story begins, Flashin' Jack has amassed the most points, but that can change quickly, easily. And a lot is at stake. The winner will achieve vast fame and fortune (though it isn't clear how!).

Other key characters include members of the fictional Boop Family. Professor Jackson Boop is a freelance chemist doing his best to concoct a powerful new fuel for Flashin' Jack's car. When the story opens, he's working against time to get the fuel ready for a big race that's only a month away. Quinnie Quinn is trying to steal the formula or, at least, prevent the Professor from completing his work.

In a laboratory in the basement of his home, Professor Boop spends a third of his time working on the new fuel. He spends another third writing his memoirs, and a final third visiting Dani, his beautiful and sexually adventurous research assistant. Edna, the Professor's wife, spends most of her time reading books and writing feminist tracts against road racing. The Boops have twin children, Bert and Mary, aged 27. Bert spends his days developing battle strategies for his thousand tin soldiers. Mary spends her days on housework; also, feeding the family tomato soup and grilled cheese sandwiches. And praying at a small shrine in her bedroom.

Unknown to Professor Boop, the beautiful Dani is also having amorous relations with both Flashin' Jack and Quinnie Quinn.

Two other featured characters are Mr. Plix and Officer Chestnut. Mr. Plix, a mysterious billionaire businessman, wants to hire either Flashin' Jack or Quinnie Quinn, or both, for his own team of competitive racers. For years, he's used a mix of promises and threats to interest them. But so far, neither has agreed to join his team. For his part, Officer Chestnut has tried for years to prosecute the road racers for their illegal activity but has never caught them *in flagrante*. Like the others, Officer Chestnut also has an amorous relationship with the beautiful Dani. Oddly, he dislikes Edna Boop, with whom he shares a hatred of road racing (and perhaps, Professor Boop.)

The book ends on the day of the momentous, long-awaited race. We aren't told who wins the race. And in the last panel of the book, Dani goes off with the mysterious Mr. Plix.

A strange book, I thought. What could Dylan have been thinking when he wrote it? Did he see a similarity between his own family and the Boop family? To get answers, I texted Garet Foster to ask if she thought Dylan would be comfortable with a conversation about her family.

28

'I don't think he'll talk to you,' Garet messaged back. 'He hardly even talks to me these days. But maybe I can help.' I didn't expect much help from Garet—she seemed a little too spaced out about her family's doings. But it was worth a try. I told her to give me a call, and she did.

"Did your brother model the Boop family on your own family?" I asked her when she called. "And if he did, who are the other characters modelled on? Like Mr. Plix or Officer Chestnut?"

"I don't know about Mr. Plix and Officer Chestnut. But yes, I do think he modeled the Boop family on us," she said. "I'm not happy with the way he presented us, but there you are. And over the years, I probably did make us too many meals of tomato soup and grilled cheese."

I asked my next question carefully, not wanting to offend

her. "What was that about you praying at a shrine in your bedroom? Was that real too?"

"That's a complicated story, Rachel. The short version is, I spent a little time in a reformatory when I was a teenager. I'd been getting into trouble—acting out—all the time. Finally, I went too far, and the authorities locked me up for a year, plus three years on probation after that. But I was lucky. I discovered Jesus while I was locked up, and He saved me."

"How did your parents react?" I asked her.

"They were terribly upset, of course. My father was especially upset when I came back home talking about Jesus all the time. Trying to get my father to change his ways—to give up his research on gangs, most of all. I told him he needed to move away from those people, especially Jonny Devlin. To think about his life. His soul. Otherwise, I was afraid terrible things would happen."

"How did your parents react?"

"My mother wasn't on board with the religious part. But she agreed my father ought to stop associating with the Devlin gang. My father just laughed and said he 'didn't believe in religious mumbo-jumbo.' Those were his exact words. So I stopped talking about Jesus. But I never stopped believing in the need for repentance. I knew my father could still find grace if he changed his ways."

"And what is your brother telling us about your father? In his graphic novel, I mean?"

"Maybe that his ideas aren't for the best? That they're dangerous. Perhaps, even wicked. As for that stuff about the research assistant Dani, I don't have a clue."

I wasn't very impressed by her interpretations. "Thanks, Garet. I'll get back to you if I have any more questions," I said finally.

There was no point contacting Dylan. I felt certain he was writing about his own family but wasn't going to fill in the gaps for me. Or identify Mr. Plix. Did Plix represent Yuri Kirilov? I wondered. And Officer Chestnut? Was that supposed to be Agent Harrison?

One thing was clear: Donny had been upsetting his family for a long time. They knew, or at least sensed, that he'd gone off the rails. And Garet was trying to save him. To reform him. But so far, he'd refused and ridiculed her views. Now, Melanie was dead. Dylan would have nothing to do with his father. And Garet worried all the time about her father's soul. I still didn't know what part he'd played in Melanie's death. But I was more and more certain he was at the root of it.

As I thought this through, Jen phoned. Yes, she was another night owl—always had been.

"Did you give Donny Foster my number and encourage him to phone me?" Jen almost shouted into the phone.

"Of course not. I don't know how he got your number, but it wasn't from me. What did he want?"

"He said he really enjoyed our conversation at Thanksgiving. Said we might enjoy getting to know each other better. Also, suggested going out to dinner on Friday."

"What did you say?"

"I told him I didn't think we'd hit it off. It would be best if we didn't try."

"What did he say to that?"

"He laughed and said he'd phone back in a week. That I might change my mind."

"Don't worry about it, Jen. He'll go away."

"I swear he'll pay a price if he gets in my face again."

"Well, on that happy note, good night, Jen. I'll talk to you when I get back from Houston next week."

I started thinking about Dylan Foster's take on his father's life again and realized only one other person I knew could confirm what Donny had told the Dean. That was Gina Wolff. So I arranged to meet her in Ottawa the next day. This conversation had to be face-to-face. I couldn't risk it being overheard. So we made an appointment and I booked a morning flight out of Billy Bishop.

The next day, I got to Ottawa before noon and went directly to Gina's home in Bytown.

Ottawa was having one of its usual winter days when I arrived. The snowbanks were a metre high and new snow wouldn't stop falling. My taxi slid all over the road as we came into town. I wasn't sure we were going to make it in one piece. But that didn't deter the Ottawa natives. Through blowing snow, I could see heavily clothed men and women jogging alongside the canal. And on the canal itself, a dozen people—they may have been young men, though I couldn't tell—were playing hockey.

"Hey, how's it going?" Gina asked me at the door when I finally arrived. Gina was, clearly, in a great mood.

"That's what I want to ask you. The Dean and I have been talking to Donny, and he keeps bogging us down in sludge. We don't think much of what he's telling us is true."

"Okay, that sounds like a good reason to visit. Tell me what he said, and I'll tell you what I think."

I repeated his latest story, trying to remember every bit of it and even using his words, whenever possible. I particularly told her what we'd found out when we cracked Melanie's cipher messages. Donny had known about the Devlin Crew's human trafficking and prostitution all along, though he'd repeatedly denied such knowledge.

"What do you think?" I asked her when I'd finished.

"Some of what he told you is probably true," she said. "But I think Melanie may have blabbed about human trafficking and pissed off a lot of people. Jonny would have told Donny to shut Melanie up before she got hurt. Donny would have passed along that message, although maybe he wouldn't. He didn't have any guts when it came to challenging Melanie. But let's say he warned Melanie, and she ignored the warning. She was on a crusade.

"Then, Jonny would have told him, 'Melanie is causing me a lot of trouble. Get her out of Houston or she'll end up dead. She's making a lot of enemies, and I won't protect her anymore. Take her back to Toronto, right away.' The question is, why Donny wouldn't take that advice."

"I agree, why wouldn't he drag Melanie back to Toronto? That's what I would have done, if my spouse was in danger," I said.

"The most likely answer isn't pretty. Dragging Melanie back to Toronto and keeping her there would have ended his work with the Devlin Crew. In effect, Jonny probably was telling him, 'Get Melanie to stay home and keep her mouth shut, or our working relationship is over.' And Donny didn't want that. So he'd have warned Melanie one last time, then stopped warning her. He knew what would happen, sooner or later."

I was shocked to imagine my colleague sacrificing Melanie in the interest of his research.

"Is it possible a member of the Kirilov Gang killed Melanie, on the orders of Yuri Kirilov? And that the Devlin Crew had nothing to do with her death?"

"Anything is possible. But I don't think Yuri Kirilov is a player in Houston, except as a real estate owner and developer. He's got more money than God. I can't see him getting involved in murdering people."

"You don't think he might have threatened Donny to get information about the Devlin Crew? And he killed Melanie to tighten the screws?"

"If Yuri had wanted information about the Devlin Crew, he would have asked Jonny at one of their Thursday night dinners. They're both on the Board of the new TXX. Good friends, I hear. Jonny's even the godfather of Yuri's grandson, Edward."

"Just one more question. Do you know anything about a person named Farid Srivastava? He's a plastic surgeon I've been dating. I want to rule out the possibility that he's connected with Melanie's death in any way."

Gina shook her head. "The name doesn't ring a bell, but I'll check the CSIS information system tomorrow. And I'll ask Harrison if he knows the guy. If I learn anything, I'll let you know. Just one thing comes to mind: Farid sounds like an East Indian name, and I think the Smith Brothers are East Indian, originally. But maybe that's a coincidence."

Nothing is ever a coincidence, I thought. "I have to go. Tomorrow's a crazy day. Sorry I have to bounce out of here."

Gina laughed and said, "No problem," waving me away with her hand. I grabbed my stuff, caught a cab a block away, and took the next flight back to Toronto.

Back home a few hours later, I got a text message from Gina's boss at CSIS. 'Someone broke into Gina's home and abducted her shortly after you left. We think she may have been taken to the US, maybe Texas. A note said she was being "taken south to get a taste of the trouble she's caused." At any rate, she can't answer any more questions. If you need information about any of her cases, please channel your request through me.'

I thought about Gina's abduction for the next three hours and couldn't stop trembling. Finally, I collapsed into bed and slept like a baby. Four hours later—certainly, sooner than I would have liked—my alarm clock let me know it was time to get up. I had to get to the airport.

Gina had reserved seats for us on a direct flight to Houston. The flight gave me and Altan time to compare notes. But somewhere over Buffalo, New York, I fell into a deep slumber. Almost before I knew it, Altan was shaking me and saying my name, over and over. A few minutes later, we were off the plane at George Bush Intercontinental Airport and in a cab to our hotel.

Houston was blazing hot—thirty degrees warmer than Toronto when we'd left that morning. Hotter than hell, I imagined. I couldn't believe a short plane ride—well, four hours—could take me into such a dramatically different climate. I felt like I was in the 'Down Country' I'd imagined—down south, down around the Gulf of Mexico, down in the semi-tropics. I was in a place I didn't know at all. A place I didn't like much.

I peeled off my overcoat and suit jacket, hoping I'd brought the right clothes. If not, I'd have to buy new ones. But that would be the least of my worries.

Gina had booked us adjoining rooms on the tenth floor of a budget Marriott hotel. Right in the heart of downtown, across the road from where the criminology conference would take place. After signing into our hotel, we checked in at the conference venue, but sessions hadn't started yet. With time to kill, we strolled around the downtown, two rubbernecked *flâneurs*, dropping into shops for retail therapy.

I bought myself a summery outfit that suited the local climate. Altan bought his partner a souvenir t-shirt. Later that afternoon, we went back to the conference venue for the opening session. Finally, drenched in sweat, we returned to our air-conditioned hotel for a quick dinner and early bedtime.

While attaching my phone to the charger, I found three

messages. One, from Farid, said 'I'm missing you like crazy. Get back here soon, sweetheart. Let me know if you need me down there.'

A second, from Agent Harrison, said 'We're on for 9 a.m. at the Federal Building tomorrow, room 805. See you then.'

The third, from a number I didn't recognize, said 'Hello, Professor Tile, we haven't met yet but I hope to correct that soon. I'll contact you tomorrow with instructions.'

That last message spooked me. Only a few people knew I'd come to Houston. That meant the message writer had a secret source at the FBI in Houston, CSIS in Ottawa, or the School of Criminology in Toronto. But what did this anonymous person want? I'd have to wait to find out.

The next morning, Altan and I met Agent Harrison at the Federal Building. He said he'd checked me out with CSIS, prior to making this appointment.

"CSIS says you're okay. They think you may know who killed Michael Coale and won't tell the police. But as far as organized crime goes, they think you're a safe bet."

He didn't have any more idea than we did about who'd sent the unsigned message, or what had happened to Gina. But he told us everything the FBI knew about the Melanie Foster case, then asked us to share the information we'd collected. He couldn't tell us much about the Kirilov gang—only that the FBI was investigating them in Manhattan.

After a quick lunch, we got into Harrison's clunker of a car and drove down Highway I-45. Inside this small, confined space, the smell of nicotine and old tobacco smoke was overpowering. Once or twice, I caught myself gagging and thought I might throw up. I tried to breathe through my mouth, then tried to stop breathing altogether. Nothing worked.

Harrison, meanwhile, told us about the fabled Killing Fields.

They took up a mere 25 acres, roughly twenty football fields. Not a big area, considering all the notoriety The Fields had garnered. And they were little more than acres of scrub and grazing land. Some of the land was fenced in and some, wide open. Here and there, I saw deserted farmhouses or barns, but few people or animals. The area felt desolate, empty.

Harrison turned off the I-45 at a poorly marked side road and drove half a mile east. Without any warning, he stopped the car and invited us to get out. The silence was eerie. Aside from a slight hum of trucks on the I-45, we heard nothing. Harrison pointed to a tree about 200 yards away and led us to it. In the distance, I saw a pair of black dogs—mongrels, by the look of them. They lurked in the bushes, watching without a sound.

"This is where they found Melanie Foster's body, in a shallow grave next to the tree," he said. "It had been chewed on by wild dogs. They're all around us here, as you can see." Harrison pointed out several pairs of dogs I hadn't noticed.

There wasn't much else to see in the Killing Fields, but we stared at the tree for a minute or two anyway. I tried not to imagine what Melanie's corpse had looked like when the police found it.

"Over there," Harrison said, pointing to a flowery bush about a hundred yards farther into the scrub. "That's where we found Lana Bond. She was buried in a shallow grave too."

I knew the flowery bush was an azalea, a hardy plant I'd rarely seen in Canada. It needed lots of heat and sunshine. Then I remembered that purple azalea bush in the centre of Melanie's painting of the Killing Fields. To judge from the painting, we were now standing right where Melanie had once stood, looking in the same direction.

Donny hadn't liked the painting, he'd said, not that I blamed him. But now that I was here, I knew Melanie had visited the same spot and wanted other people to know about it. I also knew from the inscription that Melanie had come here well before her death. And in the distance, I could see the outline of a trailer home, like the one in Melanie's painting.

I asked Harrison about it.

"No idea, Rachel. Those things come and go, all over this part of Texas. I wouldn't put much importance by it." I was surprised at his lack of interest. As for me, I was fascinated.

Even the soundscape was haunting. Nature had turned the Killing Fields into a sound vacuum. Nothing human belonged here. Nothing stayed except dogs and dead bodies. Now, I understood why people called this the Killing Fields. But they could have also called it the Dead Zone. The only living things in sight were scruffy red and purple azalea bushes and pairs of wild dogs.

"Agent Harrison, do you know who killed Lana Bond, or why?" I asked.

"The Devlin Crew may have found out Lana was giving us information. We don't have any suspects, probably never will. That is, unless a gang member turns state witness and tells us what he knows. But that's unlikely, because the Crew is very tight. It's impossible to get any information out of them."

29

By now, sweat was pouring off my face. Altan, looking faint, leaned against Harrison's car, hoping for a bit of shade. This was my vision of hell. I really hated this place. But I wasn't ready to leave it, not just yet. I felt like Orpheus in the underworld. But if so, who was I here to save?

"I have one more question, and you may find it a bit weird," I said to Harrison.

"Go ahead, I love weird questions," Harrison replied, smiling and lighting up a cigarette.

"Do you know any members of the Devlin Crew who are friends with members of the Smith Brothers gang? I know those gangs compete with each other. Maybe they're even enemies. But do any of their people spend time together?"

"Wow, that comes out of left field. Let me think." To help himself think, he walked around the field for a few minutes, head down, puffing on his cigarette.

Finally, he stubbed out his cigarette, came back over to us, and answered my question. "A lot of the gangsters in Houston know one another, Rachel. They may have gone to the same public school, grown up in the same neighbourhood, or even worked for the same boss at one time or another. Some may have even had the same girlfriend or boyfriend. Take Lana Bond. For a while, she was seeing guys in both the Devlin Crew and the Smith Brothers. Though she tried to keep it hidden, that's for sure.

"Or Conkie Rovino. Everyone knows him. He may even have friends in the Smith Brothers gang, though everyone knows he's part of the Devlin Crew. Everyone likes Conkie, because he's funny and harmless. Another person with a lot of contacts is Kim Cressy. She works for the Devlin Crew but lots of people around Houston know her. She's friends with everyone, whatever gang they work for. I could probably name a few other people like that. They do what they're told but get along fine with people from other gangs. So long as there's no gang war going on. But I have to ask you, what's with that question?"

I was shocked to hear Kim Cressy's name mentioned again.

She seemed to be popping into my world with amazing regularity. But for now, I'd keep that to myself.

"Nothing more than curiosity," I told Harrison. "You know how academics are—full of questions and not too many answers." He accepted my explanation without hesitating.

Finally, after peering at the surroundings for another minute or two, I said "Agent Harrison, I want to check out that trailer." I pointed to the one I meant, the one in the distance. The one Melanie had painted in her picture. "I have a feeling Gina Wolff may be a prisoner there."

Harrison gave me a funny look, like he thought I was crazy. "Okay, Rachel, go ahead," he said, nodding his head in surprise.

We got back into the car and drove several hundred yards across the scrubland. As we neared the trailer, Harrison cut the engine, and we coasted the rest of the way.

Altan and I slipped out of the car and circled the trailer, peering into its windows. Through one window, I could see a big guy watching TV—handsome, young, legs stretched out in front of him. It must have been a comedy show because he was laughing his guts out. And over in the corner, I could see Gina, her arms and legs tied to a kitchen chair. She was nearly naked, and her head was slumped forward on her chest. She looked almost unconscious.

I took a can of pepper spray out of my purse, hid it in my hand, and tip-toed up three steps to the trailer door. I knocked on the door and called out, "Hello, I need help," in a mumbled voice.

After three knocks, the door opened. The big guy was taller and more muscular than I'd imagined. He had to be six three or four, over 220 pounds. And he was wearing jogging shorts with an unidentifiable logo. Nothing else. He flashed me a lazy smile, visibly wondering who I was. He may have been stoned.

I said I was looking for directions back to Houston. He opened the screen door and came out on the stoop. Lazily, he looked around, wondering how I'd gotten there.

Suddenly, looking into his large, dreamy face, I couldn't control my rage. I caught him by surprise, spraying his eyes. Then I kneed him in the groin. As he sank to the ground, I smashed his nose with the flat of my hand. The guy went down heavily, but he wasn't out yet. He lay on the stoop writhing in pain, and I couldn't have him getting up. So I kicked him in the head twice, then a third time for good measure. He was out for good.

Mr. Tall Guy wasn't a pretty picture anymore, and my rage was gone just as suddenly as it had surfaced. Blood was pouring out of gashes on his head, covering the stoop and leaking on to the sandy ground.

Altan ran over and stared at the big guy. "How'd you learn that shit, Professor?" he asked me in amazement.

"All those martial arts lessons finally came in handy," I said, smiling. But my knees were shaking. For about ten seconds I couldn't control my body. I kept twitching. That's how I came to realize it's different when you really put someone down—different from anything you'll experience in a dojo.

Altan and Harrison had watched in shocked surprise. "I'm going in there," I told them. "Follow me." But Harrison wouldn't enter the trailer. He first wanted to confirm there were no accomplices around to sneak up on them.

Gina was naked except for a large men's Houston Astros' tee-shirt across the top of her body. Duct tape kept a wad of cloth in her mouth. But I knew everything I needed to from her face. She was hysterical with fear. Her eyes bugged out, almost rolling around in her head. I ripped off the duct tape and pulled the gag out of her mouth. Then I grabbed a bread knife from the kitchen counter just steps away.

"What have they done to you?" I whispered, as I cut the ropes that bound her to the chair.

She mumbled something I couldn't make out.

"Altan, cold water, lots of it. We need to wake her up. She's been drugged."

Altan looked at Gina in horror, then lowered his eyes. He was embarrassed to see her nakedness, and I could tell she was embarrassed to be seen that way. Altan ran the kitchen tap, filled a pot with water, and handed it to me. He wasn't going to throw it on Gina, wouldn't look at her again. I wasn't so shy.

Startled by the cold, Gina jumped up, then slumped back and started to cry. After a minute, she stopped crying and started talking. "They've been shooting me full of heroin every day. And that big guy has been raping me, a few times every day. I guess that's how they get women ready for sex work," she mumbled. Her lips were swollen, and she couldn't move them easily. Her face was bruised and dirty. One of her front teeth was missing.

I called out to Harrison again, and this time he came in. Meanwhile, I covered Gina with a sheet I'd found in the back bedroom.

"Where are your clothes?" I asked her, gently.

"I don't know. Check the closet," she mumbled, pointing to a dim corner of the room. I searched a heap of clothes inside the closet and found sweatpants and a sweatshirt. Probably not Gina's, but they'd have to do.

"Put these on," I told her, and directed the men to look away while Gina dressed.

"We have to get out of here," Harrison said, when Gina had finished dressing. "You never know who might show up."

He didn't care about the guy on the front steps. But he was expecting something worse, and I wasn't going to disagree.

Altan and I helped Gina stand, then helped her—nearly dragged her—out of the trailer. Mostly, we carried her. She'd started crying again and couldn't stop. We made her as comfortable we could in the back of Harrison's car and Altan fastened her seat belt. Then, Altan spied an old Ford idling on the other side of the field. Someone inside had been watching us. He—and I felt sure it was a male—had eased his car on to the field slowly and quietly, without drawing attention to himself.

Harrison put his car in reverse, turned around and headed toward I-45. Out the rear window, I could see the old Ford start to give chase. Within seconds, it was keeping pace with us, about five car lengths back. Suddenly, the Ford sped up and overtook us. Harrison pulled into the right lane, giving the Ford enough space to pass. Instead, it pulled up close behind us.

Within seconds, less than one car length separated our two cars.

Harrison pulled a gun out of his shoulder holster, slipped off the safety, and put it on the seat beside him. Time started to slow down. Scenery began to move past the car windows at a sluggish, dreamlike speed. I felt like screaming but stopped myself. From the back seat, Altan had grabbed me with his left hand. The pressure on my arm was hurting me. "Ow, let go," I yelled, scowling at him. Gina had fallen unconscious.

But none of this seemed to faze Harrison. He drove with his left hand, while pulling something out of the central console with his right.

"Craig," I shouted. "Can't you get us away from him?"

"Let me handle this. I've done it before," he answered a bit sharply.

Hoping to attract the attention of passing drivers, he flipped a switch. A siren wailed 'Whoo, whoo, whoo,' an ear-splitting noise after the silent Killing Fields. Then, Harrison dipped his right hand into the centre console and brought out a blue light. With surprising speed, he mounted it on the dashboard. Our car was a light-and-sound show.

Harrison shouted into a hand-held microphone. "Agent Harrison on Highway I-45 near State Road 31. Calling for backup. I have civilian passengers and a criminal pursuer." Then, Harrison wove back and forth across the centre line of the highway. He was trying to shake the car behind us, without any success. I readied myself for a collision or a gunfight, shaking with fear. But the Ford swerved left and pulled up next to us at seventy miles an hour. The driver—a guy of about thirty in a casual shirt and jacket—stared into our car. Smiling, he pretended to shoot at us with his thumb and forefinger.

Seconds later, the Ford sped up to what must have been more than a hundred miles an hour. Within seconds, it was out of sight.

Harrison slowed his car, then stopped and parked on the side of the road. Never having been in a car chase before, I was scared stiff. So were Altan and Gina, who had now regained consciousness. I got into the back seat, put my arms around Gina, and held her close to me. She was gasping for air. Finally, she calmed down and was breathing normally. But she had started sobbing again, and between sobs she told me they'd drugged her, then flown her from somewhere outside Ottawa to somewhere outside Houston. It was a small private jet, she said, very fancy inside.

Harrison took all this in stride. "I know that guy," he said without any expression, meaning the car driver who'd just chased us. "One of Devlin's boys, Dickie Wells. Does odd jobs for Jonny. I wonder if he had a hand in Melanie's death. Or Gina's abduction. He certainly has the skill set, and Jonny trusts him, far as I know."

From the side of the road, Harrison called in the Ford's license number and waited for an answer. In a minute or two, the officer on the other end came back on the line. The Ford had been reported stolen a week ago.

Heading back to Houston, Harrison calmed us with stories about the gangsters he'd met, including Dickie Wells. And that guy who'd been holding Gina captive—Mark Somebody. Harrison couldn't bring the guy's last name to mind. Just another of Devlin's tough guys. Bigger than average, I'd have to guess.

"Have you ever met Jonny Devlin, Agent Harrison?" Altan asked.

"Once or twice. Can't say I know him well, but he's pleasant enough when you're making small talk. I hear he can be a real joker after a few drinks. Still, he's a stone-cold killer when he has to be. I wouldn't mess with him if I could help it."

I took in what Harrison said, but didn't talk for the rest of the ride. Couldn't stop thinking about feral black dogs and what they might do to a woman's half-buried body. Whenever they found one. And what they might do to that guy I'd beaten, if he didn't recover.

Back in downtown Houston, we took Gina to a hospital emergency room, checked her in, and phoned the city police. They'd want to take her statement. We waited around the hospital for two hours while Gina was being examined. Finally, they checked her into a room for an overnight stay. I promised to return in a few hours.

Back at our hotel, far from black dogs and half-buried bodies, I felt slightly more relaxed. I knew I should visit the criminology conference for another session or two. But I couldn't concentrate on what the speakers were saying. So, after freshening up at our hotel, we headed out for an early dinner. Altan and I tried to avoid discussing what we'd seen that afternoon, but we didn't succeed for long.

After dinner, I went back to the hospital and spent an hour with Gina. They'd given her a sedative and she'd sleep well that night. I promised to visit again first thing the next morning.

Back at my hotel room, I found another text waiting. 'It's time to meet, don't you think? Please come by my office at Lone Star Investments tomorrow morning at 9. Come alone. Don't tell anyone where you're headed.' The message was signed 'Jonny Devlin'.

So, Lone Star Investments and Jonny Devlin were truly one and the same. Now things are fitting together, I thought.

I felt a rush of fear and exhilaration. At last, I was going to meet the mastermind of the Devlin Crew. The man who held the lives of so many people in his hands. The man who'd authorized Gina's kidnapping and maybe even Melanie's murder. I admit, I was scared. I didn't want to meet this guy, but figured I had to. He was the key to this entire crazy story.

I looked up Lone Star Investments on my phone. It was located in a 25-storey office building only minutes from our hotel. Ignoring the instructions I'd received, I knocked on Altan's door to tell him my plans for tomorrow.

"That sounds dangerous. Should I wait for you outside the building, just in case?" he asked, leaving the rest of his thought unstated.

"That's not necessary. I'll meet you here as soon as I get back. Meanwhile, please visit Gina. Keep her company for an hour or two. Tell her I'll be there in the afternoon, as soon as I'm able."

Altan agreed, shaking his head in mild disapproval. But I knew I had to do this alone.

Then I found a new message from Garet Foster. 'Rachel,

where are you? I'm so worried about my father. I've been phoning and phoning, but he hasn't answered my calls or any of my text messages. Do you know if he needs my help?'

'I'm in Houston,' I answered 'so I don't know what your father is up to. He may be out somewhere with friends. Relax. I'll let you know if I hear anything.'

Just before I put away my phone for the night, a message came in from Connie.

'Hi, Professor. I hear you're in Houston at the ACS meetings. I wanted you to know Professor Foster came to see me this afternoon. Said he wanted to get to 'know me better' and wondered if I was satisfied with the supervision you're giving me. I said everything was going fine, thanks for asking. Then he wanted to know if I ever felt like going out for a meal, to discuss the state of criminology, my research, his research, and so on. I told him I didn't think my partner would like that. But we could have a coffee at school and discuss those things there, if he wanted. He said he'd let me know. So, what's with that???'

I emailed Connie back. 'That's just Donny being Donny. Put it out of your mind. We'll chat about this when I get back.'

30

The next morning, I phoned the hospital to check on Gina's condition, then ate breakfast with Altan. After brushing my teeth, I strolled over to the Lone Star Investments office. The bustle of Houston was impressive, but I didn't think I'd like living here. The place was too big and hectic. Most of all, I couldn't stand so much heat, day after day. The heat sapped your brain. It sucked the will power right out of your body.

Entering the cool, air-conditioned office of Lone Star Investments, I spied a pleasant-looking young woman at a desk. "Hello, I'm Rachel Tile, here to meet Mr. Devlin." She murmured a few words into a gold-plated telephone, then got up and opened the door to her boss's office. "Please follow me."

As I peered around Devlin's dim office, my head turned toward large windows that looked out over central Houston. The blinds were half-shut to keep out early-morning glare. The décor was 'modern cowboy' style. Walls covered in sepia photographs of early Houston and its inhabitants. An old, wooden wagon wheel mounted prominently on one wall.

A grizzled-looking man rose from behind a mahogany desk at the far end of the room and ambled over. Jonny didn't look any of the ways I'd expected. He was tall and lanky, wearing a well-pressed navy-blue suit and white shirt. The oddest thing about his appearance was a Western-style bolo tie with a silver clasp to keep the strings in place. Dressed that way, Jonny looked like the Olde Tyme sheriff of a prosperous Western town. Like Gary Cooper in that classic movie, *High Noon*. Old-fashioned, serious. And I'd also find out Jonny was devilishly charismatic—downright charming, in a rough kind of way.

"Hello, Professor Tile. At last, we meet. I'm Jonny Devlin—you may have heard of me," he said, smiling, slowly pumping my hand up and down.

"Of course. Thank you for making time to see me. But how did you find me?"

"Oh, it's easy to find people these days, what with friends and the internet. Please sit down—I'll call you Rachel, if I may." He spoke softly, like an old-school gentleman.

"Of course," I said, hunkering down in an easy chair.

"Let's put our cards on the table, shall we?" he said, abruptly. When I nodded in agreement, he started talking again.

"You know something about my line of work. Maybe from

Agent Harrison. You spent time with him yesterday. He may have told you I'm a criminal—someone who does bad things." He made a spooky face, to highlight the foolishness of this belief. He had still spoken very softly. But now his voice started to rise.

"But that's only half the truth. I've invested money in lots of legitimate businesses: in real estate, stocks and bonds, a chain of restaurants, a housing complex, a chain of super-markets, and a few casinos. I've probably forgotten a few of the things I own, but you get the idea. I'm a businessman. My goal is to get rich as legally as possible. Car smuggling, the activity that interests Donny Foster, provides only a small part of my income.

"And I may give up that business altogether if my other investments turn out as I expect. I won't have any more time for cars. My golly, I already have successful Italian restaurants in Seattle, San Diego, Mexico City, Vienna—heck, even in Toronto. I also own a few gentlemen's clubs, two of them right here in Houston: Bells N' Whistle and The Johnson Rod. All my entertainment spots are very popular. Lots of times, I wake up at night and think to myself, 'Jonny, you are one very successful guy.'"

He was speaking more loudly now. And I could see where Donny Foster had picked up his lavishly boastful manner.

Suddenly, a worried look crossed Johnny's face and he spoke softly again. "My gosh, what a terrible host I am. I didn't even offer you a drink. Would you like water or coffee, or something else? Do you folks drink tea in Canada? I can't stand the stuff myself, but I can get you tea if you want."

Jonny looked over to a couch in the corner. Someone was there, reading a magazine in the shadows. "Conkie, get the lady something to drink. Chop-chop!" he called out.

Dropping the magazine, Conkie sprang to his feet. "Sure, Boss." He rushed to my side and leaned over me. "What can I get you, Miss? Would you like a coke and a Danish? That's what I always get the Boss around this time."

Conkie had a grin on his face and a big dent on his forehead. Just what you'd expect from someone who'd sustained a serious head injury. Still, my first impression was positive. Conkie wore a black and gray striped suit, with silver cowboy boots on his feet. On closer inspection, his wrinkled white shirt was missing buttons and his patterned blue and red necktie, dotted with food stains. The overall effect was sloppy. Conkie may have dressed in the dark while half asleep.

"No, thank you. I've just eaten breakfast, so I'm all set for liquids and snacks," I told him, smiling.

Conkie looked offended. His shoulders slumped. I suddenly realized he'd been waiting for a chance to please his boss, and here I was, taking it away. He might have a hard time forgetting this slight.

"You know, maybe an orange juice would be good. Could you get me one?" I asked him.

Conkie grinned and said, "Right away, Miss." He rushed out of the office in search of orange juice. There was something manic about Conkie's approach to service.

I turned to Jonny. "Why have you sent for me, Mr. Devlin? I didn't expect such hospitality." I smiled pleasantly as I completed this sentence. But inside, I was thinking, 'Why hasn't he killed me, or at least ignored me?'

"Well, Texas is a hospitable place and you're a guest here. That's part of the story—a small part, to be sure. But I've also heard about you. When I heard your Dean had asked you to investigate Donny Foster, I made a point of finding out more about you. That's another reason for our meeting. I like what

I've heard. You're smart. You're successful. You're dynamic—my kind of person. You're a good fighter too, I hear." He smirked when he said that.

"But most of all, I want you to get an idea of what I'm thinking. You need to understand what I'm about. I'm willing to take as much time as we need to get you there—I mean, to get you to understand me. Okay?" As he said this, Jonny stretched out his arms, like he was handing me a very valuable gift. Or about to pull me toward him. I didn't know which.

"So, what should I understand?" I asked, expecting the worst. Expecting he was going to punish me for beating up his goon. I had no idea what this odd, strangely amusing crime boss was about to tell me.

"I like your directness, Rachel. It makes everything much easier when you're doing business—especially, with a stranger. So, here's the thing: I'm in business to make a lot of money. As I've said, most of my money comes from legitimate activities. Gosh, I could break out last year's tax return, if you wanted proof. You're a scholar and that means looking for evidence. But I don't think you want to see my tax return, do you? Please believe me: I'm in business to make a profit, like Jeff Bezos and Elon Musk. Or your former husband? Mike Coale, wasn't it? And I want to keep my taxes as low as possible. I'm sure you feel the same way, Rachel. We all do."

Jonny chuckled. I half expected him to slap his knee to highlight the hilarity of what he'd just said.

"Okay," I said simply, nodding my head and waiting for the next revelation.

"So here's the thing. This kerfuffle with Melanie and Donny Foster has caused me a lot of trouble. It's made people snoop around. But even when the snoops are as nice as you are—and I hope you won't mind if I say, as beautiful as you are—no matter, I don't like people snooping around. It's not good for making money and keeping it."

"I get it. You don't want people snooping around," I said, standing up, straightening my skirt, making ready to leave the office.

"Don't take this the wrong way," Jonny said. "Please sit down. I don't want you rushing out of here, telling people I'm a bad host. I'm enjoying your visit. Please relax."

I sat back down.

"What do you want from me, Jonny?" I asked, more curtly than I'd intended.

"That's simple. I want you to have a nice visit to Houston, enjoy the sights, eat some tasty food, do a bit of shopping. Then head back to Canada and tell your boss she won't have any more trouble from me or Donny Foster. That, Rachel, is a Jonny Devlin 21-carat gold promise. You can take that to the bank. No… more… trouble." Jonny smiled once again, rubbed his hands together like he was dusting them off, picked up his can of cola and took a huge sip. He let out a loud "Ah!" after downing the drink.

"Is that all?"

"Pretty much. I'd also like you to stop discussing me with Gina Wolff and Craig Harrison. Or any other police. I don't want people looking into my business. Can you manage that?"

By this time, Conkie had returned with my orange juice. I thanked him and smiled. He looked like I'd just given him a cheque for a million dollars, then went back to the couch in the corner.

I paused to think about Jonny's request, then shook my head.

As I started to talk, my voice trembled slightly. I couldn't help it.

"Jonny, I'm not sure I can do what you want, so let me tell you why. My Dean wants me to find out what happened to Melanie Foster. I can't refuse the Dean—especially, since I've made this trip to Houston and talked to Agent Harrison about the case. But here's another reason: it looks like my university is getting sued for negligence. Donny screwed up the supervision of one of his students. That means a $10 million hit to the university. You can be sure the university will look at every inch of him—at least, until this lawsuit is settled. And since I'm Donny's boss, that means they'll look at every inch of me too. I can't make that go away by snapping my fingers."

Jonny stared at his hands for a few minutes. He flexed them once or twice, then started massaging the back of his neck. "That's not good. In fact, it's very bad, especially if Donny runs his mouth about me and my business. I can see you're not the main problem. It's Donny and your boss, the Dean, who I have to worry about."

Jonny rubbed the back of his neck again and flexed his shoulders, trying to release the tension. Then he looked back at me and smiled.

"Here's how we'd handle this problem down here in Texas. It would be real easy. I'd send one of my lawyers to meet with the university president. He'd bring a suitcase containing $10 million in unmarked bills and hand the suitcase to the president as a 'donation,' let's say. Then, the president would use it to settle the court case. After that, the Dean would put that numbskull Donny Foster on a research leave until he got his shit together. Oh, and by the way, I have a right to curse him out if I want to. That fancy lawyer cost me $300,000 so my nephew didn't have to go to jail. Or dip into his savings, either. I figure everything would have been fine if he hadn't invited that girlfriend of his, Gina Wolff, to visit him in Austin."

"Donny told us you were his uncle," I said, matter-of-factly. "We were surprised to hear that."

"Yeah, well, in my world everyone's related to everyone else, one way or another. But that doesn't matter now, does it? If your Dean has any sense, she'll keep Donny from supervising graduate students. Ever again. He could still teach courses if he wanted. But he couldn't send students out on those crazy missions he thinks up. That, plus the $10 million, would deal with the lawsuit. Right?"

"Sure, that might work in Canada too," I said. "But it leaves the problem of Melanie Foster's death. Also, whether Donny is a risk to the university: a guy who puts other people in harm's way. The university can't have a dangerous person around. So, I have to find out how Melanie's death fits into this picture."

I didn't mention Gina's abduction. That was a conversation for another day, nothing to do with the university. Something between me and Donny and Jonny.

31

Jonny kept rubbing his neck and twisting his torso, trying to release the tension in his shoulders. Seeing Jonny's discomfort, Conkie called to him from the other side of the room. "Can I get you anything, boss?" Jonny shook his head, then turned back to me.

Meanwhile, I'd been looking around the room. I didn't want to stare—to make Jonny feel I was putting pressure on him. He wouldn't respond well to pressure.

"Okay, I get all that," he said finally. "You're right, the problem is all Donny. Did you know I'm also his godfather? I promised my sister Bella I'd look out for him. Now that she's gone, I have to make good on that. I'll have to think about this a little longer. Meanwhile, I need you to back off as much as you can. Make your Dean think you're doing what she wants, but don't do anything that will piss me off. I could have had you and your young assistant and Agent Harrison—oh yes, and Gina Wolff—killed yesterday, if I'd wanted." He smiled when he mentioned Gina, like she was part of a joke. I didn't like that. I dug my nails into the palms of my hands to keep from saying anything.

"But I prefer to reason with people. That's what we're doing right now—reasoning together."

That idea may have sounded presidential to Jonny. Like something that great Texan, Lyndon B. Johnson, might have said in a moment of crisis. Jonny had an air-brushed photo of LBJ on the wall behind his desk.

"I wish to hell I'd never taken this job," I told him, softly, with what I hoped sounded like determination. "But the world went in a different direction. I promised the Dean—she's also a friend of mine, and you know how friendships work—I promised her I'd find out what I could. When I get back, I'll tell her I've met you and you don't want us mixing into your business. But here's how you can help me. You can tell me who killed Melanie, and why?"

"You are one tough broad, I'll give you that," Jonny said, a smile forming on his face. "No, I *cannot* tell you who killed Melanie. Or I should say, I *will not* tell you who killed Melanie, or why. Donny can answer those questions. He has all the information you'll ever need. You just have to pry it out of him. But don't try to pry it out of me. I don't like being pushed.

"So, here's the deal. Go back and tell your Dean about our conversation—all of it, mind you. Then, you two figure out how to get Donny talking. He didn't kill Melanie. I know that for a fact. But here's the important thing: don't contact me again. Above all, don't work with the FBI or CSIS—or whatever police forces may be involved—to find out who killed her. If you do, you will be messing with my business. Then, I'll have to punish you. I don't want to do that, but you'll give me no choice. Understood?"

Knowing what Gina had just gone through, I was terrified. "I understand," I whispered.

"Believe me, I know a lot about your friends. Your family too. Did I mention I own a small business in Toronto—a restaurant called Ferrari? I get news about Toronto almost every week. For instance, I know you like to visit our place. You were even asking Carla about our Wednesday night meetings. Rachel, I don't want you nosing into my Toronto business either. Do we have an understanding, then?"

"I understand," I said again, standing up to leave. "By the way, I've received letters from the Texas Stock Exchange. Are you behind those letters?"

Jonny smiled and nodded his head. "Yes, I am, but my colleagues are in full agreement. We can't have outsiders messing around in our business. Especially now that we're trying to get a major new financial institution up and running. I hope you'll take this to heart. A lot of money is at stake."

Jonny walked me out to the bank of elevators and said goodbye, full of smiles again. We shook hands and I took the elevator down to the first floor. It was nearly noon, and the sun was blazing overhead. I felt like I'd been with Jonny for days. Like I'd just made a deal with the Devil.

Back at the hotel, I checked my messages and found one from Farid. 'Is everything going okay, sweetheart? I'll come down there if you need me. Let me know. Otherwise, I'll see you tomorrow night, wherever you suggest.' I sent him a thumbs-up emoji plus two heart emojis.

I found the November issue of *Inklings* nestled in my mailbox and paused to leaf through it. As usual, Altan's column was hilarious.

Ask The Asker
By Altan Asker
Doctoral Candidate
School of Criminology
Strachan University

Happy November, everyone. I've received a lot of queries from people who are just starting their doctoral studies in Criminology at Strachan University. Below, I've answered their challenging questions to the best of my ability. Here's a sampling:

From Eager to Do Well, October 28:
Dear Asker,
I want to do well in the doctoral program at Strachan University. Which of the following would you consider the best preparation for success in this program? (1) Attending the lectures, (2) Doing the readings, or (3) Getting to know the professors?

Dear Eager to Do Well,
I suggest that, if you want to complete our doctoral program with distinction, you should start working on a Black Belt in martial arts. This will come in handy when doing field work abroad or dealing with emotional professors. Also, attend the lectures if you can find the time.

From Can Hardly Wait, October 22:
Dear Asker,
Having finished my coursework, I'm getting ready to collect data for my doctoral dissertation. The data collection may take me abroad. What preparations do you recommend?'

Dear Can Hardly Wait,
Some people would recommend you learn the language of the country in which you plan to collect data. However, far more important, in my view, is that you take out Blue Cross Extended Medical Care coverage. Also, be sure to visit the local hospitals while you are abroad. Try to find one where you are willing to spend a long time in bed.

From Want to be Prepared, October 25:
Dear Asker,
I'm about to start collecting data for my dissertation. What are the relative merits of analyzing official statistics, interviewing prisoners, and observing criminal activities abroad?

Dear Want to Be Prepared,
All these strategies have merit. However, if you plan to observe criminal activities abroad, I recommend taking out death and injury insurance. Many excellent policies are available and you're sure to find one you can afford. Loved ones will appreciate your thoughtfulness.

That's all the space I have, dear reader. This is The Asker saying TTFN. I'll be back with more advice in the next edition of *Inklings.* The Christmas edition, you might say. Meanwhile, be sure to send me your questions at TheAsker@gmail.com and I'll answer as many as I can.

Primed for humour, I met Altan to get his view of the Houston situation. But first, I told him everything Jonny had said. I included his warning that, if I talked to the police, I'd be punished.

Altan revealed that, during my meeting with Jonny, he hadn't visited Gina in the hospital after all. Instead, he'd prowled around Jonny's office building. That's right, he'd put on an HVAC repairman's outfit—I can't imagine where he found one—and come in a back door. Even bumbled into a lounge on the third floor. There, he saw more than a dozen men in suits sitting around, killing time. Dickie Wells was one of them, but didn't seem to recognize Altan. Another guy was cleaning his gun. Aside from that, Altan hadn't seen or heard anything useful.

I congratulated him on his resourcefulness. Then I begged him to, please, avoid any more life-threatening forays during this trip. I was off to see how Gina was doing, and I'd be back in an hour or two.

Gina was much better this morning. Completely conscious. Slightly bruised around the face and arms, and other body parts I couldn't see. But ready to tell me what had happened after I'd left her home. It wasn't a pretty story. She'd been chloroformed, shoved into the trunk of a car, driven to an airfield and put into a private jet, tied up in a closet for four hours. After the jet landed, she had another car ride in the trunk of a car and, finally, the start of drugging and rape. Mostly naked, most of the time.

When I got back to the hotel, Altan suggested we review what we'd learned so far. Who were the leading suspects for Melanie's murder and why did we think so? I couldn't get Gina out of my mind, but realized this was the best way to use our time.

"Tell me what you think, Altan," I said, still vibrating from his account of the morning's explorations and Gina's account of her abduction.

"Okay, Professor. First, there's Donny Foster. He's the single best bet, and I haven't heard anything that rules him out as Melanie's killer."

"Jonny Devlin said it definitely wasn't Donny and he has no reason to lie. Plus, Gina told me she was on the phone with Donny for hours, the day Melanie disappeared. Besides, she didn't think he had the guts to kill Melanie. He was too big a coward where she was concerned. Gina knows him better than we do, so I'd go with her judgment."

"Okay, my next bet would be Jonny Devlin. He had the best motive, given all the trouble Melanie was whipping up," he said.

"Yes, he had the motive. But I doubt Jonny ever gets his hands dirty in that way— not anymore. Besides, he would feel a family obligation to Donny's wife. To not kill her, I mean."

"My third bet would be Conkie Rovino. Conkie might have wanted to please his boss by killing Melanie, whether Jonny asked him to or not."

"You're right, that's something Conkie might think of doing. He's a loose cannon, for sure. But in the end, he probably wouldn't do it. He'd be afraid of riling Jonny if he killed Melanie without checking first."

"My fourth bet is that guy we saw in the Killing Fields, Dickie Wells. He looks like an all-purpose enforcer for the Devlin Crew. Jonny may have asked him to kill Melanie."

"You're right again. Dickie may have carried out the killing. But we don't know enough about him or the other guys Jonny keeps around for dirty work. So, I suggest we keep Dickie and his associates in the back of our minds for now. Leaving aside the Kirilov gang, Donny and Jonny are at the top of our suspect list. But here's another possibility: what if a combination of people killed Melanie? Let's say one person gave the order, a second person—or collection of people—carried out the killing, and a third person acquiesced."

"That's an interesting possibility, Professor. Jonny was in a good position to give the order and could have given it to any number of people. So, we still have to identify who carried out the killing. As for a third person acquiescing, I'm not sure what you mean. Why would Jonny—or anyone else—need someone to acquiesce?"

"We're looking at a network of relations between the Devlin Crew, the Smith Gang, and, possibly, the Kirilov Gang. Because of the family ties between Jonny and Melanie, they need to collaborate on her murder, or at least acquiesce. Otherwise, there's the risk of a gang war. And Donny would have to acquiesce too, if he knew about the plans to kill her."

"That means we need more information, Professor. So let's keep our eyes open and take another look at the evidence when we get back to Toronto. But before leaving Houston, I'd like to check out the Bells N' Whistle. Maybe we'll learn something useful about Jonny Devlin's business. Want to take a look?"

"Okay, let's go. But if I don't like the place, I'm leaving. And none of this goes into *Inklings*. Got it?"

"Yup, got it."

We caught a cab in front of the hotel and asked the driver to take us to Bells N' Whistle. Turning in his seat, he stared at me for a good ten seconds. "Are you sure that's where you two want to go?" he asked. "We've got a lot nicer places to visit in Houston."

"That's where we want to go," I said.

32

It was weird driving through downtown Houston on Halloween. Let's just say we saw a *weird* selection of costumes. Robots, spacemen, princesses, Taylor Swifts, and ghosts, of course. But also what would have been, by Toronto standards, an unusual number of Donald Trump costumes. And devils. Devils and demons of every size, shape, and colour. Mostly devils in shiny, fire-engine red costumes, with horns and long, pointy tails.

Finally, the taxi stopped in a dark, deserted industrial district, in front of a four-storey building. Blue, red, and green neon lights nearly two storeys high outlined two bells and a whistle. From a distance, you might have taken the image for male genitalia. Another neon sign above the front door read 'Bells N' Whistle. A Gentlemen's Club. Ladies Always Welcome.'

"That's it," the cabbie announced, "BNW." We paid the fare, got out, and started for the front door. "You may not want to stay long. Here's my number if you want me to pick you up," the cabbie shouted. I walked back to the cab and took his card.

Inside the main door, a large, bald man greeted us. His tattooed face displayed a tasteful selection of swastikas, American eagles, and Confederate flags. Next to him sat a wrinkled woman at a low desk. In keeping with the holiday, she wore a devilish eye-mask and horns that blinked on and off, red and blue, red and blue. "Hello, folks," the woman said. "There's a cover charge of $30 each, it buys your first drink. Will that be cash or a credit card?"

I gave the woman my credit card and she billed it for $60. On the other side of a draped entry, we found ourselves in a huge room. It was nearly pitch-black, and the noise shattered my eardrums.

As my eyes adjusted to the dark, I could make out bars and bartenders on two sides of the room. Three small, brightly-lit stages occupied the centre. Strobe-lights randomly searched the room. On one stage, a nearly naked woman in a devil's mask wriggled to slow, crushingly loud rock music. On another, a woman with devil's horns slid down a pole, wiggling suggestively. On a third stage, a semi-nude woman crawled on all fours, growling at her viewers like a wild animal. At tables around the three stages, men leaned forward, bloodshot eyes nearly toppling out of their heads. Men nearest the stages waved what may have been twenty- and fifty-dollar bills at the dancers. Now and then, a dancer bent over and received a donation in her G-string.

We stumbled through the room, finally landing at a table four rows back from the nearest stage. Almost right away, a young woman appeared. She wore a devilish mask. Her sequined bikini bathing suit had a Bells N' Whistle logo inscribed on the butt. "What can I get you two tonight? The first one's on the house. It came with the cover charge."

I asked for glass of red wine and, weirdly, Altan asked for a mojito. He'd never drunk one but had heard they were popular in the southwest US. The server smiled and went to fill our drink order, wiggling her logo as she walked away.

When she returned, Altan tasted his drink and scrunched up his face. "That tastes awful," he shouted over the music. "Do you have anything decent?"

"I can bring you a different mixed drink—say, a rum and coke—but that will cost you another $10. Do you want it?"

"Yeah, I'll pay the extra $10. I don't feel like going blind tonight."

"And while you're at it, bring me a different glass of red wine," I said. "The stuff you brought me tastes like sour grape juice."

"I can bring you a genuine Italian Chianti for another $10," she told me.

I nodded my agreement. "By the way,' I said, "I notice this building has four storeys. Are the upper floors for storage?"

The server smirked. "No, other things go on upstairs. Lots of customers like to take a nap while they're here, sometimes with company. So, they rent a room for that purpose."

"Who do they take a nap with?" Altan asked her, smirking back.

"We have a team of pretty young women who give massages. That helps the men fall right off to sleep, if they want to. The girls wait for clients in a room off to the side." She nodded to a nearly-hidden doorway in one of the walls.

"Mind if we take a look?" he asked. "I feel like a massage tonight. Don't you, Rachel?"

The server smiled. "I didn't take you two for the massage-type of people. But if you're interested, go right ahead. I'll serve your drink order when you get back."

I had doubts about this turn of events. Sure, Altan wanted to find out as much as possible about the BNW, even if that meant going for a massage. But he was playing with fire. Defying what Jonny Devlin had said—or at least implied— about staying out of his business. Maybe we were acting recklessly. On the other hand, we might not get this opportunity again.

We stumbled towards a door the server had pointed out. At the end of an unmarked passage, we found ourselves in a poorly lit salon. Tastefully furnished with worn-out couches and tattered easy chairs, it smelled of musk and sweat and cigarette smoke. A dozen women, aged from fifteen to thirty, sat reading magazines, talking quietly to one another. One woman was adjusting huge breasts in a too-small brassiere.

Altan smiled at a skinny, pale woman who looked about 15 and asked her name.

Obviously uncomfortable, the young woman answered in a heavy Eastern European accent. "In club, my name is Nancy. You call me that. Do you want massage?"

"Sure, I'd like a massage," Altan said.

"I give you massage upstairs. It $50 for first fifteen minutes."

"Okay, let's do it." Altan opened his wallet and handed her two US twenties and a ten.

"No, no, give it that lady there, then we go upstairs." Nancy pointed to an older woman with red hair and bright red cheeks— no longer a beauty and no longer giving massages. Altan paid her the money, then followed Nancy through another doorway.

Turning back, he called out to me, "I'll be back at the table in about twenty minutes."

I headed back to our table to drink my expensive glass of cheap wine. As I sat there feeling nervous, I wondered if I was being watched or filmed. I felt certain Altan would be watched and filmed while Nancy massaged him. That's the way these places worked, I'd heard. Watching and filming everything, maybe to blackmail people later.

Almost immediately, the server appeared with my glass of wine. "I figure you could use this now."

I said "Thanks," and asked her name.

"I'm Sadie," she said.

"I've never been in a place like this before."

"It's pretty laid back," Sadie said, smirking. "People come here to drink too much, pay too much for a thrill, and get into pointless arguments." She smiled to show she was only kidding.

"The only other place I've been like this was a casino back

home. It was shinier and brighter, but also a bit seedy."

Sadie laughed. "Yes, that's what this place is, shiny and seedy," she said laughing, then turning to see if anyone else needed her service. No one did. Eyes were still riveted on the dancing girls.

"I have to get back to work," she said anyway, nervously scanning the room. "Wave if you need anything." She clearly wasn't in the mood for conversation. Not for something a watcher might misinterpret.

I yearned to leave BNW but couldn't go without Altan. Was he really getting a massage? I couldn't imagine him having sex with the underage girl who'd taken him up that dark stairway. First of all, he played for the other team. And even if Altan was straight, would he have sex with that pale, scrawny girl? In a shabby room, on a filthy bed stained by hundreds of other men? I couldn't imagine him doing any of that.

Twenty minutes later, Altan was back at our table. "That was interesting," he said drily. "But let's talk back at the hotel." Sadie brought his drink, and he slurped it eagerly. He was thirsty, or maybe keen to get drunk.

"Can we walk there, or hail a cab along the way?" I asked him, eager to leave.

"That's not a great idea, Professor. Not after what happened to Pam Riley."

Thinking it over, I had to agree. I knew I could handle myself but didn't want anything bad to happen to Altan. "Go ahead. Phone that cabby."

I gave Altan the cabby's card, and he keyed the number into his phone. A little over five minutes later, we were speeding back to our home away from home.

We didn't talk much in the cab, still worried about being overheard. Finally back at the hotel, Altan handed me a balled-up note on a scrap of paper. "Nancy slid this into my pocket in the massage room."

The note read, 'Help me. I am prizzoner in club. Tell police to escape me.'

Nancy may have kept this note in her pocket for days or even weeks, until she could pass it to Altan. Her random knight in shining armour.

"What should we do for her? What *can* we do?" I asked him, my voice trembling.

"We can pass this along to Harrison. Maybe his people have already staked out that place."

I emailed Harrison, telling him what Nancy had written.

He wrote back quickly, saying all thirty 'massage' rooms were wired to record images and sounds, twenty-four hours a day. And, as he told us three days later, Nancy's body soon turned up in a shallow grave, in the Killing Fields. Second by second, her actions that night had been filmed and analyzed. Watchers must have seen the note change hands.

There were always consequences when this happened at BNW. And apparently, it happened pretty often.

Harrison told me later about the investigation of Nancy's death. The girl's real name was Maria, and she'd arrived in Houston only three weeks earlier. She'd probably left Moldova in a shipping container. Her plans was to find a job, get married, and have American babies. And of course, send money to her mother back home. After I told Altan all this, he felt a little responsible for Nancy's death. He knew it wasn't his fault, but the feeling lingered.

With another day to fill before returning home, we felt honour-bound to attend at least one more conference session. Then we took a long cab ride out to suburban Briggs College. Donny had kept a research office there.

33

The website told me Briggs College boasted many lawns, gardens, and playing fields. Its dozen or so structures included a Humanities Building, a Fine Arts Building, a Science Building, a School of Business, and a School of Theology. Also, six dormitories for men and two for women. Off to one side, I could also make out a construction site and work machines. A huge sign showed schematic plans for a new, five-storey science building. Gigantic letters announced 'Coming in September 2027: The Jenny Kirilov Research Centre. Watch Us Grow!'

I paid our cab driver and headed for the School of Business. Young women surrounded the entrance, shouting, chanting, and waving signs. As we got closer, I saw the women were protesting commercial research on sex robots. I couldn't tell from the signs if they were opposed to business, research, robots, or sex. Carefully and politely, we made our way through the noisy picket line. Inside, one wing of the building housed 'project suites' devoted to 'Behavioral Research.' And in one of these suites, Donny Foster had carried out his research on auto smuggling.

Inside the suite, a woman of twenty-four or so sat at a desk, in front of a laptop. She was so immersed in her work, she didn't hear us come in.

I said hello, introduced myself, then introduced Altan.

"I'm Hannah Proctor," the young woman said, smiling.

Hannah didn't look like your average doctoral student. She was gorgeous, with a face and figure that other women would have died for. Not literally, I hoped. She said she was analyzing data for her doctoral thesis on the profitability of crime. "I'm interested in the people who make a living smuggling cars," she said, telling us also that Donny was her 'outside supervisor.'

I noticed she had a framed photo next to her laptop. A picture of her and Donny. She was wearing an apron that read 'Kiss the Cook.' Donny was wearing a tall white chef's hat and holding a spatula, evidently barbecuing steaks. They were both grinning at the camera, a picture of domestic bliss.

I asked how long she'd been working on this project. I meant her dissertation—not domesticating Donny. They were probably the same.

"About three years. The work's complicated, but I've learned a lot of interesting stuff," she said. "Professor Foster is a wonderful supervisor." She radiated a smile to highlight what she was saying.

"You must know Professor Foster pretty well by now," Altan commented softly, looking at the picture again.

"Yes, and it's been great working with him," Hannah said, not noticing.

"Did you ever meet his wife, Melanie?" I asked. "She came down to Houston for a short visit last year."

Hannah scowled. "Yes, poor Mrs. Foster. What a terrible thing, her getting murdered. It shocked all of us at the Business School. Then, of course, the shock of Professor Foster going on trial for her murder. But it turned out fine in the end, with him being freed and all."

Hannah smiled and glanced at her data again, plainly hoping we'd leave.

"Did Mrs. Foster ever come here?" Altan asked.

"Only once, the day she disappeared. She was awful angry at Professor Foster. And snippy towards me too. Then she left and I never saw her again. She headed off in a rental car and I went back to work. If I remember rightly, Professor Foster went over to the cafeteria to 'cool down.' At least, that's what he told me later."

"Why was Mrs. Foster snippy towards you? That must have been upsetting."

"I wasn't upset by it. She was mad at Professor Foster, or maybe just mad at the world that day."

"Was anyone with Mrs. Foster when she left the campus?" Altan asked.

"I saw two people—a man and a woman—talking to her, maybe asking her for a lift into town. She must have said okay. They got into her car and drove off together."

This hadn't been mentioned in the trial transcripts I'd read. "Have you seen them around campus since then?"

"No, I don't remember ever seeing them before or after. Maybe they were just checking out the campus—you know, deciding if they wanted their kid to study here. Lots of people spend a day here for that reason. They look around, ask a few questions, check out a few classrooms, then leave. We don't pay them much attention.

"Mind you, those two didn't look like your typical helicopter parents. The guy had great posture and was wearing an expensive suit. He looked like a business executive or fancy lawyer. The woman was around my age, dressed very stylishly. With shades on and a dark, broad-brimmed sunhat. Like a movie star or a fashion model, not your usual college mom. They made an eye-catching couple. But honestly, I don't know any more than that. The three of them got into Mrs. Foster's car and drove away, like old friends."

"One more question, Hannah, and we'll let you get back to your research. How far is Highway I-45 from here?" I asked her.

"The I-45? Gosh, the on-ramp is only about half a mile away. Maybe less. You could walk there in five or ten minutes. Or I could give you a lift, if you want one."

We were surprised by this. Despite having looked at maps of Houston many times before, we'd never noticed the proximity of Briggs College to I-45. And the Killing Fields.

I found all this very interesting. Interesting that Hannah had seen Melanie the day she was murdered. That she'd seen her leave with two strangers. That she'd never looked into it or even wondered about it. Maybe Donny hadn't wondered about it either.

"Thanks, Hannah. You've told us everything we need to know," I said.

Altan called for an Uber, and forty-five minutes later we were back at our hotel. Now we knew how Melanie had gotten to the Killing Fields. But that left unanswered questions. Who had accompanied Melanie there? Did they kill her? Did Donny follow in his own car and take part in the killing? And what part, if any, had Hannah played in this saga? Or was the murder engineered by the Kirilov gang, as Donny had said?

"Professor, we have to add Hannah Proctor to our list of suspects. Knowing Donny, they may have been having an affair. She may have wanted Melanie out of the way, so they could get together. Permanently."

"You're right. Hannah had a motive to kill Melanie. And as the last person to see Melanie alive on the Briggs campus, she had the opportunity. Let's put her on our list, while we sort out the role Donny and Jonny played in Melanie's murder. But that big construction sign we saw today revived my interest in the Kirilov gang. There may be gang members on campus, masquerading as construction workers." Altan promised to do more research on that possibility.

Back at the hotel, we took it easy that evening. I phoned Gina to see how she was doing, then we watched a video. *The Godfather, Part II.* The next morning, Altan and I skipped the rest of the criminology conference and flew back to Toronto.

Back home in my ratty old bathrobe, I planned to do the laundry, read a book, and relax. But around four in the afternoon, I got a call from Craig Harrison.

"Police raided one of Jonny's chop shops last night. This was a tactical force—part of the Houston police—that's been watching the Devlin Crew for years. Jonny may think you had a hand in it. I'm telling you this in case anything out of the ordinary happens. So keep your eyes and ears open."

"Okay, thanks for letting me know," I said, getting ready to hang up.

"Oh yeah, and one more thing. The police also broke into a trailer home on the fringe of the Killing Fields. The one we visited, I think. It seems many women had passed through it in the last five or ten years. Bits of clothing, cosmetics, used menstrual pads, and other personal items were scattered all over the place. Traffickers had been using the trailer to store women who'd just been smuggled into the country. Imprisoning the women there, readying them for prostitution in and around Houston. They also found an injured man in the trailer, a member of the Devlin Crew. Someone had beat him up pretty bad. Probably someone from a rival gang, they said."

Harrison was very cautious in the way he described all this, in case anyone else was listening.

"Got it," I said. Ending the call, I shivered with disgust. They wouldn't be looking to pin any of this on a female professor of criminology. All the same, I shouldn't have been so rough with that guy. My rage had just got away from me.

As I'd thought, the Devlin Crew had used the Killing Fields as a halfway point on the trip from Galveston's harbor to Houston brothels. They'd been bringing newly arrived women to the Killing Fields, drugging them, raping them, readying them for prostitution. And they may have murdered Melanie to keep this location secret.

I couldn't sit still now. I kept getting up and staring out the window. But watching for what? Gangsters with guns? Naked women with devil's horns? All I saw was—pretty much nothing. Teenagers walking home from school. A few stay-at-home moms wheeling strollers. A nanny on her cellphone, bringing 'her' kids home from the park for a snack. Two taxis. Seven SUVs. A repair truck across the road. Mrs. Rothman was having her drains cleared again. Down the block, the Kreskins were moving out. Downsizing, old Mrs. Kreskin had said.

Rattled by Harrison's phone call, I poured myself a glass of club soda with lots of ice. I sat on the couch, drinking it, worrying and wondering as the day turned into night. I was deep in thought when a ringing telephone startled me back into consciousness.

"Hello, RACHEL, it's Gene Tretnikoff in London. How are you?"

"I'm fine Gene. To what do I owe the pleasure of this call?"

"Well, you may think this is ODD, but I'm phoning about Donny Foster. It seems he has developed an enthusiasm for my DAUGHTER and I may need to rebuke him."

"What do you mean, 'an enthusiasm?'"

"He has invited her for dinner, to discuss her interest in auto smuggling. I don't mind him discussing this with her in CLASS, or even in his office AFTER CLASS. But I don't think a dinner date is SUITABLE for an 18-year-old girl and her teacher. Do you?"

Remembering Gina's affair with Donny a decade and a half earlier, I had no trouble answering. "I agree, Gene, it is unsuitable. Would you like me to raise this with him? I could do it quietly but firmly."

"Yes, that would be HELPFUL. Please tell him I have spoken with you about this. If he repeats this behaviour, I will be very DIRECT."

"Of course, Gene. That will not be necessary, I assure you."

"THANK YOU. I knew you would understand."

Gene hung up the phone. Donny had made himself a new enemy.

Then, 'messages' started arriving from Jonny. First, my sister Megan showed up. Around eight in the evening, someone had keyed the side of her car and sprayed 'Rachel' on the back window in white paint.

"What's this about?" Megan shouted, almost before she was out of her car. "I didn't sign up for a car makeover."

I was terrified. "I'm not sure, but I have a suspicion. Someone thinks I backed out of a deal I made with them. Get your car fixed and I'll pay for the damage. It's all a big mistake and won't happen again." I hoped that was true. But maybe I'd violated the agreement I'd made with Jonny, when we went to the BNW, talked to Hannah Proctor, and told Harrison about the note Nancy had slipped Altan. Or when I'd beaten one of Jonny's men in the Killing Fields.

"My car is ruined. Don't I deserve a little more explanation than that?"

"Megan, I don't want to draw you into this mess. At least, not any more than necessary."

"Okay. That sounds lame to me but I'm going to let it go. It better not happen again. At least, not without a decent explanation."

Then my phone rang. Farid was on the line. "I don't know what this means, but someone has sprayed your name in white paint all over the ground floor windows of my house. Is this a joke? Who'd do something like that?"

I felt another jolt of fear. "I'm so sorry, Farid. Someone has targeted my closest friends, to punish me. They think I broke a deal I made with them, though I didn't. I'll cover the cost of cleaning all the paint off your windows. I'll even replace them, if necessary. Let me know."

"Okay. That all sounds weird, but I suppose you know what you're doing. I'll talk to you tomorrow when I'm calmer."

34

I spent a restless night remembering what had happened in Houston. Gina's abduction. That guy I'd beaten up. And especially, my conversation with Jonny Devlin. After hearing from Megan and Farid, I should've called Jonny and explained what Altan and I had been doing in Houston. How I hadn't intended to break the deal. But in the end, I didn't phone him. I was too scared.

Then, around nine the next morning, as I stepped into the shower, I got a call from Jackie Taylor. I left the shower, put my bathrobe back on, and went to talk to her.

"Rachel, members of the Workshop have been following Kim Cressy for the last few days."

"How did they find her?" I asked.

"One of them saw her on TV a week ago. So, she contacted the network and said she was a producer at CBC. They were glad to give her Ms. Cressy's coordinates. Anyway, they've been watching Kim for the last few days and just reported something odd. Maybe you can make sense of it. She was seen damaging a car that belongs to someone named Megan Tile. Is there any relation?"

"Yes, she's my sister."

"Kim was also seen spraying white paint on the windows of a home that belongs to someone named Farid Srivastava. Do you know him too?"

"He's a good friend of mine," I said, starting to panic.

"Now, here's something really odd. It seems Mr. Srivastava helped Ms. Cressy spray paint on his *own* windows. Can you make any sense of that?"

After a moment, I murmured, "Maybe."

"And here's one more bit of strange information. After decorating his windows, Ms. Cressy spent the night at his home. She didn't leave until eight this morning, after he'd already left for work."

I was surprised to learn Jonny had someone as classy as Kim doing his dirty work. I would have expected him to use someone rougher and less noticeable, someone like Dickie Wells. On the other hand, Kim was perfectly disguised for dirty work—hidden by her glamor and grace.

I thanked Jackie and hung up the phone.

What was the connection between Farid and Kim Cressy, I wondered. Were they lovers? Friends? Certainly not casual strangers. I pulled out my laptop and reviewed everything I knew about them. Points of similarity and difference. Also, points of possible contact. I'd have to add them to my list of suspects in the death of Melanie Foster.

The possibility Farid and Kim Cressy might be killers terrified me. I'd hugged Farid, kissed him, even slept with him. Yet, there was a chance he was a stone-cold killer. From now on, I'd have to be careful. At least, until I had far more information about his loyalties.

That's when I decided to take a look around Farid's home. I'd been there once before, briefly, on the way to a date, so I knew his address. I also knew he left the back door unlocked.

The risk of burglary in this neighbourhood was zero, he'd said. Much lower than the risk he'd forget his house keys at the office.

I went to Farid's place around eight that evening, when I knew he had a late surgery scheduled. All the lights were off, and I used a flashlight to explore the house. Never having been upstairs, I started there. I found nothing of interest in three medicine cabinets, the desk in his home office, the bookshelves in his upstairs TV room, or the drawers of his walk-in closet. But then, I found something quite out of the ordinary. In the end table next to Farid's king size bed, I found a SIG Sauer P320. One of the most popular and effective handguns in North America, I'd read somewhere.

I wondered if Farid had a license for the gun. Also, why he needed a handgun in this safe neighbourhood of a safe city. Should I ask him about the gun? Whether he'd ever seen a gun? Shot a gun? Possessed a gun? I wanted to test his truthfulness. But I wouldn't have that conversation, not yet. When I did, maybe I'd find out Farid had good reason for keeping a loaded gun by his bedside.

Discovering the gun had spooked me enough for one night. I put everything back where I'd found it and rubbed a hankie over the end-table to erase my fingerprints. I left the house through the same back door I'd entered.

I worried through the rest of the next day. I gave a terrible lecture, couldn't stay focused at a faculty meeting, couldn't concentrate on my rage book. But there was no point sitting around, brooding. I took a long walk, and the cool air revived me. Back home, I spent the rest of the day working on my book and preparing a report for the Dean.

The next day, I told the Dean about my trip to Houston. All about Jonny Devlin's threat. Also, about what Megan and

Farid had experienced on the weekend. I didn't mention Gina's abduction or that I'd beaten someone pretty badly in Houston.

"Can't you tell Mr. Devlin you're not to blame for the raids on his chop shops?" she asked me.

"He told me not to contact him again."

"So, what are you going to do?"

"I'll keep trying to find out about Melanie's death from Donny Foster. He's the one Jonny told me to ask."

"That's my job, Rachel," the Dean said. "Maybe I can threaten him into talking."

The Dean texted Donny to come to her office right away.

He was in the middle of a seminar and said he'd come over when the class ended. The Dean and I passed a pleasant hour scanning our emails and chatting about the fall semester. At last, Donny arrived, as promised. He gave me a weird look, then looked away.

When he was sitting down, the Dean began the interview with a direct order.

"Professor Tile was told recently—and very clearly—that you have complete information about the murder of your wife. About the person who might have killed her, and the reason. And we intend to find out the whole story today. If you have any hope of staying on at Strachan University, I want your full cooperation right now."

I'd never heard the Dean speak so harshly before. Certainly, she had ever spoken to me that way.

Donny was startled by the Dean's directness too. "Dean, I've told you I don't know who killed my wife. I've also told you I suspect the Kirilov gang, but that's only a suspicion. My suspicions won't hold up in court. The police won't take them seriously, since I have no concrete evidence. Going public about my suspicions will get me killed by the same people who killed Melanie. So I don't want to go down that road."

"There's no more time for delicacy," the Dean declared, nearly shouting. "We need to know what danger you pose for this university."

"I don't see what the death of my wife has to do with the safety of people at this university."

"You may not see the connection, but I do and so does the Provost. We can't proceed until we have a full account of what happened to Melanie. We don't want that happening here."

"Dean, I won't say any more until I have a lawyer to advise me."

"So be it, then." The Dean flipped the pages of her day planner. "We'll meet at 9 a.m. on Thursday morning. Please be here with your lawyer. Professor Tile, I'd like you to attend too. I'll make sure our lawyer is here as well."

Donny took his jacket and left the office. I said I'd attend the next meeting and left a minute later. I planned to go home, take my mind off the Foster case, and work on my rage book.

But on my way home, I got another call from Harrison. It wasn't good news.

"That tactical force in Houston has raided a second chop shop belonging to the Devlin Crew. They've also raided the Lone Star offices and taken all the computers."

"Thanks for letting me know," I told him. I dreaded what would happen next.

35

Jonny Devlin wasn't long in responding. That evening, I got phone calls from both of my children. They'd each received a sealed letter, by means of bicycle messenger. Inside each was a recent photograph of me, and each had been doctored. One showed blood dripping out of gruesome gashes on my head. The other showed my eyes blacked out, with a big X across my face.

The message at the bottom of each was the same: 'Tell your mother she's been warned for the last time.' This freaked out both of them, and especially Ellie. Just last year, she'd been beaten up by her then-boyfriend, Bobby Gupta. Ellie knew firsthand just how serious a threat of violence could be.

I tried contacting Jonny, but his assistant wouldn't put me through, "on the boss's orders." I started to panic, and it took me hours to fall asleep that night. Then I slept for ten hours straight, almost in a coma.

While eating breakfast the next morning, I learned a home in Leaside had exploded last night. It had happened minutes before the homeowner returned from work. The homeowner, Donny Foster, was reported to be a Professor of Criminology at Strachan University. Predictably, the newscaster joked that Professor Foster now had a real-life crime to solve.

I found Donny's cell number and phoned him, half expecting he'd refuse to talk to me. Yet he sounded relaxed and said he was fine. He'd stayed at a hotel while police and fire fighters sifted through debris at his home. I asked him to meet me at the office in an hour. To my surprise, he agreed.

He was already there when I arrived, so we got coffees and sat down to talk.

"What happened last night?" I asked him quietly.

"The firemen think there may have been a gas leak or bad electrical connection."

"Is that what you think?"

"No, it was arson. I'm sure Jonny was sending me a message."

"What was he trying to tell you?"

"To keep my mouth shut about his business."

"And what makes you think so?"

"I had a long phone conversation with him yesterday afternoon. Told him I was being squeezed to tell the Dean what I knew about Melanie's death. He said to go ahead and tell her what I knew without mentioning his name or anyone connected with his business. I said I didn't see how that was possible. How could I discuss Melanie's death without talking about the smuggling business—also, certain other matters I won't mention right now?

"He said, and I'm quoting, 'I don't give a crap how you spin this. You can tell her about the Kirilov family, or men from Mars, or that Martin Luther King killed Melanie. Or your memory is a blank, due to the shock of Melanie's death. The point is, don't bring my name into the discussion and don't talk about my car business. If you do, I'll have to hurt you. I promised your mother I'd protect you. But you'll put me in a bad spot if you blab about me.'"

"And what did you say?"

"I said I couldn't talk about Melanie's death without talking about the car business. And I wasn't going to look like an idiot by pleading memory loss."

"What did he say to that?" I asked him.

"Jonny said that was up to me. But I'd bear the consequences if I ran my mouth. He'd send me a basket of consequences right away, to clear my mind. I guess that was the point of the explosion at my house."

"Why is Jonny making such a big deal about all this? There's nothing you can tell us about his gang that we don't already know from your published research articles. Right?"

"That's not quite true," he said, haltingly. Then, in a rush, he said "In fact, I know everything about the Devlin Crew, though I'm going to deny I told you this."

Expecting the worst, I excused myself and went to the washroom. I sat on the toilet for a few minutes, then washed my hands and splashed cold water on my face. Even checked my email. Finally, with nothing more to delay me, I went back to my office. Very slowly, you understand. I was in no rush to get there.

Finally sitting behind my desk again, I asked him to continue. What did he know that he hadn't already told us about the Devlin Crew?

"I'm Jonny's HR guy: the keeper of his secret files. I created a human resources database for the Crew and keep it up to date. I even use AI to vet the files. That way, Jonny always knows who can be trusted, who's looking suspicious, who needs to be punished. So, Jonny's right to be nervous about what I might reveal. And that's the reason he can't afford to piss me off. I'm too valuable to the organization. The only other person who could do what I do is someone you don't know—a woman named Kim Cressy. Though I've been training an assistant, Hannah Proctor. If push came to shove, she could take over my work."

"So, what are you going to tell the Dean?"

"I'll tell her everything I know about Melanie's death. To clear the air. I can't have people thinking I killed my wife."

"Okay, Donny, but I hope you know what you're doing."

He nodded, got up, and returned to his own office.

I didn't get much work done that afternoon, thinking about what Donny had told me. When I got home, the place was empty. I thought about moving into a hotel but dismissed the idea. For reasons I couldn't name, I was convinced Jonny wasn't going to hurt me. Plus, I liked being at home. The comfort of home helped me think about the Foster Problem. So, I started at the beginning, all over again, for the umpteenth time.

I got Altan on the phone and, as usual, we started trading ideas.

"My best guess is still that Melanie was murdered by her husband. That's how most wives are murdered," he said.

"Fair enough. And maybe Donny was planning to start a new life with a brand-new partner—say, Hannah Proctor. That may have been the prosecution's assumption when they tried him for murder."

Gradually, we started talking faster, cutting each other off to add fresh insights. By now, we thought like one super-brain, every conversation a race to the finish.

"Or maybe Melanie was killed to keep her from drawing attention to human trafficking. That's harder to prove but let's keep it in mind."

"I'm still not sure we can ignore the Kirilov gang. They had good reason to squeeze Donny for information about the Devlin Crew. Maybe they're involved in human trafficking too."

"Maybe a few different gangs wanted Melanie dead. Maybe Jonny Devlin also wanted to share the responsibility for killing her, out of respect for Donny, his nephew and godson."

"Donny may have guessed they were going to kill Melanie. Maybe he even knew about that group, the Workshop?" I asked. "That's Melanie's militia, I'm thinking."

Then suddenly, I wondered if I'd leaked crucial information about the Workshop. "I just realized that everything I learned about the Workshop, I passed along to you and the Dean. I can't be sure I didn't say something about this to my boyfriend, Farid. And right now, I'm not so sure if I can trust Farid."

By now, three things bothered me about Farid. One was the gun in his bedroom drawer. Another was his mysterious connection with Kim Cressy. A third—a distant third—was his mysterious East Indian background, including his mysterious earlier marriage. There were just too many things I didn't know about him.

Spooked by this realization, I tried to remember what I'd told Farid about everything I'd learned. I hadn't put any limits on what I'd told him in bed, before bed, or after bed. And if I'd given him critical information, he may have passed it on to someone else. But to whom?

"I have to go, Altan. I have to do some thinking, alone."

Distressed that I may have compromised the investigation, I stared guiltily out my living room window. I phoned Gina to find out how she was doing. She was almost recovered now and would return to Ottawa the next morning. Police had questioned her about the gangster they found at that trailer. She'd said she didn't know anything about him. I promised I'd visit her in Ottawa next week.

Unlike the world inside my head, the world outside was quiet and peaceful. I saw young mothers pushing baby carriages down the street. Knots of teenage girls ambling by, laughing and talking to each other, free of any concern except who was dating whom these days. A few neighbours walking their dogs and chatting with one another. Most of the dogs knew each other and wrestled harmlessly, their way of saying hello.

Somehow, the evening passed. Liquids were consumed. Work got done. Dogs and their owners fell asleep in their respective beds. Teenage girls dreamed of what? Perhaps, boyfriends and popularity. How different this was from Down Country, where it was always hot. Where black dogs prowled empty fields in search of dead women. Where criminals stored women like cattle.

The next few days passed in a blur. Then, three days after our last meeting, I met Donny, the Dean, and the lawyer for a final showdown. At least, I *hoped* it would be a final showdown.

Donny hadn't brought a lawyer after all. He wanted to "make a clean breast of it all," he said. "A fresh start."

"Okay then, let's start again," the Dean said. "Tell us what you know about Melanie's death."

"Let me back up a few years, Dean. I'd known for a long time that Melanie was interested in human trafficking—especially, the trafficking of foreign women for sex work. I also knew she met regularly with a small group of women who called themselves the Workshop. They collected information, met with law enforcement, and protested businesses that exploited women. However, Melanie and I had never discussed this. It was her secret activity.

"When I started planning my research leave in Texas, Melanie finally brought up the topic. She asked if the Devlin Crew was involved in human trafficking, and I told her I didn't think so. I had no evidence they were and didn't feel comfortable asking Jonny about it. She insisted I ask Jonny right away. I told her he'd go ballistic if I did. Challenging him about it would also put my research on car smuggling at risk. My D-scores project would go out the window, the biggest project of my life blown to pieces.

"Melanie didn't want to hear that. She started snooping around, listening in whenever I spoke to anyone in the business. She rifled through my research notes. She may have even talked about trafficking with members of the Devlin Crew when she got to Houston. Maybe she flat-out asked them if their gang was trafficking women. Or if they knew any gangs that were."

"Eventually, Jonny took me aside. We were having drinks, and he said, 'Your wife noses around our business too much. I don't know what her game is, but I'm suggesting—in a polite way—that she should lay off. It will be better for her health if she keeps out of these things.' And I'm pretty sure Jonny told Melanie the same thing the next time he saw her. She had intruded into things that didn't concern her, and that made her a target. Finally, someone decided Melanie was a threat to their business, so they arranged to have her killed. But for my own health, I didn't ask Jonny for details."

Suddenly, Donny stopped talking. He nodded to us, as if to say, 'That's all there is.'

But we didn't think that was the whole story. Not by a long shot.

36

"Professor Foster, did you warn Melanie that she was in danger? That even Jonny was getting mad at her, and she needed to get out of town?" the lawyer asked.

"Yes, I warned her three or four times that she was playing with fire. Jonny warned her too, then told me to warn her again, and I did. But Melanie wouldn't back down. Jonny told her, very plainly, to get lost if she was on a crusade. He didn't have time for crusades, he said. They were bad for business. But she wouldn't stop talking about it. Then, one of Jonny's guys may have told members of another gang that Melanie was drawing attention to their human trafficking business. The Kirilov Gang probably got involved at that point."

Donny stopped to mop his face with that large, polka-dotted handkerchief we'd seen before.

"In the end, a member of the Kirilov Gang may have killed her, with permission from their boss, Yuri Kirilov. Jonny would never have had her killed, out of respect for me. And the Kirilovs were as heavily invested in human trafficking as any gang in the country. Like Jonny, they worried about drawing attention from the FBI. Maybe, Melanie would even go to the media and make everyone look bad. So yeah, probably Yuri Kirilov okayed this hit."

"And you figure Jonny didn't play a part in this?" I asked. "You don't think that, maybe, he had a chat with Yuri Kirilov and said, 'It's okay with me if you kill Melanie Foster. She's a troublemaker. But for personal reasons, I can't ask one of my own people to kill her.'"

"I don't see Jonny giving the okay, because he and I are so close. He knew I'd be devastated by Melanie's death," Donny said, looking sad and sincere.

"I don't believe what you're saying," the Dean said, bluntly. "Let's meet again in a week and start over. Mark that date in your calendar, everyone."

Donny looked incredulous. He shook his head vigorously as if to say, 'I've told you everything. Why won't you leave me alone?'

After Donny left the office, the lawyer said, "Dean, every time we meet, Foster hoses us down with a new batch of lies and half-truths. Why don't we bring an action to deprive him of tenure? We should force him to tell his stories in court, under oath."

"You may be right," she said, "but let's string this out a little longer. The Provost doesn't want this going to court. There'd be too much media attention."

"Okay, it's your call," the lawyer said, then left the office.

I left the Dean's office shortly afterward, feeling frustrated. I knew Donny had much more information than he'd given us today. As keeper of the personnel files for Jonny Devlin, he probably knew exactly who had done what to whom. Possibly including who had beaten that big guy at the trailer in the Killing Field. And that meant he'd lied to the Dean *again*.

Conveniently, he'd provided no evidence that put himself or Jonny in a bad light. But the Dean wouldn't put up with his lies much longer. She'd take them as personal insults and wouldn't stand for much more.

But Donny would soon have other problems to worry about. At home the next morning, I got quite a surprise. On the front page of my morning newspaper, a short piece directed the reader to a larger piece on page seven of the first section. An article titled 'Who Knew Social Research Could Be This Dangerous, or This Unethical?' was all about Donny Foster. Specifically, about his D-scores. Also, about his long association with criminal gangs and the grievous injuries to his doctoral student, Pam Riley.

The reporter had interviewed Pam's father, and Aaron Riley hadn't minced his words.

"We're coming after Professor Foster and the people that allowed this dangerous, useless work. There's no place in our universities for people who carelessly put other people in danger to further their own careers. This is going to cost Dr. Fiedler [the President of Strachan University] $10 million and Donny Foster's dismissal, and that's only the beginning. We're going to press the Board of Governors, on which I sit, for a review of the Research Ethics Board. I want to know how Professor Foster's worthless research could have received their approval. I can promise you, heads will roll if we find out what I think this investigation will reveal. That's all I have to say right now. I'll say a lot more in court next month."

To get another perspective, the reporter had contacted two American criminologists for comments. One, Philip Bricker, was a junior scholar who also studied car smugglers. An untenured faculty member at the University of Nevada, Bricker told the reporter, "'Dr. Foster's research on criminal gangs has received a lot of attention from the scholarly community. No criminologist in the last fifty years has done a better job studying the everyday features of gang life among car thieves. But many scholars feel he's crossed a lot of ethical lines in his work—at least as many as Julia Dent, and probably more. People think Professor Foster needs to be reined in, for the good of criminology's reputation.'"

The other source, Jonathan Rance, a senior professor in criminology at Brigham Young University in Utah, was even more direct. He said he'd always doubted Foster's findings. "It is a central principle of ethnographic research," Rance had said, "that the researcher must keep a distance between himself and the people he's studying. Otherwise, he's liable to bias his data and the conclusions he reaches. And I'm afraid that's what's happened here. In pursuit of flawed and meaningless findings—his so-called 'D-scores'—Foster has collected data in a foolish, dangerous way.

"Even worse, Foster has left himself open to the influence of Houston's Devlin Crew. They have no interest in furthering Foster's research. On the contrary, they've done everything possible to mislead him. And worst of all, I learned just yesterday that Donny Foster is the nephew and godson of the notorious Jonny (Ghirardelli) Devlin. That relationship explains not only the Devlin Crew's cooperation, it also clarifies the weird and dangerous direction Foster has taken his research.

"It's time for the American Criminological Society [ACS] to review this case and revoke Professor Foster's membership. I would support a decision to prevent Professor Foster from ever publishing his work in any journal associated with the ACS or its affiliated scholarly societies."

The article closed with an ominous suggestion that this might be the first in a series of articles about 'so-called research' at Strachan University. Later articles would discuss what such research cost, who it hurt, and who it helped.

As I finished reading the article, my phone rang. It was Farid.

"Hi Farid, what's up?"

"I should ask you the same question. I just read that article on Donny Foster. It sounds like he's in big trouble. Are you in trouble too?"

"I should be okay," I said, knowing that wasn't completely true. "But we have to figure out a way to deal with Donny. If we do that properly, we can limit our liability in this lawsuit." I wanted to put a good face on the whole thing. At the same time, I didn't intend to give Farid any crucial information. Not until I knew more about him.

So, I lied and brought our conversation to an end. "I'm getting buzzed, Farid. It may be the Dean calling, so I have to go. I'll call you back later." I hung up the line.

37

In the middle of the afternoon, my energy level always dropped, and I had to take a break. I stared out my office window at the students milling around below me. They were everywhere and never seemed to flag. God, I wish I was young again, a student full of wonder and ignorance, with my life still ahead of me. I'd never have that again. Certainly not after going to Down Country, seeing the Killing Fields.

I knew I wouldn't learn anything more from Gina. She was off the case, still recovering. But maybe Craig Harrison could fill me in, so I pulled out his card and dialed his number.

"Craig Harrison here," he said, picking up the phone.

"This is Rachel in Toronto. I need a little information and wonder if you can provide it. Gina was going to get it for me but she's off the case now, resting up."

"I know, I talked to her yesterday. She's doing better, but you probably know that. What do you need, Rachel?"

"What can you tell me about Dr. Farid Srivastava? He practices surgery in Toronto, and I wonder if he has any connection with the gangs that operate in Houston. Specifically, whether he has any connection with the Devlin Crew or the Smith Brothers gang."

"I can tell you Farid Srivastava is the youngest of the three Smith Brothers, though he doesn't go by the name of Smith."

"Is he involved in their criminal activities?" I asked him cautiously.

"We're not sure. He's never been arrested or convicted of a crime, to the best of my knowledge. We're not even sure he's involved—only that he's a brother of the two gang leaders. But here's an interesting fact: Farid has ten bank accounts under six different names in the US, Canada, and the Cayman Islands. Altogether, they contain $122 million US. That's pretty good money for someone in the surgical business. Is that the information you need?"

Seeing a rare chance, I asked him "Do you have any banking information for my colleague, Donny Foster?"

"It happens I do. He has seven bank accounts in various parts of the world, under seven different names. One of them under the name of Jackson Boop, if you can believe it. The sums total $52 million US, as of last week. I wouldn't have guessed your university paid its faculty so well. Is there anything else you need to know?"

"Do you think Yuri Kirilov arranged the murder of Melanie

Foster? In your opinion, I mean. I won't hold you to this."

"My opinion? No, he didn't arrange her murder. I don't think he's arranged anyone's murder in the last twenty years. Not since he's become a real estate gazillionaire."

"What about his criminal activities in Manhattan? Doesn't the Kirilov gang kill anyone there?"

"I don't know. But that wouldn't involve Yuri in any way. He gave over control of the Manhattan gang to his son Byron about fifteen years ago. And the Byron Kirilov gang is not active outside Manhattan, so far as I know. Anything else? Remember, this goes no further than us."

"No, that's all I need. Thanks for your help, Agent Harrison. It means a lot."

"If you learn anything about Mr. Srivastava that we should know, please pass it on to me."

"I will," I said, and hung up the phone.

I marveled at the money Farid and Donny had squirreled away. It sounded—no, smelled— strongly like the earnings of organized crime. It also made me wonder why Donny had borrowed a measly $300,000 from Jonny to fight his court case. Maybe, he was afraid of drawing attention to hidden accounts while he was on trial. And maybe he intended to repay Jonny but hadn't gotten around to it yet.

After calming down, I figured I'd better phone Farid. I didn't want to give him any cause to worry.

"Sorry to hang up on you before. I'm pretty jumpy these days. You've probably noticed that."

"No problem. You're under a lot of stress. I wanted to talk about the newspaper article: now and then, something like that happens at the hospital where I do surgery," Farid said. "Someone leaves a sponge or scalpel inside a patient's body and all hell breaks loose. Usually, someone loses their hospital privileges, even their license to practice. Are you in danger of anything like that?"

"I don't think so. This lawsuit could hurt our reputation, but I'm not about to lose my job. After all, I never approved Donny Foster's research project. Nobody asked my opinion when his proposal was being reviewed. But sure, Criminology could lose a lot of funding if this continues. It won't be good for my School. There may be ripple effects for years to come."

"That's what I was afraid of. Do you need my help? I could come over, if you need me."

"No, Farid," I said. "I'm fine. I'll phone you later." Then I hung up.

I knew I had to get Jonny to call off the attacks on my friends and family. But I was terrified about phoning him. What to say? How to say it?

Then I realized if he'd wanted to hurt me, he would have done it already. Besides, I had a funny feeling that Jonny and I understood each other, even though we stood on opposite sides of the law. So I found the business card for Lone Star Investments and phoned Jonny's number.

"I'm sorry, but Mr. Devlin is out of town today," a secretary told me. "In fact, he's in Toronto for a car auction. I've been authorized to give you his cellphone number. You can contact him there."

I dialed the number and got Jonny on the line right away.

"What the hell, Rachel, why are you phoning me again? You must like flirting with danger," he barked. Yet he sounded oddly light-hearted.

"Mr. Devlin, good morning to you too. No, I hate flirting with danger. Also, I assure you, I haven't broken our agreement. I haven't been blabbing about your business. Do you have a moment to talk?"

"I'm at Ferrari having a bite to eat. Why don't you stroll over here? I reckon it's less than half a mile from where you live." With that, he hung up his phone.

When I got to Ferrari ten minutes later, Jonny was seated at a table for four, near the back of the restaurant.

"Pull up a chair, and tell me why you need to disturb a man who's trying to eat the best goddam bowl of ziti God ever created," he said, smiling. With a large white linen napkin, he carefully removed pinkish pasta sauce from around his mouth. Then he stared attentively, waiting for me to talk.

"I'm sorry to interrupt your meal, Mr. Devlin, honestly, I am. But your nephew Donny Foster is going to bring a firestorm down on our university."

Jonny slowly and carefully put his fork on the table, then stared into my eyes. "I don't give a single gold-plated shit about your university, Rachel. It doesn't affect my life even a little bit. More than that, I warned you not to contact me again. Can't you take a warning? I don't like that, not at all."

Jonny scowled at me, his eyes bulging out of his head. I knew Jonny meant every word he'd said. I was genuinely terrified.

"I g-get it, Jonny," I stammered. "But here's the thing. This may end up affecting you too. I mean, it will affect your business, your bottom line. And I know you care about that."

I silently gulped as I finished that sentence, wondering how Jonny would react.

His reaction was uncontrolled laughter. Jonny shoved away the bowl of ziti and laughed for what seemed like thirty seconds straight. I thought he'd fall out of his chair or have a stroke, he was laughing so hard.

"You are one hell of a woman, Rachel. I need a good laugh and a gutsy woman around, every now and then. Anyway, you're right, I do care about my business. I don't want anyone screwing it up—not you, or your university, or my nephew, the famous criminologist Donny Foster. What do you suggest?"

"It's simple. You should give Donny a job as Research Director for Lone Star Investments. That way, he can continue his research in a friendly environment. What he finds out might even help your business, if those D-scores are worth anything. And by the by, sometime you might tell me why you're willing to have him work on that D-score project. I don't see how it helps you. Anyway, Donny won't teach any more—at least, not at our university. But he'll feel important and well-paid as your consultant. Best of all, he can study criminal gangs till the cows come home."

I felt mildly embarrassed at using a cliché like 'till the cows come home.' But somehow, the situation called for a bit of folksy, down-home plain speaking.

Jonny took a moment to reflect on what I'd said, idly chewing on forkfuls of ziti while he thought.

"Give me a second. I have to visit the little boys' room," he said, coyly. He moseyed over to a door off to the side and, ever so slowly, walked downstairs to restrooms in the basement.

When he was finally back at the table, Jonny sat down again and said "You're right. That's the way to go with this. I won't like having him around all the time. Donny gives me a major headache after a while. But I have to make good on what I promised Bella, and that's the best way to do it. Now we have to find out if he'll go for this idea. I'll talk to him and let you know."

"Should I leave while you do that?" I asked him.

"Not necessary. I'll phone him from upstairs. I have an office there. Carla, bring Professor Tile something to drink, and a dessert if she wants it."

I drank a glass of club soda and nibbled on chocolate biscotti while thinking about my next lecture. At last, I heard Jonny clomping down the stairs from his office, once again ever-so-slowly. After sitting back down, he took a sip of his wine and started to talk.

"I finally got through. He was on the phone with a lawyer for the longest time. Anyway, I suggested he work for me as Research Director, like you said. He was pleasantly surprised. Said he'd try it for six months, if he could get a leave from the university. Then, if we were both happy with the arrangement, he'd stay on, more or less permanently."

"Does that mean Donny would resign his job at the university?"

"He didn't say so, but I guess that's the way he's leaning." And then, Jonny leaned to one side and pretended he was about to fall out of his chair.

38

Sure, that was corny, and Jonny was a bit of a joker, but I've always been drawn to people with a sense of humour. Problem is, Jonny did a lot of not-so-funny things too. So I smiled but didn't laugh.

"Okay, Mr. Devlin," I said, "do we have a deal? Can I tell the Dean that Donny has accepted a job with your company, and she should give him a six-month leave to try it out?"

"Okey-dokey, Rachel. You do that. Let me know what she says, especially if you run into snags. Otherwise, I'll deal with Donny myself from here on in. Oh, and two more things I want you to know."

"What, Jonny?" I asked him, now eager to get out of there.

"First of all, you need to watch your temper. You put one of my men out of commission the day you visited the Killing Fields. You owe me for that, but I won't collect. Not just now. Maybe never. Second thing: when I talked to Donny just before Melanie's death, he was very blunt. He told me, 'Uncle Jonny, do what you have to. I'm always on your side.'"

I was relieved to hear I probably wouldn't have to pay for beating up one of Jonny's men. But the second bit stunned me, though I tried not to show it. Donny had been willing to go along with anything Jonny decided.

"Oh yes, and one more item, since you asked," Jonny said. "About the reason I tolerated Donny's research in Europe. The research that landed one of his assistants—Pam Riley, right?— in the hospital. The fact is, Donny was doing that work for me. He was monitoring the Smith Gang, so we could steal their cars and put them out of business. And the strategy just about worked."

That came as a surprise. Also, a vote of confidence in Donny's abilities.

"Thank you, Mr. Devlin—Jonny. You've been very helpful," I said, getting up to leave. "And thank you, Carla, for the delicious biscotti," I shouted across the room. "I always love eating here."

Jonny Devlin was easy to deal with, once you figured out his wavelength. Back in my office, I dialled the Dean's number and got her on the line.

"I think I've solved our problem," I said, grinning so hard I figured the Dean could sense it from across the campus. "Jonny Devlin will hire Donny as his Research Director for a six-month trial. That's if you give him a leave from teaching. Then, after six months, if they decide to continue the arrangement, Donny will probably resign from the university. Oh, and by the way, it was Jonny Devlin who paid for the trial lawyer, so that's another lie Donny told us."

"Thank you!" the Dean shouted. "I'm so relieved. Of course we'll give him the leave he wants. Ask him if I should date the leave from today or another date. And Rachel, is this supposed to be a paid leave or unpaid leave? An unpaid leave would be easier, but at this point, I'll even pay him to go away."

"I'll tell him you've offered an unpaid six month leave. If he balks at that, I'll bargain with him. Maybe get him to accept a $10,000 research allowance or relocation grant, something along those lines."

"Perfect. Email me the details after you've talked to him. And thanks again for finding a solution. You've saved our lives."

I got up, walked down the hall to Donny's office, and knocked on his door. After an abrupt "Come in," I entered.

"I've been on the phone with the Dean. She's happy to give you a six-month unpaid leave so you can try out that research position with Lone Star Investments. When do you plan to move?"

Donny, ever cagey, saw an opportunity to improve his well-being. "Do you think the Dean would cover my moving costs? I'll need to take clothes, maybe even furniture when I move to Houston, even if it's only for six months. Would the Dean come up with $3,000 for moving expenses?"

I knew the Dean would come up with $20,000 to get him out of her hair. Instead, I told him, "I don't know, Donny, but I'll ask her. Let's assume she says yes. When would you leave? I'll need to hire sessional instructors to handle your courses."

"I'll drive to Houston this weekend with my immediate needs, plus my new dog. I've named him 'D-score'—'D' for short. First thing I have to do is rent a place to live, and I'll get on that right away. The rest of my stuff can arrive the following week. Although, I've been thinking I have too many books. Maybe I'll give them away, or even burn them, before I head south."

He said this last part with a weird smile.

"I'm going to make a fresh start, Rachel. Do new things. I've always wanted to try skydiving. Or auto racing, that would be fun too. And I may marry again. Start all over, with a new family. Everything is possible, Rachel. Everything, if you set your mind to it."

These plans to create a 'new Donny' struck me as weird. And the idea of burning his books struck me as especially strange. Was he renouncing his past life as a scholar? I didn't know and didn't trust him to tell me the truth. I just wanted to wrap this up.

"Whatever you think best, Donny. It's all fine with us. I'll get sessional instructors to cover your courses as soon as tomorrow. If necessary, I'll teach them myself for the rest of this week."

He looked earnestly into my eyes. "So this is goodbye, at least for now."

"Take care of yourself, Donny" I said, turning to leave his office.

I grabbed my coat and briefcase, switched off the light, and headed home again. It had been a good day, I thought. Finally, just a fine, straight-up good day.

Back home, I texted the Dean. "Everything's set. Donny's accepted your offer of an unpaid leave, plus $3000 for moving expenses, effective midnight tonight. You can email him the offer for signing. I'll teach his classes until I've lined up sessional instructors to take over."

I texted Connie, Maribeth, and two other doctoral students, asking if they wanted to cover any of his courses, starting tomorrow. I heard back almost immediately from Connie, who said she could take on all of his research methods courses. That left his introductory course on theft, the one Irina had joined. But that course only had a dozen registered students. If I couldn't find anyone to teach it, I'd cancel it altogether.

Now in great spirits, I got into my pyjamas and settled down to watch *The Great British Baking Show*. I was rooting for a young woman with the hearing problem. Or, failing that, the young man in funny glasses. He reminded me of a student I'd once taught. When my phone rang, I paused the show to answer it.

"Rachel, it's Jackie Taylor. I'm sorry to bother you. Do you have a minute?"

"Jackie. How nice to hear from you. I'm watching *The Great British Baking Show*. Do you know it?"

"Of course. Who are you rooting for? I'm going for that young woman with the hearing aid. What about you?"

"She's adorable, isn't she? What's up? I'm sure you didn't phone to talk about baking."

"No, I wondered how you're handling the big lawsuit that's coming down the pike. I wouldn't like to be in Donny's shoes. I wouldn't even like to be in your shoes today."

"Of course. As for Professor Foster, I can tell you he's soon going to be called simply Dr. Foster, or maybe even Mr. Foster. He's leaving our university for a job in Houston as Research Director at Lone Star Investments. He'll continue his work on D-scores at that impressive location."

"Oh, that's very interesting," Jackie said softly. "But he hasn't paid the price for Melanie's death, has he? He's gotten off scot-free, and she's in the ground. My best friend ever."

"But he's been tried for Melanie's murder and they've let him off. Why do you hold him responsible for her death?"

"He *is* responsible, even if he never held the gun that shot her. I know that for certain."

"That's a serious accusation. What evidence do you have to support it?"

"Why don't I pop over and tell you what I know?" she asked.

I gave her my address and pulled on jeans and a sweatshirt. Twenty-five minutes later, she knocked at my door.

After pouring drinks, I sat us down at the kitchen table and Jackie took a wad of papers out of her purse.

"By now, you may have guessed the Workshop that Melanie led involved a group of women who met regularly to discuss human trafficking. They modelled themselves on an earlier group who'd called themselves 'The Furies.' Their goal was to end human trafficking in Canada and, eventually, all of North America.

"You may have also guessed I'm a member of that group, and you know a few other members, though you may not know they're members. Roxy Duncan and Gina Wolff were both early members of the group, and in fact, they're still members. Your friend Jen Coale has joined us too. Right now, Roxy's chairing the group until we can name a new leader, though Melanie's shoes will be hard to fill. Oh, and by the way, thanks for saving Gina's life. She's the heart and soul of our group now." She smiled and clutched my hand in hers.

It dawned on me that I'd recently seen Gina wearing that silver Celtic ring I'd first seen on Jackie.

"Why haven't I heard more about this group?" I asked.

"We've kept the group secret, for our own safety. And we've kept people in authority—people like you—out of the loop. If you found out, you'd feel pressured to tell your boss, the Dean. Then she'd be conflicted about whether to tell her boss, the Provost. If he knew, he'd try to control the group, and maybe even tell other people about us. So we didn't want to put you or the Dean in that position."

"In short, we know a lot about the Devlin Crew and the Smith Brothers. That's mainly thanks to the work Melanie did over many years. Whenever Melanie found out things of interest, she brought them to the group for discussion. And whatever Gina or Roxy learned from their police contacts, they passed along to the group as well.

"Finally, Melanie decided it was time for a closer look at Jonny Devlin's Houston operation. Of course, she'd visited Houston several times, on her own without telling Donny. Finally, she encouraged Donny to take his sabbatical leave in Texas, then announced she'd visit him there. We warned her that would be dangerous, but she insisted on going anyway. She owed it to the women Jonny Devlin had turned into sex slaves, she told us.

"Gina cleared the way by meeting Donny in Texas a few weeks before Melanie arrived. She rooted around in his notes and drew him into conversations about the Devlin Crew. She also contacted the local FBI branch. She and Craig Harrison quickly became friends, and Gina funneled a lot of FBI information back to us.

"While she was down there, we used a code Melanie had devised. You've probably found two of the coded messages. They told us Donny knew the Devlin Crew was smuggling in women every week. That he'd even visited the Bells N' Whistle as a customer. Jonny Devlin called the women there 'dancers' and 'waitresses.' In fact, they were sex workers. They each handled as many as ten customers a night, at $50 or more a time. Some of them, for $1000 a night.

"So, Melanie knew the Devlin Crew smuggled women into the country and forced them to work in brothels. Donny knew it too, and though Melanie tried to get him to admit it, he wouldn't. He refused to confront Jonny about the trafficking and refused to break off his connection with the Devlin Crew. That connection was too important for his research, he said. And he considered his research more important than anything else.

"He even threatened Melanie with divorce if she kept bugging him about the Crew. In fact, he did everything he could to make her return to Toronto. Finally, Melanie blew her top. At lunch with Donny and Jonny one day, she blurted out what she thought about the Crew's activities. She couldn't help it, she was so frustrated with Donny's reluctance to confront Jonny.

"Jonny told her she should mind her own f–ing business and said she should leave town right away. Said he couldn't guarantee her safety if she stayed on. Melanie went back to the hotel and sent us a coded message telling us exactly what Jonny had said. Also, what Donny had failed to say.

"That was the last time we ever heard from Melanie. I was due to meet her the next day in New Orleans, but she never showed up. Eventually, as you know, police found her body in the Killing Fields. So you see, Donny was aware of the danger facing his wife. He'd failed to protect her. Whether that was out of cowardice or self-interest or another reason, I don't know. But that's why I hold him responsible for Melanie's death."

39

I watched Jackie's face as she told me this long, sad story. And I saw lines in her face I hadn't seen before. While she told this story, she looked old and frail. The death of Melanie, her best friend, was the worst thing that had ever happened to her.

Then, her expression shifted. Anger flashed across her face. She was set on getting revenge, like those Furies of a century ago, or maybe the Furies of two millennia earlier. Jackie wanted justice.

"That's the most complete version of a story I've heard several times before, once from Gina and several times from Donny," I said, between deep sips of club soda. "But before today, I'd never heard much about Melanie's clash with Jonny. Clearly, she knew what was going on and Jonny knew he couldn't have her around. So he gave Donny an ultimatum: get Melanie out of here or something bad will happen. Donny ignored the ultimatum and Melanie dug in her heels." I shook my head in sorry disbelief.

"Here's a bit more information to top it off, Rachel. Shortly before leaving her hotel room, Melanie texted to say we should make plans for the following week. After a short break in New Orleans, we'd come back to Houston and confront Jonny together. She knew things had come to a head. But she didn't know Jonny had already signed her death warrant."

"I have the feeling you plan to avenge Melanie's death," I said, after a minute or two of silence.

"I can't tell you any more tonight, Rachel. I'm all talked out. Go watch your baking show. We'll talk again in a week or so. Meanwhile, I have things to do."

Time passed uneventfully for the next three days, and I got a lot of writing done. Then, finally, a message arrived from Jackie. It said simply, 'Check the *Houston Herald*'s website and pull up today's article by Alethea Zeto, on page 3.'

Online, I found a half-page article titled "The Sex Slaves of Houston." It described the lives of six sex workers Zeto claimed to have interviewed in Houston bars and brothels. They'd risked their lives to give her this information, she wrote.

All they wanted was to stop the smuggling of sex workers and other 'slaves' through the Port of Houston.

The article described how both the Devlin Crew and the Smith Brothers smuggled cars out of the country and sex slaves into it. Zeto also reported having interviewed Agent Craig Harrison of the FBI and CSIS investigator Gina Wolff.

Both Jonny Devlin and Kris Smith had been invited to comment but declined to do so.

Finally, the article reported on research by the "noted smuggling researcher Dr. Donny Foster." He couldn't be reached for contact either. However, his research had revealed an "intimate familiarity with car smuggling personnel, and presumably, also an intimate familiarity with sex slavery." One woman told Zeto she'd even 'serviced' Professor Foster at the Bells N' Whistle during his visit a year earlier. Foster had allegedly boasted about his close ties to the owner of the Club, Jonny Devlin. Also, about his knowledge of artificial intelligence and his value to Jonny Devlin for that reason.

Foster reportedly told the same woman he probably knew more about car smugglers than any other researcher on earth. The journalist suggested Foster probably also knew a great deal about the human trafficking business. If so, police ought to have a 'long conversation with the expert.'

Nice turns of phrase, I thought: every sentence a stiletto aimed at Donny Foster's heart. I guessed Jackie, Gina, Roxy, and a few other members of The Workshop had gotten together to craft this icy bit of journalism. Good for them, I thought.

The article called for a Governor's Task Force on human trafficking. "The time for silence and inaction is over. Women are not cattle, to be locked in Houston's sex barns so they can service wealthy men for hefty fees. The Governor of Texas should close down these all-too-well-known sex clubs and brothels. Federal Immigration officials should ensure that, after they are freed, these sex slaves get safe lodging, work permits, and visas that allow them to stay in the country. Most important of all, the Houston police should crack down on the Devlin Crew, the Smith Brothers, and smaller gangs that copy them. A failure to act will tell Houston voters it's time for a new Governor, a new Mayor, and a new Police Chief."

I messaged Jackie back. 'Nice article,' I wrote. But I couldn't guess how this article would affect the lives of all the people involved.

Three days later, teenagers found Donny Foster's body in the Killing Fields and reported their discovery to the police.

His body wasn't far from the spot where police had found Melanie's body. And like Melanie, Donny was in a shallow grave. But there was a difference. Someone had used a metal rod on him—maybe a tire iron. His ribs, arms, and legs all were broken.

The police claimed to have no idea who'd murdered Donny. However, they admitted his death may have had something to do with the article by Alethea Zeto. Inside Donny's jacket pocket, they found a piece of paper that read "$300,000 IOU paid in full." The police also claimed they didn't know what this message meant. But I did. It meant, "You lost the bet, sucker!" At least, that's how Christopher Marlowe, author of *Doctor Faustus*, would have read it.

That evening, the Mayor of Houston went on television to denounce the murders in and around his town. He specifically mentioned the murder of a "world famous criminologist and researcher," Professor Donny Foster.

A day later, Garet brought her father's body back to Toronto for burial, then phoned me. "Thank you for your help, Professor Tile. I know you did your best. I just couldn't keep my father safe. He should never have returned to Houston. I warned him not to go but he wouldn't listen."

I heard Garet weeping softly on the other end of the line. After ten seconds, I told her, "You're a good daughter. You did everything you could have done and I'm sure your father knew you loved him."

Garet's weeping got louder. She gasped "Thank you," and hung up the phone.

It was November 28, Thanksgiving in Down Country. I tried to imagine how they celebrated the holiday in Houston. Say, at the Bells 'N Whistle. I imagined strippers wearing Pocahontas outfits—then, stripping them off to loud music. Lots of turkey-themed decorations. Thanksgiving-themed drinks. Maybe even a special activity event at the BNW called The Gobbler. God help me, I didn't want to further imagine what that might be.

The next day, long before my December deadline, I gave the Dean my final report. I kept it brief and informal. No paper copy survived our meeting.

"Dean, I don't have much to tell you that's new. I understand the Riley lawsuit is off the table. All the Riley family wanted was an apology and Donny Foster's departure, and they got both. We know almost exactly what happened to Melanie Foster and, more recently, to Donny Foster. They both put themselves on the wrong side of criminal gangs in Houston. Melanie did this by threatening to call attention to their role in human trafficking. Then, a newspaper article by Alethea Zeto did precisely what the gangs had feared. That was the last straw. Jonny Devlin held Donny responsible for the article, and in a sense, he was.

"The article, incidentally, was engineered if not written by Melanie's old friend Jackie Taylor and a former Strachan student, Gina Wolff. They gathered the evidence for that article and put it in Ms. Zeto's hands. They may have even written it for her.

"We may never know exactly who murdered Melanie Foster. My best guess is someone in the Smith Brothers gang pulled the trigger, after getting a go-ahead from Kris Smith and Jonny Devlin. What we know for certain is that Donny Foster didn't care enough about his wife to keep her safe. When he refused to cut his ties with the Devlin Crew, Melanie had to die. In the end, they both had to go.

"Why were their bodies left in the Killing Fields? I suspect that, whoever killed the Fosters, or approved their killing, was sending a message to law enforcers. Something like 'We will not tolerate anyone or anything that interferes with our activities.'

"Melanie had wanted to stop the human trafficking more than anything, more than life itself. And Donny had wanted to complete his D-score research and make a fresh start. But in the end, neither got what they wanted. Houston will probably never find the political will to end human trafficking. And there's probably no criminologist who'll pick up Donny's work where he left off. So, both Fosters may have both died in vain."

"But the Foster case helped us change the way the Research Ethics Board vets research proposals, and that's a good thing. In the end, we saved the university $10 million and plenty of bad publicity. That's another good thing. Finally, one of our graduates, Gina Wolff, did a great job investigating the Devlin Crew, as we would have wanted. That's a third good thing. So, in the end, things turned out as well as we could have hoped."

I avoided telling the Dean anything about the Workshop, Gina's abduction, or the guy I had to beat up. After presenting my report orally, I tore up the paper notes, took my coat, and left the Dean's office. I planned to take a good, long break from D-scores, sex workers, and Donny Foster. But my story wasn't over yet.

40

Tonight was a scheduled date night with Farid. I had a plan and could hardly wait to see how it turned out. At seven sharp, Farid showed up with another mammoth bouquet of roses. I hugged him and said we had to go. I'd reserved a table at Ferrari.

After the wine arrived, I asked Farid to tell me about his family.

"I have two brothers. They're both married with children and they're very American. You'd like them, Rachel. They've even changed their names. They call themselves Kris Smith and Victor Smith."

"Why did they change their names, but you didn't?"

"I knew staying with my original name would please my mother. Life in the US is easier if you have an American-sounding name like Smith. In Canada, it doesn't matter as much."

"What do your brothers do, Farid? You've never said much about them."

"Kris and Victor own a lot of real estate. They also have shares in other businesses: car repair shops, nightclubs, restaurants, even small banks and finance companies. They're very rich, though you wouldn't know it to meet them. They're still down-to-earth people."

"How come you didn't go into business with them?"

"Actually, I did. I've invested a lot of my own money in their businesses, but I don't get involved in their everyday operations. I guess you'd say I'm a silent partner." Farid smiled as he said that.

I hesitated for minute, then blurted out the question I knew I had to ask.

"Farid, when I investigated Donny Foster, I kept hearing about the Smith Brothers, how they were at war with the Devlin Crew. Your brothers aren't the famous Smith Brothers, are they?"

Farid paused. "Yes, Kris and Victor are the famous Smith Brothers. And though they have a lot of holdings in Texas, they live in Maryland near my mother."

I knew it was time for a showdown. "When Melanie Foster died, a few people thought the Smith Brothers may have been involved. Do you think your brothers had anything to do with Melanie's death?"

Farid pulled away from the table, a look of dismay on his face. "How can you even think that?"

"I need to know the truth. If your brothers were involved in Melanie Foster's death, and maybe Donny's death too, I want you to tell me. We can't keep seeing each other if we can't be honest. Even about things that are hard to face."

Farid stared into space and considered what to say next. Finally, in slow, measured tones, he said "I can't tell you a lot about my brothers. They may or may not have had something to do with the deaths of Melanie and Donny Foster. If they did, it was because Jonny Devlin had asked them for it. My brothers aren't violent people. But the Fosters had become a nuisance to everyone in the car business. Melanie wouldn't shut up and go home, no matter how many times Jonny asked her to."

"How do you know that, Farid?" I whispered.

He hesitated for a moment, then blurted out, "I talked to

Melanie myself. Gave her one last chance to go home and mind her own business. But she wouldn't do it."

"So you were the guy who hitched a ride with Melanie at Briggs College on the day of her death, right?"

"Yes, that was me."

"And the woman with you was….?"

"Kim Cressy, a member of the Devlin Crew. She was there to do the shooting. I was there to watch, on behalf of my brothers. They were as unhappy as Jonny Devlin about Melanie's interference."

"And did you kill Donny Foster too?"

"No, that was Kim on her own. She made a dinner date with Donny—he thought it would be romantic—and killed him that night. Then she left his body in the Killing Fields. At least, that's what I heard. I guess that was done on the orders of Jonny Devlin too."

"And now, tell me why you moved to Toronto and made a point of meeting me," I asked angrily.

"Meeting you and falling in love was a complete accident, I swear. As to why I moved here, it was to keep an eye on Donny, the car auctions at Ferrari, and Jonny Devlin's new business, Bespoke Vehicles—the one Kim was helping to set up. Also, to keep an eye on the Smith family businesses in Brampton. They're going to compete with the Devlin businesses in downtown Toronto. Both gangs are building up their holdings in Canada."

I kept nodding as Farid unfolded this information. I'd suspected something like it for weeks but had dreaded finding out for certain. Now, finally, Farid had confirmed the worst.

"I have to be by myself, Farid. Please go."

Reluctantly, Farid got up, collected his things, and left Ferrari. I paid for the wine and walked home very slowly, wondering if Farid had targeted me in the gym that day we met. So he could spy more easily on Donny, perhaps. I'd never find out.

But I had completely solved the mystery. Jonny Devlin had ordered Melanie's death. She had threatened to draw media attention to the trafficking of sex slaves. And media attention, as Jonny would have pointed out, was bad for business.

Plus, Melanie had discovered a half-way house—that black trailer—in the Killing Fields. The Devlin Crew had been using it to prepare newly smuggled women for prostitution in clubs and brothels like BNW. This information, when passed to police authorities, significantly interfered with Jonny's business.

The public never learned anything about my efforts at detection. But I was lavishly praised and celebrated by members of the Workshop—among them, Jackie, Roxy, Jen, Gina, and most affectionately, my own daughter—the newest member of the group. No praise meant more than the hugs and kisses I got from Ellie that week.

A day after breaking up with Farid, I debated whether to tell Agent Harrison about Farid's confession. I'd promised to share everything so, finally, I phoned him. Harrison listened without surprise.

"Thanks, Rachel. We suspected someone from the Smith Brothers might have paired up with someone from the Devlin Crew to kill Melanie. You've confirmed it. But for now, that's merely hearsay. Not admissible in court. Farid probably knows it, too."

After hesitating for a moment, I asked him, "Would you like to scare the person who killed both of the Fosters? I have a plan."

Harrison listened to my plan, then nodded. "Do it. I'll fly in and meet you tomorrow if everything works out."

I called Roxy next. She liked my plan too and agreed to set it in motion.

The next afternoon I walked to Ferrari from home, about six blocks away. It was a gorgeous winter day, clear and crisp. My breath froze each time I exhaled. Still, I exhaled deeply and rhythmically as I strode towards the last act of this little play. This Faustian story in which I played a small but important role.

When I arrived, Roxy was already seated, chatting with Kim Cressy. The two women looked like old friends, heads close to each other, laughing and smiling.

"Hi, ladies," I said, sitting down beside them.

"Kim, this is Rachel Tile. She's a professor of criminology, an old friend of mine," Roxy said.

Kim smiled. "I feel like I know you, Professor Tile. But I can't think where I've heard your name. It will come to me eventually."

Then a man came into Ferrari and approached the table. It was Agent Harrison, gray and tired looking, smelling of cigarettes, as usual.

"Mind if I join you? I hear the pasta's excellent," he said, pulling out a chair.

"Agent Harrison," Roxy said. "Do you know Kim Cressy?"

"Oh, we go way back," he replied, smiling. "We've watched each other for years, from a distance. Kim, I hear you've been busy in Toronto."

Kim tensed, her polite smile wavering. "I don't think we've met formally, Agent. But it's nice to put a name to a face."

"Yes," Harrison said. "And today we'll have a good, long conversation."

Kim glanced at her diamond-studded watch. "I just remembered an appointment across town."

She started to rise, but Roxy grabbed her wrist. "You're not going anywhere, Kim. I'm arresting you for vandalism. Agent Harrison also has questions he wants to ask about the Foster murders and the Devlin Crew's personnel system."

Harrison stood. "We can go now, or you can enjoy lunch first. Your choice."

Kim hesitated, her eyes darting around the room. Finally, she sighed. "Let's eat first."

We ate in silence. When plates had been cleared, Roxy stood up and handcuffed Kim.

I walked home from Ferrari feeling completely satisfied. Now, the Foster case really was over. As for Farid? Well, he was never the guy I'd thought he was. And that was over too.

Two weeks later, I met Garet Foster socially for the first time—lunch at the Faculty Club. She looked much better—happier—than when I'd seen her before. Over salads and tea, we talked about the past. I had another bandage on my forehead—this time, the result of my collision with an errant kitchen doorway. I'd have to slow down, I promised myself.

"I know this will sound awful," Garet said, "but I feel like a huge weight's been lifted. I don't have to worry about my father anymore."

"That makes sense, Garet. He was a complicated man. Maybe an unhappy one too."

We talked until the pub had emptied and they were vacuuming the carpet. I felt like I'd gained a sister.

I invited Garet and her family to a holiday dinner in December. I'd repeat my Thanksgiving extravaganza with a different menu and several new guests. Maybe this time Megan could come, and Jackie too.

Garet smiled, her hands warm in mine. "We'll be there," Garet said, smiling.

These had been grueling but gratifying months. I'd solved the mystery of Melanie's murder. I was glad to get back to plain, ordinary everyday life. And to my book on rage.

Epilogue

The breakup with Rachel didn't come as a complete surprise to Farid. After all, he'd known all about her search of his home—even, that she'd found his gun. He'd also known about her role in the beating of Mark Fenton, the guy who'd guarded Gina in the trailer. That kind of information got around. People were pretty impressed by Rachel's martial arts skills. And her rage.

So no, Farid wasn't entirely surprised when Rachel dumped him that night. Or by all the stuff that happened afterward. With Donny dead, Jonny Devlin canceled the car auctions at Ferrari and tightened security around the gang's data system. He interviewed Hannah Proctor for the personnel job and planned to take a little time deciding. Replacing Kim would be harder, as Farid also understood.

He left Toronto within a week of breaking up with Rachel. Closed his surgical practice, sold his house, and moved to Long Beach, California, on his brother Kris's advice. Before leaving, he buried his gun in the backyard. It was risky crossing the border with a weapon and he could easily get a new one in California.

From the get-go, Farid felt comfortable in Long Beach. Soon, he was dating Delilah—he called her Lil for short—a brilliant Moldovan graduate student he'd met at the gym. They did everything together—went out for dinners, hiking in the hills, snorkeling off the Mexican coast. Farid quickly developed a strong affection for Lil. This could be the real thing, he started to think.

She wore a silver ring with a ruby atop a heart and when Farid noticed it, she said it was a gift from a 'dear friend.' She wore it in her friend's honour. Farid didn't remember having ever seen a similar ring. Or if he did, he never said so. And Lil didn't say anything more about it either.

That would come later.

ACKNOWLEDGEMENTS

As usual, many people read and commented on the drafts that, finally, produced the book you have been reading. I want to thank all these readers for their patience and help.

My friends Julie Doyle, Rachel Rosenberg, Charles Tepperman, Joe Tepperman, Tony Thomson, and Jeannette Wright read early drafts and offered useful comments. Spoiler alert: my friend Lorna Marsden also read it and offered a single pithy comment. I won't share it here since it's a tipoff and I don't want to spoil anyone's fun. But it was a funny comment and I'll share it with you in private, after you've read the book.

I want to thank Patricia Westerhof, from whom I received a wonderful course on creative writing while I worked on this book. Patricia provided lots of food for thought, food I'm still digesting. She also put me in touch with Janice MacDonald in Alberta, who kindly read and critiqued a draft of the book, then read and critiqued a revised version shortly afterward. Janice's direct, unsparing comments were extremely helpful.

Patricia recommended that I also seek help from one of the professional mentors who offer advice under the auspices of the University of Toronto School of Continuing Studies. One such mentor, Michel Basilieres, kindly read and commented on the first third of my book and, like my other readers, provided useful advice. Here too, I am still digesting much of the excellent advice Michel provided, but I followed his suggestions as well as I could.

Finally, I want to thank Elizabeth Sheldon, who did the line edit for this book. She did a lovely job and called a few more issues to my attention. So thank you, Elizabeth.

One thing that has struck me about all the comments I received, from the earliest to the latest, is that they were all quite different. Different readers found different things to like and dislike—to criticize—in my book. And that was the case for my first mystery novel, *Deadly Donation*, as well.

I think there's a message in that fact, something to do with 'eyes of beholders.'

As odd and unlikely as this book may seem, the story is loosely based on an actual murder trial in which an actual Canadian academic was tried and released after the murder of his wife. I have taken huge liberties with that story, and by no means should you read this book as an attempt to 'solve' that earlier, actual case. Nonetheless, my book is concerned with an incompletely answered question posed by an actual case: why was the academic accused, tried, and then released for a murder many people felt sure he'd committed. And what happened when that academic returned to teaching and research—to normal, everyday life—after the trial?

I continue, in this book, as in others I have written and am currently writing, to be fascinated not by the question 'Whodunit?' but rather, by 'Why did he/she/they do it?' And as I plumb this question, I continue to learn about myself, other people (real and fictional), and the world at large. In particular, I continue to learn about the poisoning effects of socio-political inequality—effects that are currently roiling Donald Trump's United States and, increasingly, the rest of the world. So, you might find it useful to keep Donald and Elon and their facilitators in the back of your minds as you read this book.

Finally, I want to thank my old friend, mentor, and publisher David Stover for the excellent help and advice he's given me over the years. Thanks, David. Please know that I'm endlessly grateful for what you've done for me.

Lorne Tepperman
Toronto
June 2025

A Tale of Three Covers

Down Country, the second book in the Rachel Tile Mysteries series, is being published in three versions, each with a different cover (the interior of the book, of course, remains the same in all three versions). The idea is to highlight the different themes embodied in the book.

The image on the first cover is of sunset in a deserted area outside Houston. Houston is, of course, where Rachel carries out her investigations. With a population in its metropolitan area of more than 7 million, it is the largest city in Texas, famous as the home of NASA's Mission Control. It is home to such major industries as petrochemicals, health care, shipping … and organized crime.

The second cover also depicts Houston, this time with Hurricane Francine looming in the background in September 2024. Houston and the Texas Gulf Coast have suffered through numerous hurricanes over their history. Catastrophic weather seems an apt analogy for the events of the novel.

The third cover eschews geography to tackle one of the novel's key motifs—that Donny has sold his soul to the Devil. We all know what happens in the end to those who sell their souls, as the famous image by a follower of Hieronymus Bosch so terrifyingly illustrates…

9 781772 443707